Lincoln's Doctor's Dog

James O. Long

Published by Bottlefly Press, 2020

Lincoln's Doctor's Dog

Published by Bottlefly Press
Boise, Idaho
www.bottleflypress.com

Edited by Jenny Niemeyer
Cover illustration, layout and design by Jenny Niemeyer

Print edition ISBN 978-0-9848-113-4-2

Library of Congress Control Number 20200900047
Long, James O., 1937-
1. Humor 2. Fiction

eBook ISBN 978-0-9848-113-5-9

This is a work of fiction. Although some characters really did exist
and some events really did happen some names, characters, businesses,
places, events, locales and incidents are either the products of the
author's imagination or used in a fictitious manner.

Designed and printed in the U.S.A.
10 9 8 7 6 5 4 3 2 1

For Susie

T. L. Pettigrew
Historical Research
Library of Congress
Washington City

Dear Mrs. Pettigrew,

I am writing in hope that some reliable source may exist that would give me information about a dog that President Lincoln supposedly kept at the White House. I don't think this dog, which may have belonged to his doctor, has ever been mentioned, and I would like to include it in a forthcoming biography.

The few references I have seen to a Lincoln dog are hazy as to whether the dog actually belonged to the President or someone else (again, the rumor is that it was his doctor's). I am uncertain even as to what the dog looked like. I think his name was Nipper.

Yours truly,
Sandburg

Dear Mr. Sandburg,

I took the liberty of forwarding your inquiry about the dog to Mr. John Hay, who is Mr. Lincoln's former secretary. His wife, Mrs. Jenny Lou Hay, sent the enclosed reply. Hope this helps.

Faithfully,
T.J. Pettigrew
(Mr., not Mrs.)

P.S. - Attached please also find a note from Mr. Harry Lincoln.

Dear Mr. Pettigrew,

I am writing in response to the letter you sent addressed to my late husband. In it you enclosed a letter from a Mr. Sandburg and also an account by a relative of Mr. Lincoln's regarding a dog.

I am sorry to tell you that my husband, Mr. John Hay, died two years ago. However, I do remember a dog named Culver who lived at the White House, although my memory fails me on details. Therefore, I am unable to comment on the accuracy of the account you sent from Mr. Lincoln's cousin, Mr. Harry Lincoln, although in my personal opinion it seems rather fanciful. President Lincoln was a considerate man who never would have introduced an innocent animal to the vile habit of chewing tobacco.

I do seem to recall that Mr. Hay mentioned that the President's dog had some strange appetites and upon one occasion swallowed a salesman's watch.

Sincerely,
Jenny Lou Hay

Enclosure from Abe's cousin, Harry:

Dear Mr. Pettigrew,

First time I seen that dog was right there in the White House. I do remember Abe called him Kupper and taught him to do all kinds of tricks and I can tell you that Kupper was a right smart dog.

One time I called on Abe, and Abe was settin in one rockin chair and Kupper was in another. They would both rock and spit tobacco in a spittoon. I don't recollect how Abe taught Kupper to chew.

As for your other questions, I don't remember exactly what color Kupper was. I think he was a spotted dog and had some hound in him.

Sincerely,
Harry Lincoln

Enclosure from Harry's uncle, Aubery:

Dear Nephew Harry,

In hopes that I find you and your family well, I write regarding your question from Mr. Sandburg about Kipper. I can state positively that I seen the dog, Kipper, chew tobacco.

Abe would set that dog in a rocker they would both rock and spit. Abe had done taught that dog how to spit clear across the room. I never seen a dog that could spit, much less one that could spit as far as Kipper.

Abe would get him a chaw, and he'd work it around and give Kipper a chaw and Abe would say, "I'll go first," and he'd go "pat-too" and put it dead smack in a brass slop-jar clear over by the door. Ten foot if it were an inch. "Shoot!" Abe would laugh, and Kipper would go "pat-too" the next time the rocker came fro, but of course he wouldn't spit as loud as Abe.

Now, ever once in awhile either Abe or Kipper would miss and hit the wall or the floor and I can tell you Mrs. Lincoln was fit to fry eggs. She didn't like that spittin one bit and she used to get so mad at Abe she could cuss, although I never did hear her cuss. But she would get mad and try to make Mr. Hay do something, but Mr. Hay didn't know what to do. I don't know if Mr. Hay ever said anything to Mr. Lincoln.

And I'll tell you the time I was there with Abe and that dog a-rockin and a-spittin and General Grant come by in his full dress uniform with a great long sword in a silver scabbert and a feather in his hat. The general couldn't help getting tickled when he saw that dog aimin at the spittoon, and said he never seen nothin to beat it. Now that really tickled Abe and he give General Grant a chaw and drug up a extra rocker, and pretty soon the general was rockin and trying to out-spit Kipper and Abe. Well, Lord, Mr. Hay about died because he knew was going to catch the dickens from Mrs. Lincoln.

I don't remember exactly what color Kipper was. I think he was kind of a brown dog, if I recollect right. Maybe a sooner of some sort.

Yours Faithfully,
Aubery R.L. Lincoln

Department of Veterinary Medicine
State College, Pennsylvania

Dear Mr. Pettigrew,

    In answer to the question you posed on behalf of Mr. Sandburg,
it seems highly improbable that a dog could be taught to spit. If you wish
further details, I will be happy to provide them, but I hope this answer suffices.

        Sincerely,
        T.L. Arnold
        Professor of Canine Anatomy
        Pennsylvania Agriculture College

Now, a letter supposedly from Harry's Aunt Cora:

To: Mr. Sandburg
From: T. J. Pettigrew

So far, our research about Mr. Lincoln's (doctor's?) dog has produced mixed results. For whatever it may be worth, I am forwarding to you an unsolicited note from a Mrs. Cora V. Johns, whom I understand is the sister of Aubrey (he spells it Aubery) Lincoln:

Dear Mr. Pettigrew,

I can state definitely the following facts: Mr. Lincoln's dog's name was Cooper.

Cooper was either the second youngest of three pups or the second oldest. Whichever way you want to look at it. Cooper, although old for a dog, was eternally young, like an orphan. He was mostly terrier, with a hound-like heart, although not self-pitying like a hound. No, indeed, he was more like a terrier, or a Spitz, if there is such a thing as a Spitz.

He had a longer neck than most terriers. He wore his head earnestly always, stretching up to reach the nearest hand. His hair was impossible. It grew every which way, and was woolly. He had a patch over one eye. Not a real one, of course, but it looked like a patch, because it was brown. It made Cooper look so dear, if a bit stupid.

Cora

(Note: the "o" in Cora is drawn like a heart.)

Now, an unusual note to Mr. Pettigrew from General Grant:

Madam:

    Col. Cartwright here at the Home read me the letter you sent that was written by Mr. Aubery Lincoln.
    I would beg to correct the record in this regard: When I called on Mr. Lincoln I never wore a hat with a feather in it. That sounds like another dandy fellow, an officer of rank, whose name I won't sully this page with. Seems like I do remember the dog, though.

       Faithfully,
       U.S. Grant

And a note from General McClellan:

Dear Mr. Pettigrew,

Your associate, Mr. McIntyre, showed me Gen. Grant's reply to your inquiry.

The general's poor memory is not surprising, considering his continuation to this day of his Abominable Habits. I will not stoop to comment further on the matter of the general's hat, but I have seen him actually call on the President while quite unsteady on his feet, and while wearing not only a hat and feather, but a sword, if you can believe it.

Mr. Lincoln's dog's name, in case you are not aware, was actually Culpeper, if I recall correctly. Or possibly Culpepper.

Your servant,
McClellan (Maj. Gen., USA, ret.)

From Sandburg to T. J. Pettigrew:

Dear Tom,

Let's just forget the dog research.

Thanks,
Sandburg

Then, three months later, an unexpected dog letter from Pettigrew to Sandburg:

Carl,

　　I just got this from Mathew Brady. I was surprised to learn he was still alive. I'm sure you will be delighted with it.

- Pettigrew

The letter from Brady as enclosed:

Dear Mr. Pettigrew,

　　I certainly do remember Mr. Lincoln's dog, Cooper, because I was present when Cooper ate the original Gettysburg Address. That story is quite true. (I can shed no light, unfortunately, on the amusing incident claimed by Aubery Lincoln in which the dog supposedly was taught to chew tobacco.)
　　In the Fall of 1863 I had made an appointment to capture Mr. Lincoln's portrait on a new type of French camera with an adjustable lens. We - meaning Mr. Lincoln and myself - were to meet in his study at the White House, but our plans were changed at the last moment by his decision to go to Gettysburg. We all know the reason for that. I think the President really was amazed and awe-struck at the sacrifice of so many youngsters. These were only children, most of them, who had saved the Union.
　　At any rate, Mr. Lincoln could not keep the original appointment, so he arranged through his military aide, General Abernethy, to have me accompany him on the train from Washington to the battlefield where he was to deliver an address.
　　I remember I had difficulty steadying the camera because of the movement of the coach. Mr. Lincoln was greatly distracted and yet he was quite courteous, as he always was, about sitting for a portrait. (I should add that I did search my photographic negatives for one showing Cooper with the

President, but so far haven't found one.)

Probably the reason I remember Mr. Lincoln's dog so vividly is the outlandish event that took place as the President was distracted with getting his picture taken. For some reason, the dog got it in his head to chew up and actually eat most of the President's speech, which the President had rolled into a tight scroll and left unattended on a table. Perhaps the dog mistook it for a bone, I don't know. I didn't know what the paper contained, and nobody really noticed what was happening until the deed was practically done. I think General Abernethy managed to contest Cooper for a scrap the size of a post-stamp, but it was of no use.

That is why, with the train practically pulling into the station, Mr. Lincoln had to sit down and very quickly write a much shorter version of his speech on the back of an envelope.

Mr. John Hay (the President's secretary) was much upset, but I do not recall what the President's reaction was. It's too bad Mr. Hay is no longer among us, for I am sure he could have supplied many interesting details.

Sincerely,
Mathew Brady

1.
The President and His Doctor

From a distance, silhouetted against the sunlit Potomac, the two men looked like locomotives meeting, their tall hats nodding toward one another and blending at times into a sort of arch. The dog grew out of Dr. Hunt's considerable eclipse. There was a muzzle and fuzzy eyebrows and a hint of teeth and tongue, all protruding from Hunt's frumpled knee. Farther down, wagging cheerfully in silhouette from the doctor's ankle, was a raggedy tail. With the pale winter sun so low, it was impossible to judge whether the dog was on this side of the doctor or the far side. It was also impossible to tell to an absolute certainty whether it was Mary Lincoln who pronounced the word "shit," very distinctly, as she struggled to bang shut an upstairs window at the White House.

Then she opened it again. She let go of the window and cupped her hands over her brow, brushing a curl from her fine cheek and squinting at the scene taking place on the riverbank. All at once, glee and vindication flared her nostrils into shapes of triumph. As she adjusted her hands against the glare she thought she saw...oh yes, yes! There they were! Right there at the bottom of the doctor's raggedy trouser cuffs! Gifts sent from heaven to rejuvenate the faltering ill will she felt toward the doctor. Why, the man was wearing spats! Spats! In the daytime! And with that dreadful checkered suit!

Mrs. Lincoln could not understand why her husband continued to see Dr. Hunt. "That man," she would say, "never washes his hands, and he's always petting that nasty dog. And I declare, father, have you looked closely at what he calls his medical implements? *Medical implements?* Antiques is more like it - antiques gone to rubbish! And nasty old bottles of who knows what. Father, I do declare, I just do declare. That man does not know any more about doctoring than I do!"

"Now mother," Mr. Lincoln would say.

And she would start all over again.

Mr. Lincoln did think once or twice about getting another doctor, but he never did.

2.
Winter

A snowflake landed on Cooper's nose.

Joyfully he barked.

His tracks followed him all around the White House.

Mr. Odegaard, the Norwegian ambassador, came sliding down the street with boards fastened to his feet. Cooper circled him, barking, leaping. Mrs. Lincoln opened a window and told Cooper to quit.

"He ain't botherin' nobody, Mrs. President," called Ole Odegaard. Abe appeared at the window, still wearing his nightcap.

"What brings you so early, Ole?" called Mr. Lincoln.

"These here is skis, for de snow," called the ambassador.

"Well, I'll be," laughed Mr. Lincoln.

Cooper barked again.

"Come on down and I'll let you see how they work, Mr. President," called the Norwegian.

Cooper could hear Mr. Lincoln and his wife arguing as they shut the window.

Presently Mr. Lincoln appeared on the front lawn, taking big steps with his big feet, his angular body clad in a coat that fell to his knees. On the Great Emancipator's head was a stovepipe hat, with a green plaid scarf wrapped around his ears and tied under his chin.

Lincoln stooped and grabbed a fistful of snow, packing it in a ball and flinging it toward Cooper who leaped and tried to catch it in his mouth.

The Norwegian laughed.

"Wait where you are, Mr. President," called Ole Odegaard. He unstrapped the boards from his feet and made his way up the lawn. Behind Mr. Lincoln, coming out of the White House, were General Abernethy and Mr. Hay and two young blueclad sentries whose chatter was etched in white on the cold blue air, and young Amy Lincoln in a winter bonnet and wool stockings under her skirt, and all of them followed by Mr. Brady hugging the wooden box of a new Foucault camera that trailed stiff legs like a confused octopus.

"Just a minute, Mr. President, oh, just a minute, sir," Brady was calling.

"Hurry up, then," Mr. Lincoln teased. "I'm about to slide clean from here to Norway, ain't I Ole?"

"I wouldn't be surprised, by golly," laughed Ole. "Hold these here poles in your hands and give a push when you're ready."

"Look out, Cooper," said Mr. Lincoln. Unsteadily he began sliding down the hill.

"Wait," called Mr. Brady, running for the White House. "I forgot something."

"I cain't stop! Whoopee!" called Mr. Lincoln. Cooper sped between his spraddled legs.

Lincoln's wobbly figure came apart like the works of a broken clock, a whirlwind of flailing parts, of spinning sticks, angular elbows, hitches and jerks, and finally a pile of President and slat-boards. General Abernethy huffed and puffed down the gentle slope where presently he stooped to inspect the wreckage as Cooper ran around with Lincoln's stovepipe hat. The sentries chased Cooper, who dodged them.

"Mr. Lincoln!" said General Abernethy, reprovingly.

Lincoln, prostrate in the snow, only chuckled and shook his head, finally accepting the help of the general and the two sentries who had given up the chase long enough to set the Great Emancipator back on his feet.

Amy got Cooper to give her the hat. "Here, father," Amy said. "Cooper chewed the brim a bit."

Lincoln smoothed the teethmarks and put the hat absently back on his head. His face, suddenly somber again, was toward the silent war in Virginia.

"Are you all right, Mr. President?" General Abernethy inquired, after a spell.

"Sure enough, Horatio," Mr. Lincoln said. Then he gave a whoop and a holler and fell down again. "Horatio," he said, "this here foot-sleddin' beats all. I want you to try it. Won't that be all right, Ole?"

"Oh, you betcha, Mr. President," the Norwegian ambassador said, pushing the skis into the hands of General Abernethy who sputtered and protested all the way back up the hill.

Amy laughed into her knitted scarf. Cooper, running in joyous circles, barked at his own tracks.

***

Beginning in the spring, Dr. Hunt had taken to coming to the White House with "that dog," as Mrs. Lincoln called Cooper.

The first time, Cooper was just following along behind Hunt, who seemed not to notice until Lincoln did.

"Here, boy!" the President said. Later, he asked Dr. Hunt where he got Cooper. Hunt said he didn't get Cooper at all. He couldn't remember exactly, but he thought Cooper showed up at his office one morning, or maybe it was one afternoon, but he couldn't remember which one it was, exactly.

"Well, whose dog is it?" the President said.

"Mine, I reckon," Hunt grunted.

"Well, did he have a name to start with, or who named him Cooper?" Lincoln asked the doctor.

"I never named him that," the doctor said. "I thought you did."

"Well, no, I never named him," Lincoln said.

"I thought I heard you call him Cooper."

"Well, I did, but that's because that's what his name was, or so I thought," Lincoln said.

"Why, no."

"Well, then, what's his name?"

"Cooper, I thought," the doctor said.

One day Dr. Hunt left Cooper with Mr. Lincoln, and Cooper stayed overnight. Then he stayed two days. And then a week. And then it seemed like he was just there.

Mrs. Lincoln studied Cooper carefully. She could find nothing objectionable about him, although she was sure there was. She bided her time. She expected Dr. Hunt would take his dog home any day, but Hunt never did.

One day, to her own surprise, Mrs. Lincoln brought Cooper a treat from the kitchen. She let him eat the treat from her hand, but was careful not to let him lick her fingers.

***

Much of Mr. Lincoln's conversation with Hunt was taken up with explaining how smart Cooper was, and how he would feel lost without such a good companion.

"He ain't worth a plug nickel," Hunt would say, pounding the dog like a drum.

Every once in awhile, Mr. Lincoln would ask Dr. Hunt again where he got Cooper, or whose dog he was, and what his name was, but the doctor seemed confused about the whole subject. Mr. Lincoln never did get the story straight.

Half the time, the doctor would drop off to sleep as he sat in the cane-bottom rocker in Mr. Lincoln's study.

Sometimes Mr. Lincoln would go back to his papers, but, more and more, he would tiptoe quietly out of the study and take Cooper for a walk. The walks grew longer, sometimes to the river, young sentries trailing, where Mr. Lincoln would throw a stick for Cooper, and Cooper would get it.

The walking and the throwing made Mr. Lincoln feel much better.

Hunt sent Lincoln a bill for five dollars for his professional services, which Mary complained about but paid.

***

One day General Abernethy asked Lincoln, "Did Hunt give you that dog?"

"Not exactly," the President said. "Cooper ain't Hunt's to give." He adjusted his glasses looking at Cooper whose left hind leg paused in mid-scratch of a flea.

"Well, he ain't good for nothing," Abernethy said. Lincoln continued to say that Cooper was the doctor's dog. Mary kept saying to give him back to the doctor tomorrow, to which Mr. Lincoln kept agreeing, because Mary refused to have a dog. And that is how Cooper came to live at the White House.

***

By and by, Cooper took to visiting General Abernethy. Abernethy smelled like maps and horses. Cooper felt the general's callused fingers tousling his head, pulling on his woolly ears. "You ain't worth a nickel," Cooper heard the general say.

Even though Mr. Lincoln was walking with Cooper every day, General Abernethy didn't like the way the President looked. His eyes were bleary. Dark circles grew under them.

Some days, the President wouldn't even pay attention when Cooper brought him a stick to throw.

"You got to get more rest, Mr. President," General Abernethy grumbled.

"All right, Horatio," the President would say.

But try as he might, Mr. Lincoln never seemed to rest just right. At the morning staff meeting, he would yawn, and his eyes would roll around in his head, and soon he'd be nodding in his beard while people were trying to talk to him.

"I'm sending for Dr. Hunt," General Abernethy said.

That afternoon, Cooper barked excitedly as the familiar portly figure of Dr. Hunt filled Mr. Lincoln's vestibule. "Hey, hey old boy!" greeted the doctor, removing his top hat and setting down a satchel.

Mr. Lincoln opened his eyes wearily. He'd been trying to doze in his rocking chair.

Hunt looked sideways at the President, "Abernethy tells me you're not feeling good."

"Abernethy carries on like an old hen," said Lincoln.

"Uh-huh," Dr. Hunt nodded. "Why don't you just step out of them pants and set on the edge of that table. And unsnap that shirt, too."

Dr. Hunt went to examining Mr. Lincoln. Lincoln was talking about army boots. He said the boot factories weren't making enough. "We need more and more, and the factories make less and less. The boys will soon be barefooted."

"Uh-huh," Hunt nodded, not paying attention.

Lincoln said, "Seems like I'm too tired and sleepy to even think about it."

Cooper wagged his tail, poking his nose among the strange smells of Dr. Hunt's bag.

Lincoln forced himself to brighten, "Say, Hunt, did I ever tell you about the short little congressman we had back home that got beat for re-election, and had to get a job tending elephants in the circus?"

"I don't think I recollect - " Dr. Hunt said. "Coop, fetch me my listenin' stick out of that bag."

Cooper nosed around and did as directed. He watched as the doctor put one end of the listening-stick against Lincoln's chest and pressed his ear against the other end.

"What are you aiming to hear?" asked the President.

"Hush," Hunt said.

"Anyway," Lincoln went on, "this short little

congressman lost the election, and he kindly disappeared for awhile and then somebody heard he was tending to the elephants in the traveling circus - "

"Thunderation!" Hunt interrupted, taking the stick off Lincoln's chest, "I couldn't hear a wagonload of bullfrogs with that big trap of yours runnin'. Now quit talkin' and wigglin' around. Your bones creak."

"My bones always creaked," said the President. "And they been creakin' worse ever since Mr. Stanton informed me that our soldier boys are going to need ten thousand pairs of boots per month this winter, and our contractors can't cobble up but about five thousand."

"Hush. I ain't studying boots."

Cooper waited beside the bag. Finally Hunt handed him the listening stick and said, "Put that back, Coop, and get me my knee-tapper."

Cooper found Dr. Hunt's knee-tapper, and Hunt tapped smartly on each of Mr. Lincoln's knees. Each time he tapped, one of the President's legs would fly up, and one of Cooper's ears would fly up, too.

Tap.

Leg up.

Ear up.

"Uh-huh," Hunt said.

"You figured something out?" asked Mr. Lincoln.

"You can put your pants back on."

Lincoln put on his pants. Hunt stood and thought, his fist on his chin. Lincoln poked around in Hunt's satchel and took out the listening stick and listened to Cooper.

"How fast is a dog's heart supposed to beat?"

Hunt shook his head distractedly. He twiddled his eyeglasses and made several adjustments of his bushy sideburns. He mumbled things that could not be understood, and finally puffed out his round cheeks and reached in his coat for a snuff box.

"Care for a pinch?" Hunt flipped open the pewter lid.

"I don't dip," Lincoln said.

"Tell me one more time," Hunt said, letting a little snuff dribble on his shirt, "why you can't sleep."

"Well," said the President, "I never did sleep much at night, as you know. I always cat-napped here in my rocker."

"In your rocker."

"I'd doze off three or four times a day."

"Three or four."

"But here lately I just barely get to sleep, seems like, and something wakes me up. An awful sound, like an awful groan or an aargh like somebody dying, or a loud screech or a squawl and I'm wide awake and my heart is knocking itself right out of my chest."

"Uh-huh," Hunt repeated, taking another pinch. "And you wake right up."

"Wide awake."

"Kind of an awful squeal, you say."

"More like a groan."

"Or a screech."

"Or sometimes 'aargh?'"

"'Aargh,' that's right. What do doctors call such a thing?'"

"I never heard tell of it," Hunt said. He stood and thought some more.

"You positive you don't want a pinch?"

"I don't dip," Lincoln repeated, and sat down wearily in his rocker.

Just at that moment Cooper decided to jump in the President's lap. He jumped so swiftly that the President rocked far back in his tall rocker.

GRRoooaNNN! went the rocker. And when it came forward again it went *AaaarrrGGH!*

GRRoooaNNN! AaaarrrGGH! is how it went on the big rocks and *Screeeech!* on the little rocks.

Hunt looked at the rocker. His eyebrows twiddled like a hawk flexing its wings.

"Cooper, get down off the President and fetch me that middle-size bottle of medicine and my eye-dropper." Cooper did as asked and poked eagerly in the bag and handed Hunt the bottle. "Aha," Hunt said, "this ought to do it."

"What have you got there, Hunt?" Lincoln said.

"Castor oil," Hunt said, whereupon Lincoln froze stiff and said, "Wait a minute, doc, I don't think I need castor oil!"

"Hush," Hunt said, and got down on his hands and knees and squeezed a few drops of castor oil into each of the dry wooden joints of the rocker. Then he gave Lincoln's rocker a push.

At first the rocker went *GRRooaoaNNN!... AaaarrGGH!* Then it went went *Grnnn Arrrh,* and then *Grnn Rrrgh* and then *grr rrrrr* and then... nothing.

Lincoln rocked in silence.

Hunt re-packed his bag, with Cooper helping. Then he made out a bill for ten thousand dollars for the castor oil and five thousand dollars for Cooper's assistance, knowing that Mary wouldn't pay any of it.

Later, when the doctor and the dog tiptoed out of the study, the President was sound asleep in his rocker.

3.
December Fly

A fly was buzzing around General Abernethy's office all morning.

Cooper snapped at it, but the fly was too quick, causing Cooper's teeth to click in mid-air.

After the fly pestered Cooper, it flew over and pestered Abernethy. Abernethy tried shooing it away. "Shoo!" he said to the fly, but the fly paid no heed. Abernethy then started slapping at it, but the fly was full of tricks, and Abernethy ended up slapping everything but the fly.

Slap.

Bzzz!

Slap!

Bzz. Bzz.

Slap!

Bzzzzz,zzz,zzzzz!

"Confound it! Sergeant!" Abernethy called the guard outside his door. "Sergeant, get in here!"

Sergeant Clancy ran in, dragging his musket. He was an Irish lad from New York.

"What's that fly doing in here, sergeant?" said Abernethy.

"Flying, sir, I'm sure of it," said the sergeant, watching the fly fly around the room. "Why, back home, all our flies would crawl in a crack for the winter and sleep til spring and never bother a soul."

"Well, this fly's awake," Abernethy grumped. "Take care of it."

"Yes sir!" said the sergeant. He unslung his musket. Abernethy's eyes widened, but the sergeant tossed the musket on the divan and seized Abernethy's copy of the *Washington Star*. With a cry, he charged after the fly. But the fly was too nimble.

It zigzagged smartly away. It lit on the ceiling. It lit on the doorknob. It lit on the spittoon. It lit on the general. First his nose, then his bald head. Then it turned three full flips and - *zzzzz,zzzzz!* - landed on the general's desk.

WHAM! the sergeant struck hard with the newspaper, missing the fly but startling Cooper who had been asleep underneath the desk. Cooper jumped up quickly, banging his head so hard on the desk that it knocked over Abernethy's ink bottle and spilled ink, which the fly instantly tracked all over the general's new maps.

"Stop that fly, sergeant!" Abernethy shouted, but the fly flew away as the sergeant spun around with the tattered newspaper.

Bzzz...zzz..zzzz....

The fly buzzed up to the tin ceiling and the sergeant stood on the chair and tried to swat it but he wasn't tall enough, so Abernethy climbed on the chair himself, rolling up the battle maps into a club.

WHAP! WHAP! went Abernethy with the maps, getting ink all over his ceiling and showering the rug and Sergeant Clancy.

"Maybe if we sang a hymn, sir," suggested the sergeant.

Abernethy swung again with the maps but lost his balance and fell backwards on the floor. A table lamp toppled. Cooper took cover behind the divan, and the fly zzzzzzzed away, pursued by Clancy with the newspaper. "Durned thing's getting away!" Abernethy cried.

"No, sir, he ain't," the sergeant said, and chased the fly around the room and swung at it with all his might, but missed, and the fly looped up to the tin ceiling which the sergeant soon filled with dents as he lashed out with the *Star* -- *WHHOPP! WHOPP! WHOOOPPP!* and so forth. But the fly kept hopping out of the way. Small pieces of the *Star* fluttered all over the room, and the front page of the newspaper began tearing from the roll, making the sergeant's club resemble a tattered battle flag.

Zzzzzz...zzzz...! The fly sailed away, and Abernethy once more joined the pursuit with a swagger stick this time, with which he whammed more dents in the ceiling and knocked a portrait of Mr. Jefferson off the wall and brought small pieces of ornamental tin down from the ceiling, which landed with a shower of dust and a long-dead mouse and a peculiar *PLONG!* sound such as tin ceilings make when they are being knocked down.

WHACK! BAM! WHOP!!! Plong! Bzzzzz...zzzz....

BAM! WHOP! Bzzzz! Plong! All accompanied by words such as "drat" and "damnation" and one or two others.

And *PLONG! PLANG!*

Cooper found a safer refuge under a chair that had reputedly been sat on by Governeur Morris during the framing of the Constitution, or at least that's what the dealer said who sold it to the White House, and whose Duncan-Fyfe legs bowed out to give Cooper a view of the battle taking place in front of him, the progress of which was marked by four blueclad legs chasing about, jitterbugging, jumping, changing course, skidding, and dancing, all to the rhythm of oaths and imprecations and an anvil chorus of *WHAMS!* and *WHOPS!* and occasional *WHACKS!* and *PLONGS!* some of which were followed by a tin shower.

The combatants were thus engrossed when Cooper's ears lifted to another sound - the small quick overhead thunks of Mary Lincoln's footsteps in the upstairs hallway and then the quick, determined clop of her feet on the stairs. They went *clop,clop,clop, clop,clop, clop,clop,clop*(pause)*clop,clop,clop*, and were soon coming down the hall. Cooper could imagine the tight curls of her hair springing up and down with each purposeful step.

Clopclopclop.

The combatants now heard it.

"Uh-oh," Abernethy said. The sergeant froze with the newspaper in his hand, or what was left of it.

Mary Lincoln appeared in the doorway. Her eyes were calm, but not her curls. They sprung up and down, as Cooper could see.

PLONG!

One more piece of ceiling fell.

Her eyebrows arched.

"It's a fly," Abernethy explained.

"Flying around, your ladyship," the sergeant added.

Mary held out her hand. The sergeant handed her the rolled-up newspaper, or what was left of it. Mary squinted one eye. She zeroed in on the fly that now cowered on the wall, and - *pow!* - she smacked it.

The small corpse fell to the carpet, its legs sticking theatrically in the air. Mary Lincoln studied it for a moment, thrust the *Star* into Abernethy's hands and marched out.

Cooper remained under the chair.

Abernethy stared at the newspaper. He cleared his throat. "Carry on, sergeant," he said, giving him back the *Star*.

Clancy tried to repair the tattered newspaper, but it was no good. He used it to scoop up the body.

Abernethy did not say two words the rest of the morning. Around noon, he said, "Many people do not seem to realize that flies carry germs."

That afternoon, Abernethy told the sergeant to tuck in his shirttail. Then he bawled him out for having dust on his musket. Then he threatened to court-martial him for not being able to recite the Ten General Orders of the Army.

"They're right on the tip of me tongue," the sergeant claimed.

"Learn those orders by oh-eight hundred," Abernethy ordered.

"Aye aye, sir," Clancy saluted. "Now, would that be oh-eight hundred in the morning, your generalship, or oh-eight-hundred in the evening?"

"Clancy," Abernethy said, "are you by any chance a member of the Navy?"

"Oh, no sir, I never could swim. Me cousin, Liam, now,

he can swim like a fish, so maybe it's him you're thinkin' of, because we do look an awful lot alike. Did you say there's ten of them general orders? Seems like an awful lot."

Abernethy sighed. "All right, sergeant, let's forget the orders."

"All ten? Done! And I'm thankin' you for it."

"Now, sergeant, what about the tin all over the floor?"

"Stacked up just like you told me, sir," Clancy said.

"Any hope of fixing it?"

"Oh, sure, sir. Private O'Rourke from me neighborhood's a fine tinsmith although he's only an apprentice. He says the hardest part will be fixin' the corner pieces with all those little rosettes."

"What about the fly?"

"Oh, we could straighten the legs out a bit, but I'm afraid the poor thing's dead, sir."

4.
Unusual Guest

Flapflapflapflapflap....

Cooper heard it again.
It came from upstairs.
He felt his hair stand on end.
The White House was dark. And still.
And a board creaked.

Creeeeeeeak....

Cooper felt his ears stand up.
Was Old Bill, the night watchman, making his rounds?
Maybe he'd stepped on a loose board.
Cooper hoped so.
It was quiet for a second or two, and then the noise came
again, clear as a bell. Or clear as whatever it was.

Flapflapflapflapflapaflapaflap...!

Coming from upstairs.

Gulp! It wasn't Bill.

Cooper's eyes got big.

Gathering his limbs under him, and his courage, Cooper crept up the stairs. At the top, looking down the long hallway toward Lincoln's study, Cooper could see a faint light coming from the doorway.

Cooper's legs took him toward the study, shaky as they were, it being a known fact that a dog's curiosity will beat the curiosity of any cat when it comes to strange noises.

So, there he was. The door was barely ajar.

Carefully, Cooper peered inside. He wanted to bare his teeth but he was afraid they'd chatter.

The study was empty!

Cooper's eyes bulged toward the flickering oil lamp whose wavering flame threw wicked shadows on the wall. He thought he heard his knees knocking, but he paid no heed, or very little heed, or maybe half a heed, at most, because being part Spitz his nosiness had the upper hand, casting aside all fear, all prudence, all instinct for self-preservation and even propriety, causing his feet to take charge and tiptoe him around Mr. Lincoln's desk to see what was making the noise.

FLAP FLAP FLAPFLAPFLAP!

A growl escaped Cooper's throat. His eyes fastened on the tall green window shade that should have been covering the window behind Mr. Lincoln's rocker. But it was up at the top of the window. It was spinning fitfully on its wooden spindle and slapping its gold-threaded pull-string against the window frame.

Flapflapflapflapflap!

Cooper watched as the shade spun and flapped for some time. Then came a muffled voice.

"Mon Dieu!" the voice said with unmistakable

annoyance. "Would you le mind, Monsieur Coo-pair, to be of some assistance instead of standing there like an idi-ot? This is most inconvenient!"

Cooper was so surprised to be addressed by the shade that his tongue fell out of his mouth. His eyebrows wriggled. His left hind foot rose to scratch a flea, not bothering to verify first whether he was standing or sitting. Since he was standing, he almost fell over.

Flapaflapaflapaflapa-flap!

"Sacre Bleu!" the voice despaired in French. "I am getting dizzy from all this turning around. Do something brilliant at once, Coo-pair! Pullez le shade!"

Cooper leapt on Mr. Lincoln's rocker and stood on his hind legs so that he could get the shade tassel in his teeth. He pulled it down carefully, allowing the French general to tumble out in full dress uniform.

Cooper felt his hair stand on end again. He could see straight through the Frenchman, whose swallowtail military coat was deep blue, with gold brush epaulettes on the shoulders. The coat opened in front to show a gleaming vest crossed by a red sash. Cooper was surprised that the Frenchman had two black eyes and assorted other scrapes and bruises, making him look much the worse for wear.

"That crazy woman almost killed me," the visitor complained, dusting himself off. "It is absolutely the last time I ever impersonate a fly, although it was quite brilliant, I thought."

The visitor glanced hotly at the shade, then stood for a moment staring at Cooper, one hand brushing aside the stringy hair that had fallen across his forehead.

Cooper crept as close as he dared. He stretched his nose, or, rather, his neck. He tried not to sniff too loudly.

The ghost gazed at the dog, bemused. He allowed his large head to droop until his chin almost rested on his chest. "So, Coop-air! So now we meet. And yet you are so impolite that you are smelling me. You want to see if I am real or not?"

The visitor clasped his hands behind his back, fixing

the dog with a dark gaze. "Reality," the visitor said, "it is a trés complicated concept."

Cooper followed the visitor over to the pile of war maps that Abernethy had sent Lincoln. Carefully the visitor picked out the map that Abernethy had taped back together after chasing the fly with it. Donning a set of spectacles that Mr. Lincoln had left lying on his desk, the Frenchman sat poring over the map, pausing after awhile to mutter to himself and shake his head.

"They didn't see my fly tracks," the visitor complained. "I didn't make them big enough, I suppose."

The visitor found a pen and an ink bottle and looked for something to write on. "Coopair," he said, "I must give you a most urgent message. Trés sérieux, how they say. And you must give it to Monsieur Lincoln, for the Union itself is in grave danger - "

Suddenly the ghost looked up. Cooper was startled; he had heard nothing, but now he lifted his ears and could hear the faint stirrings of footsteps. There were footsteps plainly now on the stairs.

"Ten thousand curses!" the ghost said, rolling the map up quickly and disappearing into the shade, which flew again to the top of the window.

Flapaflapaflapflap!

The footsteps were right outside the study now, and in a moment Mr. Lincoln appeared in his nightgown, wearing a nightcap and carrying a candle. Old Bill followed, his pistol at the ready. Mary followed in her robe.

"Great Caesar's ghost," sighed Mr. Lincoln, "it's only you, Cooper."

The shade still flapped. Mrs. Lincoln looked at it. "What's wrong with that thing?"

Cooper watched nervously as the President got the shade tassel and tried to pull it down.

"Guess it's stuck. I'll have to get it fixed."

"Can't be fixed when they do that," Mary shook her head. "Take it down and we'll give it to the junk man."

"I'll have somebody take care of it in the morning," the

President said.

Mary left, and Old Bill uncocked his pistol and left, too, just as General Abernethy showed up, his sword buckled over his robe.

"Everything all right, Mr. President?"

"I guess so. Looks like the window shade flew up and made a racket. I expect it woke Cooper up and he thought it was a bugger just like I did."

Abernethy reached down and scratched Cooper's head. "With old Coop awake, we don't have to worry."

Although Mr. Lincoln drank liquor only on special occasions, he decided this was one of them. He found a brandy bottle and two glasses and poured himself and Abernethy a little Napoleon.

5.
The Christmas Party

Cooper saw the Christmas tree walking down the hall. It was walking on two legs. The legs belonged to Ratliff, one of the servants. Mrs. Lincoln was behind Ratliff. She was fussing. She said it was the ugliest tree she ever saw. She wanted Ratliff to throw it out.

"Missus Chief Justice Bantom give this tree to Mr. Lincoln," Ratliff said for the third or fourth time.

"I don't care," Mary Lincoln said. "I won't have it."

So Ratliff put the tree out with the trash.

Later that morning, Mr. Hay saw it. He told Ratliff to bring it back at once. Ratliff explained that Mrs. Lincoln had ordered him to throw it out. Hay told Ratliff to put it in his office and that he'd speak to the President.

Later, Mr. Lincoln told Ratliff to put the tree in the East Room.

Mary Lincoln saw the tree in the East Room and started threatening to fire Ratliff for not throwing it away. Ratliff went to see Mr. Hay who went to the President who spoke to Mrs. Lincoln. Mr. Lincoln said he could not afford to offend the Supreme Court just then, particularly Chief Justice Bantom. Mrs. Lincoln told Ratliff to take it away anyway, that what the Chief Justice thought was neither here nor there because she was not the only person in Washington who could not stand Marcia Bantom and that she could not understand, at all, why Mrs. Hannibal Hamlin, the vice President's wife, could stand her when it was so obvious to everyone in Washington that Mrs. Bantom was over-fond of every man she met.

Cooper was listening to all this. He got up and left. Ratliff had to keep standing there with the tree.

Mrs. Lincoln told Ratliff to leave the tree where it was. Mr. Lincoln went back to his office and shut the door. Mrs. Lincoln went upstairs and shut the door.

Later, Mrs. Lincoln came downstairs again and called Ratliff and made him move the tree to a different corner of the room.

6.
Cinnamon

The business about the Christmas tree happened on the afternoon of the party. Mrs. Lincoln always got upset when she was expecting guests, which is why nobody was surprised when she tried to fire Ratliff. Ratliff told the man who was there to fix the window shade that he could not be fired, because he was a free man is why. Mrs. Lincoln overheard this and marched out of her room and marched back down the hall, march, march, march, then marched back to her room and went in and slammed the door. Ratliff went down to the kitchen and got a cup of coffee from Florence and told her all about it.

"Um-hm," Florence said.

Later on, Mrs. Lincoln came to the kitchen and told Florence she had changed her mind about firing Ratliff and had also changed her mind about serving anisette cookies at the party and wanted sweet potato pie instead. Florence told Mrs. Lincoln she couldn't make sweet potato pie because the White House didn't have a speck of cinnamon. Mrs. Lincoln raised her voice.

She wanted to know who was responsible for keeping the White House amply supplied with cinnamon, and Florence said she had ordered cinnamon twice, but the man in the store said there was no cinnamon in all of Washington because the Confederates stole it with their blockade, and stole the nutmeg, too.

Mrs. Lincoln said, "Florence, there is no such thing as a Confederate blockade. It is *we* who are blockading *them*."

"I don't know nothin' bout that," Florence said. "I just know we ain't got no cinnamon."

"Well use vanilla or something!" Mrs. Lincoln said, and spun on her heels and stalked out of the kitchen.

Florence just stood there staring, with her hands on her hips. She muttered a few things, wiped her hands on her apron, picked up a pot, threw it down, and rummaged in the spices.

"I can use vanilla," she called out, hoping Mrs. Lincoln could hear her, "but it ain't gon' be fit to eat."

No answer.

"That woman!" Florence said to Cooper, who had just wandered into the kitchen. "She gets herself all worked up about some no 'count Christmas tree and then she wants some sweet potato pie without cinnamon."

Florence wondered if she could borrow a little cinnamon from somebody and sent Ratliff out to see if he could borrow some. Ratliff came back in less than an hour with enough cinnamon to bake ten pies.

"Miz Bantom say you welcome to more, if you ain't got any," Ratliff said.

Florence looked at the cinnamon.

"Ratliff," she said, "you did not get this here cinnamon from Miz Bantom."

"Course I did," Ratliff said.

"No, you didn't!" Florence raised her eyebrows, pointing at Mrs. Lincoln's room overhead.

"Oh," Ratliff said.

Florence lowered her voice. "Miz Lincoln find out about this cinnamon, she have a hissy and I ain't got time for none of her hissies right now. I got pies to bake."

Ratliff went out of the kitchen with Cooper. They walked

around the house to see that everything was in order. Cooper could hear Mr. Lincoln asking Mrs. Lincoln where to find his collar buttons. Then Mrs. Lincoln was asking Mr. Lincoln if he thought her blue shoes looked all right with her gray dress, and Mr. Lincoln said he thought they looked fine. Mrs. Lincoln said she thought the black shoes looked better and Mr. Lincoln said he thought the black shoes looked fine.

Mrs. Lincoln would say something and Mr. Lincoln would say, "Uh-huh."

Talktalk.

"Uh-huh."

Talktalktalk.

"Um-hmm."

Talkydetalk.

"Uh-huh."

Talktalk.

"Uh-huh."

"What on earth do you mean, Father?" Mary Lincoln said at last.

"Mean by what?"

"By what you just said."

"What did I just say?"

"You just said 'uh-huh.'"

"Well, I guess I was just agreeing with you."

"Tell me what I just said."

"You mean you don't know?"

"You know very well what I mean, Abraham!"

Mrs. Lincoln said she thought Mr. Lincoln only said "uh-huh" to disguise the fact that he was paying absolutely no attention to anything she said, and it made her mad to be agreed with all the time.

Mr. Lincoln was about to say "uh-huh," but stopped himself. He wondered if she'd seen his turquoise cufflinks, which she had threatened several times to throw out and was so adamant about it that he wondered if she had not, in fact, thrown them out. This got him riled. "You can wear whatever shoes you feel like wearing," he said so sharply that she dropped her pearls, "and I can pick my own cufflinks." Whereupon he went over and rummaged in the other dresser, muttering that he still couldn't find them. Nor his tie pin. Which incidentally he didn't much care for, either.

Cooper and Ratliff went downstairs. The other servants were building a big fire in the fireplace. Marcia Bantom's fir tree gave the room a Christmas-y smell, to go with the cinnamon.

Soon the room was full of people.

7.
More Party

Oh, my Lord, she dyed it red!"

Cooper woke up as Mrs. Stanton tittered this to Mrs. Hay in the East Room. Cooper looked where the women were looking. He saw Mrs. Bantom at the door. Marcia Bantom was saying hello to Mr. and Mrs. Lincoln. She was a head taller than her husband, Chief Justice Bantom, and looked elegant in a green silk dress with her hair, pale orange, above a lacey collar.

The women looked on as Marcia Bantom curtsied to the President, her tawny temple-curls bobbing alongside her cheeks.

"Oh yoo-hoo, Marcia! Yoo-hoo!" Mrs. Stanton waved her fan at Mrs. Bantom.

The young woman glanced around, smiled, and brought a hitch to every conversation in the room in which men were participants as she strode toward the horsey wife of the war secretary. Cooper felt a thrill as Mrs. Bantom touched his head in passing.

"Marcia!" Mrs. Stanton said immediately, fluttering her

fan, blushing, "you are just too beautiful."

"And we love your hair," said Mrs. Hay, getting an immediate, covert elbow in the ribs from Marguerite Abernethy.

"Why thank you," smiled Marcia, looking sweetly at Mrs. Stanton. "And I've always admired your lip rouge."

Mrs. Stanton sucked in her breath, not sure what to think.

Flapflapflapflap flap!

Behind Marcia Bantom the chief justice approached, strutting stiffly like an old bent rooster. He carried a beribboned poinsettia.

"For your hospital, Mrs. Hay," the chief justice crowed, peering curiously at the young woman. Mrs. Hay was dark-complected, half-Creole according to some, her dark eyes undercut by circles nearly as dark, giving her a serious look. "I've got other poinsettias in the hall, not quite so large, for all the rest of you ladies," the chief justice said.

"What a beautiful plant," Marguerite Abernethy exclaimed. "You do have a green thumb I declare, Judge Banty, er, Bantom."

"Oh, this is all Marcia's doings," said Bantom. "She's wonderful. I've never seen a woman who could make a thing grow like she can."

Mrs. Stanton and Mrs. Hay blinked.

General Abernethy, his florid face glowing, marched up to Mrs. Bantom and swept down in a low bow and kissed her hand without once taking his eyes off her. "My dear," Abernethy said, "you are ravishing!"

Marcia laughed, "And you are a shameless rogue, sir," she said. "How ever does your wife manage?"

Marguerite took it as a compliment, laughing and pinching her husband playfully, but not all that playfully.

"May I be a rogue also?" Mr. Hay stepped forward and took Mrs. Bantom's hand in turn.

"A rogue does not ask permission, John," said Marcia, slapping him on the back of the head with her fan as he studied her pretty knuckles.

"Then I withdraw my request, madam."

"You may proceed."

"Ah." Smack. Hay kissed Marcia's hand very lightly, inhaling the lilac smell of her knuckles. He puckered up for another kiss but missed her knuckles entirely and kissed his own thumb as she withdrew.

Secretary Stanton jostled to be next but was intercepted by Mrs. Stanton who, showing her teeth, suggested they retire to the hall to view the other lovely poinsettias the Bantoms had brought.

Meanwhile across the room, Mr. Lincoln had started to play the piano. General Abernethy, seeing an opening, stepped up again and extended his arm to Marcia Bantom and suggested they sing Christmas carols. Mrs. Hay repossessed Mr. Hay, firmly taking his arm and steering him over to the group at the piano in time to hear Judge Bantom say, "have you all heard Marcia play?"

The group took up the cry, calling on Mrs. Bantom to sit with Mr. Lincoln and play a duet. Mrs. Bantom protested that she enjoyed the President's playing more than her own, but sat with Mr. Lincoln anyway and began to finger the keys, drawing a beautiful sound from the piano. They sang 'O Tannenbaum.'

Cooper came and sprawled near, keeping an eye on Mrs. Bantom. She leaned and swayed as she began to play, her hands moving confidently over the keys and her small feet tapping expertly on the pedals. Cooper was close enough to see the tiny veins in Mrs. Bantom's ankles.

As the last note sounded, to a clap and a cheer, Mr. Lincoln rose from beside Mrs. Bantom and bowed to her deeply, as if to concede the bench to her.

"Oh, no," Mrs. Bantom demurred, "You must stay, sir! We must play our duet!" But the President only smiled and shook his head. The crowd wondered, of course, what that duet might be, and applauded and cheered until Marcia Bantom, cheeks flushed, sat down with the President and fingered the keys, murmuring "no, really," a protestation that did not stop some of the wives from forming battle lines behind her.

"Just listen to her!'" Mrs. Stanton whispered to Mary Lincoln, behind a fan while pretending to applaud. "'No, really! No, really!' Hah. She loves every minute of it!"

Abernethy spilled brandy as he waved his glass around, calling for 'The Twelve Days of Christmas.'

"Well," Marcia tested the keys again "it really has been ages."

After a false start, Marcia soared into the tune, playing with strength and jaunty confidence. They all sang, every one of them, including the President. And even Mrs. Lincoln who had not wanted to. At all.

Later, Mrs. Hay and Mrs. Lincoln stood at the edge of the crowd, talking. "Did I see the Stantons leave?" Mary whispered to Mrs. Hay.

"I think they went into the hall to look at the poinsettias," Mrs. Hay whispered.

"Oh yes," nodded Mary Lincoln. "And give her a chance to box his ears, I imagine."

As the party was breaking up, Mary Lincoln told Mrs. Bantom for the third time how much she enjoyed getting the beautiful Christmas tree.

8.
Miz Fesmire

You've got the day off," John Hay told Mr. Lincoln.

"What?" Abe was startled. "No such thing, John."

"There's only one appointment on your book, and I cancelled it."

"Cancelled it with who?"

"The dreaded Miz Fesmire."

"She must not have heard," the President said, "because she's already waiting out in the hall."

"Why did she want to see you, sir?"

"I don't know for sure. She didn't say when she wrote me."

"And you gave her an appointment anyway?" Hay raised a brow.

"She sort of hinted what she wanted."

"What kind of hint?"

"She said she wanted to slap my jaws."

"And you still agreed to see her?"

"Well, she could scarcely slap my jaws without an

appointment, Hay."

"I assume it's just her manner of speaking, sir, but what does she really want, do you think?"

"It's sure to be some kind of blackmail. I heard she's threatening not to support me for re-election, and wants to remind me she controls sixteen votes in Dayton, Ohio."

"Seems like you're putting up with a lot just for sixteen votes, Mr. President."

"Well, it could be something else," Lincoln sighed, "whatever it is, the election's going to be close and we'll need every vote we can get."

Hay twiddled his pen. He looked at his large watch, then at his small watch, and then muttered something that Mr. Lincoln could not quite hear, and went and got the dreaded Miz Fesmire.

"Have a seat, Miz Fesmire," smiled the President.

"I prefer to stand. This won't take long."

"Just let me say it's a delight to see you, as always!" The President offered her a glass of water. "And how is your husband faring since I appointed him postmaster in your fair city, as I see here in my Patronage Book - "

"That was clean back a year ago," Miz Fesmire interrupted.

"Yes, so it was," agreed Mr. Lincoln. "But it looks like I also made you assistant postmaster at a nice salary, isn't that so?"

"That was six months ago," Miz Fesmire said.

"Uh-huh," agreed Lincoln. "And I also appointed your oldest son to West Point, just like you asked me."

"That was back when I got the post office job!" said Miz Fesmire.

"And I also got your youngest son a draft exemption for flat feet?"

"That was months ago!" Miz Fesmire said.

"And it looks like I got your other son appointed as an assistant horse inspector for the Army," Lincoln said.

Miz Fesmire frowned. "That was over four months ago!"

"Well, let's just look at the big picture, Miz Fesmire: Didn't I appoint your oldest son to West Point and get your youngest son a draft exemption from the Army for flat feet, and get your other son a job as an assistant military livestock inspector, and get your husband appointed as a postmaster, and get you a job as an assistant postmaster with a nice salary?" Lincoln said.

"All right," Miz Fesmire said, "but what have you done for me lately?"

9.
The Author

Mr. Lincoln peeped through the keyhole at his visitor. He peeped and then Cooper peeped.

Secretary Seward declined to stoop so low as to peep. He sat in the President's chair, twiddling his thumbs. "Why doesn't that man leave?"

"That's what I said."

"You have to say it to him, not to me."

"Dang it, Seward...."

Lincoln peeped again, hoping. The lobby was dark. The clock struck seven.

"Look, sir," Seward said, "If you don't want to see this man, simply tell him to go away. We've already got more postmasters than postage stamps."

"Oh, he's not looking for a job," Lincoln despaired.

"What else then?"

"He's from my publisher."

"A literary man?" Seward got up, intrigued.

"Take a look for yourself," Lincoln stepped aside.

Seward moseyed to the keyhole and grasped the tails of his frock coat so he could bend down and peep.

"There must be some mistake," Seward fumbled for a cigar. "The only personage I see in the vestibule is a rough character in a derby, digging wax out of his ears with an ice pick. I do not see a literary man."

Lincoln groaned. "I didn't say he was literary man, Seward. I said he's from my publisher. And I have to pay him a thousand dollars, or else."

Seward's gimlet eyes lit with delight. "Why, Lincoln, you're like every low-down weaseling excuse-making writer who ever lived! You accepted a handsome advance from your publisher to write your memoirs and you haven't delivered! Am I right?"

Lincoln nodded miserably. "The publisher wants my first five chapters - or the thousand dollars back."

"And I'll make a guess and say you've written just three," Seward said.

"Sort of."

"OK, just two, then."

Lincoln moaned.

"Don't tell me just one!"

Lincoln lay on the floor alongside Cooper.

"Please say you've written at least one!" Seward searched his pockets for a match.

"Uh..."

"Surely you don't mean - one page?!"

"Uhhh," Lincoln said.

"Great jumping catfish man, not a single word?!"

Lincoln sat up with a silly grin.

"Splendid!" Seward lit his cigar and stretched out on Lincoln's couch. "A publisher," he reminisced, blowing a smoke ring, "once advanced me five hundred dollars for a memoir I never got around to writing. I thought it would be sufficient to explain that I wasn't inspired."

"And the publisher was very understanding and gave you more time?"

"Well, no," Seward beat out a small fire in his beard. "He

sent two of his literary men with brass knuckles and I immediately wrote them a check. So, my advice is to return the money."

"I can't," Lincoln drew a breath, "I already spent it."

"On what?"

"Mrs. Lincoln."

"Oh."

Seward kept puffing his cigar. "Well, don't let the fact that you spent it stand in your way. Write them a check anyway. That's what I did."

"You wrote your publisher a hot check?"

"Flaming."

"Who was your publisher?"

"Something like 'Cadaver & Koot' or 'Cavender and Kooties.' One of those publisher names."

"You mean Cavendish & Koople?

"That's the one," Seward blew another smoke ring.

"Dang, Seward," Lincoln said, "that's my publisher, too!"

Seward began beating at a fresh emergency in his beard as Cooper trotted over to the door and watched a note being slid underneath.

"What is it, Coop?" Lincoln gulped.

Cooper fetched it to him.

Seward sat up. "What's the news, Lincoln?"

"It says, 'I know you're both in there!'" Lincoln said.

"Only one thing to do now, Mr. President!" Seward declared. "We go on the offensive! We put our foot down and take a stand."

"A stand on what?"

"On principle!"

"Well," Lincoln said. "what principle do you think we ought to stand on? Just to start with."

"Well," Seward ruminated, flicking a spark off his shirt, "this literary man must be reminded, first of all, that you are the President and I am not just any Tom, Dick or Harry! I am the United States secretary of war!"

"Of state, Seward," Lincoln said. "You're secretary of state."

"My bad," Seward said. "We remind him that you are

the President and I am the United States of America secretary of state and therefore entitled to deference as third in line to the presidency!"

"Fifth in line, actually," Lincoln said.

"Fifth? The secretary of war is fifth in line!"

"The secretary of war is not in line."

"I always thought he was fifth."

"No, you're fifth. Or fourth."

"That's what you said, I'm fifth."

"Dang it, Seward. Get a grip. You're fourth, remember that."

"So, who's third?"

"The Senate president pro-tem is third. The vice president is second."

"Then who's first?"

"There isn't any first. I'm first. I'm the President."

"You can't be first if you're already the President!" Seward said. "If you're first, I must be third and not fourth. Anyway, if I were you, Lincoln, I'd march out there and remind that literary man of a thing or two."

"Good advice, Seward."

"Remind him that you are the commander in chief with a two million man army at your disposal and that you are utterly and totally ruthless and have not hesitated to wage total war against a third of the country, arrest insurrectionists on the streets of Baltimore, suspend habeas corpus, and throw an entire state legislature in jail and threatened to clap the Supreme Court in irons, and that you have in your itchy fingers the keys to every gruesome federal penitentiary in the country - I'd emphasize that point if I were you - while he, on the other hand, is a mere knuckle-dragging literary man."

Lincoln blinked. "I think he'll still say I owe the publisher five chapters or the thousand dollars back," Lincoln added. "And what about you, Seward, and that hot check you wrote?"

Cooper looked from one man to another.

A few minutes later, Seward and Lincoln were seen by a guard, climbing out a window and down a trellis to the back lawn.

***

Lincoln was back at his desk. He toiled in shirtsleeves and suspenders, his wastebasket running over. Wadded-up balls of paper were all over the floor. Again, he dipped his pen in the inkwell and started over.

With malice toward few, if any, and charity for the rest –

It still didn't seem right.

"Durn."

He wadded up the paper and threw it on the floor where Cooper chewed it to small bits while Lincoln started over. "How did that opening phrase go, Coop?" muttered the President. "The first one I wrote?"

Cooper nosed around the floor and found Lincoln the right piece of paper.

Lincoln straightened it out.

Copying the first words onto a smooth new sheet, he let his pen fairly fly over the paper.

With malice toward none, his pen scratched the words out. The pen seemed to move by itself. *...With malice toward none and charity for all...* the words were flowing now! They were powerful! Direct! Visionary! The kind of cadence that would go down in history!

History! Think of it!

Beads of sweat popped out on Lincoln's brow. *And charity for all.* The words were magic now, racing to the tip of his pen from some deep wellspring beyond the resources of ordinary mortals!

Quickly he dipped his pen and made sure of the phrase that all mankind would remember from now on -

So with malice toward none, and charity for all, he hesitated and thought of his publisher. *And in sickness and in health, forsaking all others, til death do us part....*

"Dang!"

He threw the paper on the floor and started again.

10.
Larceny Joe

"How's the book coming, Mr. President?" asked John Hay.

"Thought I'd just write a speech instead," the President said.

Cooper was chewing wads of paper on the floor.

"Is it all right for Cooper to eat your drafts, sir?" Hay frowned at the dog.

"I don't think he can hurt them any," Lincoln groaned.

Hay nodded. "In case you need a break, sir, I brought the patronage book. You've got an appointment to make."

"What hungry mouth are we feeding this time?"

"Joseph Worthington Sprague III of Indiana."

"Larceny Joe from Kokomo?"

"Indianapolis, sir."

Lincoln slumped. "You know, Hay, what I said about the man who was so crooked that the only thing he wouldn't steal was a red-hot stove?"

"The governor of Pennsylvania?"

"The difference between him and Larceny Joe is that

63

Larceny Joe would steal a red-hot stove."

"He just might," Mr. Hay said. "But he does control the Indiana delegation."

"Which I need."

"Which you need. Yes sir."

"And he's out in the hall right now?"

"Afraid so, sir."

"Well?"

"Lord, Hay, I think I can find a way to finance the war, but I don't know if I can finance all these politicians."

"Yes sir."

"What jobs do we have left?"

"Ulysses Grant has several openings for buck private in Mississippi."

"What else?"

"How about a job catching mad-dogs in Moline?" Hay leafed through the book. "Or collecting Customs in Charleston, South Carolina."

"Behind Confederate lines?"

"I admit it could be a problem, sir. But if Larceny objects to the inconvenience, we could move the office to Rochester, Minnesota."

"I never heard of a Customs office in Rochester, Hay."

"That's because there's no port there. Larceny wouldn't have to do a bit of work even if there was any work to do, which there isn't. And since everybody in Minnesota is either a Swede or a Norwegian, all he'd have to do is say 'you betcha' and eat pickled herring."

***

Hay went out and gave Larceny the job.

"That takes care of it," he sighed to Lincoln.

"Anybody else out there?"

"Just one other fellow. The blind man."

"Who?"

64

"The blind man. I thought you knew him."

"No," the President said slowly. "I thought you did."

Hay shook his head.

Lincoln went over and stooped to the keyhole again. "He does look familiar, but I can't place him. He's got patches over both eyes and a white cane. Did I promise him a job, Hay?"

"Not that I can tell," Hay said, flipping pages in the appointments book.

"Am I supposed to give him an award?"

"Might just be," Hay snapped his fingers and went over to the Awards Drawer and rummaged around in the Awards. "Well," he said, "here's one for the King of England in case he ever shows up. And here's one for the French ambassador to keep him from getting huffy if we honor the King of England. And here's a great big award for Jay Cooke, the banker."

"Great big award for what?" Lincoln asked.

"It's not too specific, Mr. President."

"I guess we better keep it that way 'til Chase lets us know. I think Cooke promised to unload a bunch of Chase's newfangled war bonds on Wall Street, but he's being a little shifty on how many he's sold. Who else are we honoring?"

"Well," Hay said, "we've got an all-purpose award here that still doesn't have a name on it."

"Dust it off while I think," Lincoln said. "You say it's an all-purpose award?"

"We could have it say something like 'to so-and-so with humble gratitude for whatever it is we're being grateful for.'"

"We're bound to need it, but we better make it say something else because we already used 'humble gratitude' three or four times. Word gets out. How about 'heartfelt gratitude?'"

"'Heartfelt' is on Cooke's award, sir," Hay said.

Lincoln held up a hand. "Before we go 'round and around, Hay, let's find out who that blind man is that's sitting out there."

"Yes sir. I might have to ask."

"Name's right on the tip of my tongue." Lincoln said.

"Woof!" Cooper said. "Woof!"

The President's eyes brightened. He snapped his fingers and sprang out of his chair. "Woof - that's right!" he said, tousling Cooper's head.

Hay looked bewildered.

"Octavius Woof," chortled the President. "W-o-l-f! Our triple-double-agent from Natchez. I didn't recognize him with the patches on his eyes."

"A Natchez Rebel - here?"

Before Hay could say another word, Lincoln flung open the door.

"Captain Woof!"

"Mr. President!" Triple-Double-Agent Wolf rose and turned his head in Lincoln's direction. "Suh!"

Hay watched apprehensively as Wolf took several short steps toward the President, groping with a hand and shifting his white cane with the other. Lincoln gave Wolf his arm and showed him a seat on the divan while Hay sat in the rocker. Cooper sniffed Captain Wolf politely as Mr. Lincoln poured mugs of tea and started swapping riverboat yarns with the visitor.

Wolf, Hay gathered, had been a boat captain on the Mississippi. How he'd gotten acquainted with Lincoln wasn't clear, but apparently it was when Lincoln was lawyering for the Illinois Central Railroad.

"So," Mr. Lincoln said at last, "you joined the Rebel side."

"I'm afraid so, yes suh," the captain said.

"But then you joined our side!"

"Yes suh. A double agent."

"You intended to spy on us?"

"Yes suh, but then I turned around and spied on them."

"Then what?"

"They caught me, so I had to turn around and spy on the Union, or else."

"So, you spied back on us again?"

"Yes suh, but I was supposed to get caught spying on you and pretend to turn around and spy on the Rebs when I was really spying on the Union for the Rebs, but then I'd be a Union spy triple-spying on the Rebs."

"Wait a minute, Woof, how do we know you're not a triple-double agent spying for them?"

"Cross my heart, suh!"

***

That night, Cooper sat in the hall scratching a flea.

He paused with one hind foot in the air, watching a shadow pass back and forth in the President's study.

But it wasn't the President, it was Hay. Pacing back and forth.

Then...*clomp clomp clomp clomp!* Lincoln came down the hall in his nightshirt to see what was going on.

"What in the world's got into you?" the President asked Hay.

"Sir," Hay said, "This Woof thing is a farce. We can't give an award to a quadruple-triple-double-agent who might turn out to be somebody who is not who he says he's not when he might turn out to be just the opposite."

Lincoln said, "You're right, Hay. So how can we make sure?"

"That he's who he says he is?"

"Or isn't."

Lincoln poked a finger in the air. "Only one way to find out, Hay! Get Woof and bring him down."

Hay went and got Wolf. Lincoln sat Wolf down on the settee and took the rocker himself.

"Where's your chaw, Woof?"

Wolf reached in his pocket and held out a plug of tobacco. Lincoln took it.

"One nation, indivisible," the President said, solemnly taking a chaw and handing the plug back to Wolf.

Wolf took a chaw and handed the plug to Hay.

Hay looked at it.

"Go on," Lincoln said, "you're the witness. You have to chaw."

Hay bit off a piece.

They all sat and chawed. Mr. Lincoln started to give Cooper a chaw, but Cooper hid behind the desk.

Next day, after the President and Wolf chawed and

spit and swannied and declared three times, Wolf left with the heartfelt appreciation award tucked under his arm. Or it might have been the sincere appreciation award.

***

All was silent in the mansion that night. A time that any writer could be inspired.

Striking while the iron was hot, Lincoln drew out a sheet of paper and started once more on his memoirs.

With malice toward none, Lincoln wrote, *and charity for all, for one nation, indivisible...in liberty and in health, for richer or for poorer, with amber waves of grain....*

"Dang."

He threw the paper down and started over.

11.
Intelligence Intercepts

Stanton hurried over from the War Office to give Mr. Lincoln a midnight briefing. His square spectacles jiggled as he ran. He ran as fast as he could, which was not very fast, but very fast for Stanton. His secretary had to huff and puff to keep up with him, her dimply arms loaded with intelligence papers - Confederate communiques confiscated in the Carolinas, Lee letters latched onto in Lynchburg, telegrams tapped in Tupelo, and most secret of all, a pile of penciled parchment procured by Stanton's personal plant on General McClellan's staff.

Stanton was dismayed to find Seward already sitting in Lincoln's office.

"My report can wait, Mr. President," Stanton said nervously, eyeing Seward.

"Nonsense, Edwin!" Seward said, lighting a cigar. "We're all gentlemen here! Now, whose mail have you been reading this time?"

"Mr. President - !"

"Now boys," Lincoln wagged a finger. "Go on, with your report, Stanton."

"Well," Stanton said, reading from a stack of messages, "we've had another Irish draft riot in New York."

"Uh-huh," the President said. "Go on."

"And the Germans in St. Louis burnt you in effigy."

"Better than the alternative," Lincoln smiled wanly.

"Anybody got a match?" Seward said. "My cigar's gone out."

"Do you have to smoke that thing?" Stanton said.

"I'll open a window," Lincoln said. "Keep reading, Mr. Secretary."

Stanton nodded.

"The New York Times has called you a baboon again."

"How did they spell baboon this time?"

"B-a-b-b-o-o-n."

"I've seen it spelled so many different ways that I don't know which way is right," Lincoln said.

"I think it has one b," Seward stroked a cigar ash from his beard.

Lincoln took off his glasses and polished them on his shirt sleeve. "I think you're right, Seward. It's like spelling banana. You have to know when to stop."

"Is something burning in here?" Stanton said as Seward beat on his pants to put out a small fire.

"What's next, Stanton? Lincoln said.

Stanton straightened up his square spectacles and assumed a grave expression. "The polls, Mr. President, are against us."

"Who cares who the Poles are against?" Seward tapped an ash, "as long as they stay in Poland!"

"Polls, Seward, not Poles. And for your information, Professor Muntlepech guarantees that his poll of voters is one hundred percent scientific and accurate."

"Hah!" Seward said. "I'll give you a one hundred percent scientific poll right now. I just asked me, myself, and I what I think about polls and I think that I think polls are a hundred percent bull."

Lincoln sighed, "All right, but let's please be civil if you don't mind. I want to be on your side on this, Stanton, but I do wonder myself how your Professor Mumbletepeg is so sure he's right."

"Muntlepech," Stanton said. "Professor Muntlepech! And he has 99.23614 percent confidence in his calculations because he uses nothing but the latest integrals to prove that pie are square when served exponentially infinitesimally, which allows him to reciprocate cube roots differentially. That's how."

"Oh," Lincoln said.

"So that clears it up," Stanton declared.

"But what does his latest poll actually show?" Lincoln asked.

"Well, sir, it's trouble. It shows that eighty percent of the most likely voters are wishy-washy regarding the direction you're taking the country. Thirty-eight percent are more wishy than washy, but the washy ones are inclined to vote you out of office right now while the wishy ones are still wishy."

Lincoln nodded thoughtfully. "Well what are we supposed to do about it?"

"Nothing," Stanton said. "Just take it into account."

"Oh, I see," Seward snorted, closing his eyes and stretching out in his chair.

"What are you doing?" Stanton said.

"Taking the wishy-washy poll into account," Seward said.

"All right, now," Lincoln sighed again. "What else does Professor Mumbletepeg tell us, Mr. Stanton?"

"Well," Stanton smoothed the papers, "you have to watch your negatives, sir. Fortunately, when the professor took a deep dive into the underlying demographics on that one, he found that your negatives are less positive than they appear. Pi analysis minus the cube root of the perimeter of the isosceles shows that half the voters are of above-average intelligence while the other half are below-average, and that half of the below-averages are way below-average or way, way below-average. The good news is that the 'belows' don't make much difference because eighty percent of them don't understand the question and the other twenty percent are split between un-decideds, don't-cares, and the ones who believe you really are a baboon and would like to see a picture."

"What else did Mumbletepeg find?" Lincoln sighed.

"Well," Stanton said, "twenty-five percent of the likely voters vote while drunk, twenty percent vote while half-drunk, fifteen percent can't afford to get drunk but would like to, and another ten percent are insane or undecided. Of course there's a little overlap in those figures."

Seward nodded. "What I think I'm hearing from this Mumbletepeg report is that the President can appeal to the ten percent of voters who are intelligent, well informed and not drunk or crazy and will lose by a landslide, or he can appeal to the majority and win."

Cooper barked.

"Do I smell smoke?" Lincoln said.

Seward jumped from his chair, beating at his vest that seemed to be on fire. Lincoln joined in, swatting away with the Mumbletepeg report which set it afire as well. Stanton tried to grab the report, but it hit the floor in a shower of sparks.

"That's my only copy!" cried Stanton, as Cooper rushed in and lifted a leg on it. Sssss.

Stanton left for his office in a huff. Seward left to change his vest and get a fresh cigar. Lincoln spread what was left of the report on his desk and tried to read it.

"I think it says 'four percent approval,' but I can't tell what it's approving," Lincoln said to Cooper. Cooper got up on a chair and looked, but he couldn't tell, either.

12.
Reconnaissance

Abernethy finally got so mad at General McClellan that he rode a horse out to see him. Cooper trotted along.

The whole way, Abernethy imagined the things he was going to say. "Sawed-off little two-bit runt," Abernethy muttered. Mutter mutter mutter.

"Sir?" said Lieutenant Harkness, riding along in tandem, carrying the map case.

"Two-bit banty-rooster...."

Cooper barked.

At McClellan's headquarters, a polished honor guard snapped smartly to present arms, with bayonets fixed, as Abernethy trotted up.

"Reggggimmeent! Tennnn-hut!" cried a sergeant major. McClellan touched a gauntlet to his hat.

Abernethy reined in his horse and, attempting to dismount smartly, caught a spur on his saddle blanket and landed in a somersault at McClellan's feet.

"Well done, Horatio!" McClellan exclaimed. "Are you all right? Didn't break your flask or anything, did you?"

"Corporal," snapping his fingers at an aide, "a pot of coffee for the chief of staff!"

Abernethy opened his mouth to deliver every cussword he knew, but the only words that came out were: "Sir, the President sends his compliments."

"Compliments! From the President? You don't say! And you rode all this way to deliver them to me personally? Why, I'm touched, Horatio."

McClellan exchanged a glance with his aide.

"And did the President send anything else, Horatio, besides his compliments?"

"One or two helpful suggestions."

"Ah," McClellan said. "Well."

Abernethy pulled a paper out of his pocket. "The first thing the President wants - "

"Cigar, Horatio?"

"Thank you."

"Now, what the President would like to see - "

McClellan took a drag from the cigar, and suddenly frowned at Cooper. "Isn't that Lincoln's dog?"

"Cooper?" Abernethy looked around. "Yes. Well, no. Actually, he's the doctor's dog. I believe."

"I trust he doesn't chew on things. The dog, of course." McClellan put the cigar back in his mouth, keeping an eye on Cooper. "Excuse me for interrupting. Please go on, general."

"Well, the President - "

A tremendous cannon blast shook the trees, sending Abernethy and Lieutenant Harkness ducking to the ground and their papers flying. Cooper chased the papers.

"What was *that*?" Abernethy said.

"Fourteen-hundred," McClellan pulled out his pocket watch.

"Fourteen-hundred?"

"Two p.m. The two o'clock signal."

"Signal for what?"

"The signal that it's two o'clock, Horatio. The Army must always know the correct time."

Abernethy straightened out the paper he'd been holding. "General McClellan - "

"Egad Horatio!" McClellan exclaimed.

"What now?" Abernethy said.

"I think my watch is a minute fast! What time do you have?"

"Two-oh-three."

"Let's split the difference. Two-oh-two."

McClellan raised a handkerchief in his right hand and dropped it.

BLAM! The cannon went off again, causing Abernethy to crouch, in spite of himself. Cooper had to chase a new bunch of flying papers.

Abernethy looked at his watch again and eyed the cannon. "The President - " he began again.

"One moment," McClellan said.

A photographer appeared from nowhere and set up an elaborate camera, giving directions to the two generals.

"I think it's better if you stand on my left, Abernethy," McClellan said. He guided Abernethy into position "Historians in the future will treasure this great moment in the war! 'General McClellan receives General Abernethy who presents the President's compliments to General McClellan at sunset!'"

Abernethy looked at his watch again. "Sunset? It's the middle of the afternoon, McClellan."

Cooper ambled over and sat down to scratch a flea.

"Stout fellow!" McClellan said. "Do you know, Horatio, that the faithful dog is a symbol used everywhere in art? In the Louvre alone, dogs appear in 6,283 paintings and portraits. Cooper will convey, for this occasion honoring me, a powerful impression of my virtues of physical and moral courage, steadfastness, humility, bravery, loyalty and perseverance. I may have left one out. Be that as it may, let the picture be titled, 'Cooper and Abernethy convey the President's compliments to the supreme commander of the Army of the Potomac at sunset!'"

"Sunset's not for six hours!" Abernethy said. "And after 'compliments' you could add that the President wants to know why you have been lollygagging, pussyfooting, procrastinating, backtracking, marching sideways and up and down and camping

75

in circles and using your entire Army for everything but fighting for the past six months."

BLAM! The cannon went off again, making Abernethy hit the dirt.

"Three bells!" McClellan said, checking his watch. "Three o'clock already!"

"Three bells is not three o'clock, McClellan!" Abernethy hollered. "It's one-thirty Navy time!"

"This is the Army, Horatio. Three bells is three o'clock Army time. We skip one-thirty entirely in the interest of efficiency. Please put that in your report."

McClellan turned on a well-polished heel and strode into his tent, leaving Abernethy and Cooper standing there staring at the camera.

"I think we can stop," Abernethy told Cooper.

Later, one of McClellan's aides came out and told Abernethy that McClellan was taking a nap.

***

It was starting to get dark. Abernethy and Lieutenant Harkness had been riding for three hours. They were still a little deaf from the cannon going off. They had decided not to wait for McClellan to wake up from his nap. They crossed a river that Cooper didn't remember, and came to a crossroads.

"That way," Abernethy pointed with his saber. "Um, no, that way." He pointed his saber other way.

They made camp in the dark, and Cooper kept one eye open as a party of owls hooted from the trees. On the road near their grove, several horses galloped by, around midnight.

"What's that?" Harkness whispered.

"McClellan's cavalry, I hope," Abernethy said. "But it could be Rebs. I hope we rode the right way."

In the morning, Abernethy lounged on a stump while Harkness got the horses ready.

"Bring the map, Harkness," Abernethy said. "I need to

find out where we are."

Harkness came and spread out the map.

Abernethy pulled out his spectacles, but they were bent and cracked.

"I must have broken them at McClellan's," Abernethy said. "You'll have to read the map."

"Geography was never my strong suit, sir."

"Harkness - "

"Yes sir." He peered at the map.

"Well?"

"I'm looking, sir."

"Harkness, I want you to take your index finger and point to our location on the map."

"Yes sir."

The lieutenant hesitated.

"My right hand or my left hand, sir?"

"Whichever one suits you."

Harkness used his right hand, but his finger soon began to shake, so he used his left hand.

"Well? Where are we?" Abernethy fussed.

"I'm still looking, sir."

Harkness's left hand began to shake, too. His finger pointed every which way.

"Thunderation," Abernethy mumbled.

"Maybe we could just ask somebody," Harkness suggested.

"Criminy," Abernethy said. He held one side of his broken eyeglasses to one eye and leaned close to the map.

"Dang it, this can't be right! It looks like we're close to Scranton."

"Yes sir!" Harkness said. "That's Scranton, all right."

"It says Scranton?"

"Right, sir."

"Harkness," Abernethy drew a deep breath, "Scranton is in Pennsylvania!"

"We're in Pennsylvania?"

"No, you numbskull! Pennsylania is south of Washington! Virginia is north of Washington. We are in Virginia, Harkless."

"I always thought Pennsylvania was north of

Washington, sir. Did you call me Harkless? It's Harkness, sir."

"Of course it's Harkness! I never said whatever I didn't say, and I did not say Pennsylvania is north of Washington."

"You think it's south?"

"South? Virginia is south, Harkless."

"I thought you said north."

"I was talking about which way we must go to get to Washington."

"We're south of Washington sir, I'm definite about that."

"Then how could we be in Pennsylvania?"

"It doesn't seem possible, sir."

"It's not. We're not there."

"Yes sir. We left."

"We're here."

"Right here, yes sir."

"Get me another map."

"Any particular state, sir?"

"Harkless...."

Just then, Cooper, who had been racing up a side road and bringing out sticks to play with, brought back a small sign.

"What's that, boy?" Abernethy said. "Read it, Harkless."

"Richmond: five miles," Harkness said.

13.
The Masterpiece

Lincoln finally got a chapter of his memoirs done, but Cooper ate it.

"Lordy," Lincoln said. He sent for Dr. Hunt.

"Cooper ate all pages!" Lincoln hollered.

"I don't think it'll hurt him none," Hunt said. He laughed and pounded Cooper affectionately on the ribs.

Lincoln cried, "but I need those pages, Hunt! That literary man will be after me again. Couldn't you, uh, s-l-i-p Cooper a little of your, uh, b-e-a-n?"

"B-e-a-n?" Hunt spelled back.

"You know," Lincoln wiggled his eyebrows meaningfully.

"Know w-h-a-t?" Hunt said.

Lincoln cut his eyes at Cooper who was looking suspiciously back and forth from him to Dr. Hunt.

"Oh," Hunt said, "you mean c-a-s-t-o-r o-i-l?"

Lincoln nodded.

Cooper began edging toward the door.

"I can t-r-y to g-i-v-e him some," Dr. Hunt said, "but you'll have to h-e-l-p."

Hunt, trying to act casual, got the bottle of castor oil out of his bag. He kept his back to Cooper so that Cooper couldn't see him pour some into a spoon. "S-e-e if y-o-u can h-o-l-d his mouth o-p-e-n."

Cooper bolted out the door and disappeared.

"Well," Hunt said, "I guess he c-a-u-g-h-t on."

"Cooper's an awful good s-p-e-l-l-e-r," Lincoln groaned.

Hunt looked at Lincoln. "How have you been feeling, yourself, lately?"

"Me? Just finer than c-h-i-c-k-e-n hair," the President said hastily, eyeing the spoon.

"You mean finer than f-r-o-g hair," Hunt said. "What about your insomnia?"

"Insomnia?"

"You told me last week you couldn't s-l-e-e-p."

"I can't recollect s-a-y-i-n-g that, Hunt. Absolutely n-o-t. Must've been somebody e-l-s-e."

Cooper tiptoed back into the study.

"Is he telling the t-r-u-t-h, Coop?"

Cooper sat down and scratched his left e-a-r.

"See there," Hunt said, "your own d-o-g says you're fibbing."

"Well he's just a d-o-u-b-l-e d-o-g fibber!" Lincoln said.

"And whoever heard of c-a-s-t-o-r o-i-l making you sleep? And why are we still spelling, Hunt?"

"Step over here and open your m-o-u-t-h," Hunt motioned with the spoon.

"Hunt - !"

"Wider," Hunt said.

" - I'm telling you the honest truth -"

Hunt shoved the spoon in.

"Nnnnh," Lincoln went. "Gaaah!"

"He might need a double-dose," Hunt stared at the bottle.

Lincoln ran out of the room. Cooper stayed.

"R-u-f-f," Cooper said. "Ruff!"

"You're right about that," Hunt told the dog and put the bottle away. "And you can stop spelling now."

14.
Another Draft

Lincoln rose before dawn.

He'd been thinking about his memoirs all night.

He couldn't sleep. He tossed and turned.

"Will you quit tossing and turning?" Mary Lincoln said.

He tried but he couldn't stop.

He dressed and went to his study and lit a lamp. Cooper wandered in and sat down.

"Writing is not hard to do," Lincoln reminded himself. "All you have to do is put one word in front of another."

He got ready to work. He picked up his pen. He set his jaw with determination. He noticed that the stack of paper he was going to write on was not stacked up right.

He put down his pen and stacked it right.

"There," he said.

He set his jaw again. He drew a sheet of paper from the stack. He dipped his pen and wrote at the top: *Page Number One - My Biography.*

"No, no!" he muttered to himself, "Biography is what somebody else writes. This is 'Autobiography.'"

He thought about it, twiddling his pen. "Pretty sure that's right...."

He wadded up the paper that had *Biography* on it and threw it away.

He took a new sheet and began, *Autobiography of Abraham Lincoln*.

But that didn't look right.

"If it's my autobiography," he said to himself, "I just sign it. I don't say it."

He threw that sheet away, too, and got a fresh one. "Maybe if I just word it a little different."

Memoirs of Abraham Lincoln, he wrote carefully. Then he wondered, "Memoirs or Memoir?" "'Memoirs,'" he decided. "But maybe I need to put a 'The' in front of 'Memoirs.'"

He got a new sheet and wrote *The* in front of *Memoirs*. But now the words were off-center. They didn't look right.

Taking a fresh sheet of paper, he wrote the title out again, *The Memoirs of Abraham Lincoln*. Hey! He held it at arm's length and studied it. Then he read it aloud to Cooper who was just then busy with a flea.

But after he read it the third time, something didn't sound right. "Maybe I shouldn't have put that period after Lincoln?" He chewed on his pen.

Cooper yawned and stretched out for a nap.

Lincoln made some tea and thought about the period. He decided to just scratch it out instead of starting with a new piece of paper, but his pen tore a hole in the paper.

He reached for a new piece but didn't have any. He didn't much like the paper he had, anyway. "Some real good bond paper would make things easier," Lincoln told Cooper. "Let's walk over to Treasury and borrow some good dollar-bill paper from Salmon Chase."

Secretary Chase was gone, and there wasn't any dollar-bill paper, but an assistant found a box of war bond paper and gave it to him.

"Much obliged," Lincoln said.

When he got back to the White House, Lincoln stacked the war bond paper neatly on the left-hand corner of his desk. Then he changed his mind and stacked it on the right-hand corner.

"Maybe I should put it in a drawer," he said. But he couldn't find a clean drawer and had to clean one out so he could put the paper in it.

Drawing a sheet of war bond paper out of the drawer, he put it in front of him and dipped his pen and was about to write when a sudden worry came over him: he was about to use government bond paper. Was it legal?

"I better check," he mumbled to Cooper. "I can't afford a scandal right before the election."

The President and the dog went over to the Justice Department to talk to the attorney general. The attorney general hemmed and hawed. He wanted to study it and consult all his lawyers.

"Forget it," Lincoln sighed. "I'll take the paper back to Chase's office and borrow some regular writing paper from John Hay."

Back in his study, Lincoln sat down with a box of Hay's paper.

The he wrote. Then he looked closely at his pen nib. It looked dull and might leave an ink blot.

Guess I better sharpen it," Lincoln muttered to Cooper. "In fact, I better get some fresh nibs."

He went back Hay's office and borrowed a dozen new nibs and two new staffs.

The clock struck fifteen minutes to noon.

The Memoirs of Abraham Lincoln he wrote at the top of the first page, forming the letters carefully.

Hay stuck his head in the office.

"How are the memoirs coming, sir?"

"Splendid, Mr. Hay. I've been at them all morning."

"Glad to hear it, Mr. President."

Hay left. Lincoln dipped his pen, pursed his lips, and got down to business. With a firm hand he wrote: *Call me Ishmael.*

"Dang!"

He threw the paper away.

15.
Mr. Lincoln's Nap

Every day at about four o'clock in the afternoon, Mr. Lincoln would take a nap. He did not mean to take a nap, but he did it anyway. He would sit in his rocker with a bunch of papers to read. Pretty soon his chin would drop down to his chest. His eyes would shut. His glasses would slide to the tip of his nose. Sometimes they would fall on his lap. They would fall on the papers where the war seemed to sleep, too, for awhile, under the President's stilled fingers.

Cooper would watch this. He would watch the President's large ears move in a lively rhythm while the rest of Mr. Lincoln slept. Up and down the ears would move. Sometimes they would move in circles, all in perfect harmony with the President's snores, wheezes, gasps, hitches, sputters and explosions, and occasionally with buzz-saw imitations and other noises so varied and original that Cooper would have enjoyed them except that they made him nervous.

Every time Mr. Lincoln's ears would go up, Cooper

would feel his own ears rise, as if pulled by strings.

When Mr. Lincoln's ears deflated, Cooper's would deflate.

Up.

Up.

Down.

Down.

Mr. Lincoln's children used to tiptoe to the study and peep around the door at this.

16.
Snow Day

The afternoon of the day it snowed Florence let Cooper out the back door. Cooper sniffed the steps. He sniffed the bushes. One bush he sniffed three times, and lifted a leg on it.

Then he ran down to sniff the apple tree that Mr. Washington had planted. He lifted a leg on the apple tree. Then he trotted along with his nose snuffling tracks in the snow. He followed them eagerly in circles until he found where he started. Then he loped toward the Supreme Court.

Chief Justice Bantom and Marcia were just heading out for a walk. Cooper felt his nose gladden as he planted it against the soft wool sock on Mrs. Bantom's ankle.

"Yet another admirer, Marcia!" crowed the banty chief justice.

Marcia took Cooper playfully by the ears.

"Curious," the chief justice said. "Wonder what he's doing here? Is he Hunt's or Lincoln's?"

"I don't know. He's usually with the President."

Chief Justice Bantom looked around. "Well," he said, "I don't see either one."

The white hair on Bantom's head seemed to leap perpetually. His sharp face took on a canny look as he eyed the dog. "I wonder why he'd come here?"

"I'm sure I don't know," Marcia said lightly. "Maybe he got lost."

"Well then," the chief justice said, "maybe you should show him back home."

17.
Knock Knock

Knock knock.

"Come in," said Mr. Lincoln, looking up from his rocker.

The flushed, pretty face of Marcia Bantom appeared around the door of Lincoln's study.

"Well, Mrs. Bantom," the President said, getting to his feet.

"No, please," Marcia said, "don't stir yourself on my account. I was, ah, looking for Dr. Hunt."

"Hunt?" Lincoln was surprised. "Was he supposed to be here?"

"I don't know. His dog - "

"Cooper?"

"He showed up suddenly at the Court."

"Arguing a case?"

"No," Marcia laughed. "Chasing snowballs."

"You brought him back?"

"Yes."

Lincoln smiled. "Well, set down a spell, as long as you're

here. I'll get us some tea."

"But Mr. President - "

"Oh, fiddle-faddle, just set." He motioned the young woman to a chair.

Lincoln busied himself at the kettle that simmered over a gas ring. "I'm always burning myself on this durned thing," he laughed. "Ouch!"

"My word, Mr. President, can I help?"

"No, no, it's just this old kettle. Makes wonderful tea, though. Takes the iron out of the water."

"There's iron in the water?"

"That's the least of it," Lincoln said. He added devilishly: "The water used to come from a well, but now it comes in a pipe that goes underneath the Capitol, so the water can get a little complicated."

Marcia laughed. "Senator Hogan you mean!"

Lincoln chortled with some amazement. How on earth did Marcia Bantom know about Happy Hogan?

"I'm a friend of the senator's wife," Marcia smiled gaily. "We had lunch on Thursday."

Lincoln shook his head. "And is Mrs. Hogan now happy also?"

"Not at all. She never wanted John - Senator Hogan - to get involved with this rogues' gallery of land grant speculators. There's bound to be a scandal, she thinks."

"Do you?"

Marcia pursed her lips, looking at Lincoln sideways. "If I said yes, would you veto the bill?"

Lincoln shook his head. "No."

"Because you need Hogan's committee for something else."

"Yes."

"And, when you give in on the speculators, you'll have the senator over a barrel! You really are a rascal, sir!"

Lincoln grinned in spite of himself. Quickly he turned to check on the kettle - hoping she did not see the look of admiration on his face. It gave him a great deal of pleasure to talk to this unusual woman who seemed to know everything he was thinking.

"I think he's gone to the dickens," he heard her say, and turned to see her examining the books on a shelf near his desk. His eyes fell on the tight, orange curls on the back of her head.

"Look in *A Tale of Two Cities*," he said.

"Oh - it's autographed."

"Mr. Dickens gave it to me."

"I'm a great admirer of his."

Lincoln walked over and took the book from her. He closed it and handed it back to her. "This will be yours."

"Oh no, Mr. President," Marcia said, flushing. "I couldn't accept your signed copy."

"It would please me if you did."

"Then you must inscribe it also."

Lincoln got out his spectacles and took the book to his desk. He dipped a pen and hesitated.

"What shall I write?"

"Whatever pleases you."

He nodded. The pen quivered over the flyleaf.

Presented to my - to my what? My good friend? Great and good friend? Lord no! Esteemed friend?

He wrote, *to my esteemed friend, Mrs. Bantom.*

From A. Lincoln? Sincerely A. Lincoln? Or?

His heart sank and his glasses slid down his nose as he bent low to keep track of the words. His pen quivered again. Instead of signing with his first initial, as he usually did, he wrote his name out in full. *Abraham Lincoln.*

The kettle sang.

Lincoln handed Marcia the book and she inspected what he wrote. "You are too kind, Mr. President! This book will be in my family forever. Abraham Lincoln and Charles Dickens, all on one page!"

Lincoln gave an embarrassed wave and used his coat tail to pick up the kettle. His glasses were all but falling off his nose.

"Let me help," she cried, using a forefinger to push his glasses back into place. He found the small intimacy exhilarating.

"Do you take milk?" he said, looking around. "Come to think of it, I don't have any."

"I will drink it the same as you," she said.

Their eyes met as her lips tested the cup.

Lincoln cleared his throat. "But getting back to the railroad grants," he watched her, "the legislation really is not as bad as it sounds. Any lawyer could make a case that it is not grand larceny if looked at in a patriotic way."

"Now there's a standard to which Congress may aspire," Marcia said with a straight face.

Lincoln had to smile. "But seriously," he said, walking over to a continental map, "the grant does make a certain amount of sense, in terms of manifest destiny."

"Manifest destiny?"

Lincoln craned his head at the map, and traced with a finger the Canadian border from Lake Superior to the Pacific. "The British," Lincoln put his hand on Canada, "are up here. North of the forty-ninth parallel. And they're still sore over losing everything below it to us in the boundary treaty of 1846."

"Because we threatened them with war," Marcia agreed.

"And only because we threatened them with war," Lincoln adjusted his spectacles. He slapped his hand on the map. "And now they have their eye on this land again. And since we're a right smart busy with other things right now, they might be tempted to make a move."

"Do you believe that, personally?"

"There are people in this country who do believe it."

"I can think of about sixty-seven of them," Marcia raised a brow. "They're all in the Senate."

Lincoln seemed about to smile, but didn't.

"Mrs. Bantom," he twirled his glasses, "it is a strange fact that the British have not yet abandoned their imperial dream to rule our continent. I know, personally, that London is doing all it can, right now, to help the Confederates win the war, short of breaking relations with us. What they're hankering for is to get the thirteen colonies back."

"So to speak."

"So to speak. I believe that if we had a serious reverse right now, and it appeared we might lose the war, it's not unthinkable that Britain would put troops over our northern border."

"We would be hard-pressed to stop them," Marcia agreed.

Lincoln shrugged. "That's why Congress is willing at this time to give away an unimaginable fortune to a railroad company - Wall Street men - to build a railroad up there and draw settlers. And give us a way to transport troops."

"Only one problem with that plan," Marcia laughed.

Lincoln nodded. "I know. The British threat will be over and forgotten before the first spike is driven."

"But the financiers will still get rich on the public land."

It was Lincoln's turn to laugh. "But with the Union victorious, the British will be our loyal friends again! More tea, Mrs. Bantom?"

"If you have time, Mr. President."

"I'm enjoying our talk."

Cooper came in and lay on the floor. They discussed him as Lincoln gathered up his coat tails and tried to pick up the tea kettle again.

"Dang!" he waved his fingers in the air, put them in his mouth. "I'm always doing that."

Marcia went over and blew on them. "They look a little red. Do you have any butter?"

"Butter?"

"We used it on burns when I was a child."

"Really? Did it work?"

"No, but it made our fingers taste better. What home remedies did you use?"

"Pear preserves."

"Really? For burns?"

"No, the whooping cough."

"Did it work?"

"No, not that I recall. But my grandmother did have a cure for the chickenpox."

"What was that?"

"She'd set you in the doorway of the hen house and then she'd go in and scare all the chickens out over your head."

"Seriously?"

"She was right serious about it, yes. When I got the chickenpox, that's how she cured me."

"My grandmother had some remedies. But mostly she would cast spells."

"Spells?"

"Different kinds of spells, depending. She got my grandfather to marry her by casting a spell. I know it sounds funny, but she could also cast a spell to keep potatoes from spoiling."

Lincoln sat back in his chair. "Mrs. Bantom, this is the most amazing conversation."

"I was just thinking so, myself," Marcia said. "Here, let me help with that butter."

Lincoln allowed Marcia to work on his fingers, studying the serious expression on her face and the orange curls on top of her head.

"That feeling any better?" She glanced up.

"Yes."

It was strange, feeling the grasp of Marcia Bantom's pale hands.

"Better?" She asked again.

"Much," he said. "You know," Lincoln cleared his throat, "I've been thinking about that Dickens book - "

"It's all right if you changed your mind - "

"No, no, I was just thinking that the book is part of a leather-bound set - "

"You can't break up a set - "

"No. I mean, I don't want to break it up. I want you to have it."

"Not the whole set, Mr. President! I couldn't possibly."

"It would give me the greatest pleasure, Mrs. Bantom. A set of old books just gathers dust; a set given to a friend - I guess it gathers friendship."

Cooper barked.

***

Nearly a week later, Marcia Bantom came back to the Executive Mansion with a book that had been included by mistake with her Dickens set. He put it back on the shelf.

"I put a new handle on the tea kettle," Mr. Lincoln said.

"I'd like a cup," Marcia said.

"What shall we talk about," Lincoln said. "Manifest destiny again? The eternal friendship between Congress and mammon?"

"Speaking of friendship," Marcia winked, "have you heard the latest?"

She told him about the scandal involving Mr. Justice Hoover and the widow of ex-congressman Howe. A dozen witnesses had seen Mrs. Hoover take an umbrella to Mrs. Howe in the lobby of the Willard.

"Mercy sakes alive!" Lincoln merrily threw back his head as if he were going to howl. "Did the newspapers find out?"

"No, but they're snooping."

"And Judge Hoover?"

"That's what got the press on the prowl. He showed up in court with a big black eye. He's told at least three different stories about how he got it."

Lincoln threw back his head again in merriment.

He and Marcia sat there for an hour, exchanging gossip. Lincoln filled in Marcia on Seward's card game. Then Marcia shocked him with the information that he, the President, was the subject of speculation by women around the capital.

"You cannot be serious!" Lincoln said, not knowing whether to laugh.

"But I am!" Marcia said. "They find you extremely handsome."

Now Lincoln did laugh. "If that's so, could I have it in writing? I want to send a testimonial to the *Star*."

In the midst of their third cup, Cooper rose wagging his tail and looking at the door. Mr. Hay appeared shortly, carrying satchels of paper.

"Mrs. Bantom!" stammered Hay. "What a pleasant surprise."

"I came to, ah, deliver some invitations," Marcia said. "You are invited, of course."

"Why, uh, thank you," Hay said, glancing at Lincoln.

Lincoln lifted an eyebrow. What invitations?

Marcia rose, "I have taken far too much of your time, Mr. President."

"No need to rush!" Hay said quickly.

"Come back and see us," Lincoln smiled, getting to his feet. "Anytime at all."

Hay dashed after Mrs. Bantom to open the door for her, intending to do it with an impressive flourish but only succeeded in banging himself in the forehead, which Mrs. Bantom pretended not to notice.

When she was gone, Hay avoided eye contact with the President as he spread out a pile of papers on the commander in chief's desk. There were three legislative bills, one for veto and two for Lincoln to sign. Then a stack of new postmaster appointments, commutation orders for sixteen military prisoners, and an Army order for one hundred thousand pounds of pork bellies from a company in St. Louis that Miz Fesmire had something to do with.

"Find out which brother-in-law of hers it is this time," sighed Lincoln, throwing his pen down.

He motioned Hay to a chair and they sat there with the flotsam, their feet on the desk.

"Still a lot of stuff to sign," Hay said.

"I know."

"What did we get invited to?"

"Invited to?"

"Mrs. Bantom said something about invitations."

"I think she forgot them. Brought the wrong ones, or something. She will have to come back or send them over."

"I plan to go, don't you?"

"I hope so."

They sat there.

Hay spoke again.

"Mr. President, don't you think Mrs. Bantom is a remarkable woman?"

Lincoln glanced at Hay.

"I mean," Hay stammered, "in a remarkable sort of way."

Lincoln removed his glasses, waiting.

"I mean," Hay went on, "she's fairly - unusual."

"Yes," Lincoln smiled very slightly. "She had a grandmother who could cast spells."

18.
Old Ben

You'll never guess who just showed up!"

John Hay was excited.

Lincoln looked up from his papers.

"All right, who?"

"Ben Franklin."

"Lord help us, Hay. Franklin's been dead for sixty years."

"This is Ben Junior, I think."

"Well, please thank Mr. Ben Junior kindly, but I'm right busy."

"You ought to see him, sir! I mean, he looks just like the old man. Square glasses and everything. And every time he says something, it's one of his quotations."

"Mr. Hay - "

"And he's wearing a get-up like they wore in old-timey colonial days. Why, your eyes will pop right out, sir, because you'll swear you're meeting the real Ben Franklin."

"All right, Hay," Lincoln sighed. "Show Ben Franklin in."

Hay went out and came back presently with an old

gentleman who, as he said, was the very image of Franklin: shiny knickers and buckle shoes. Lace at the coat cuffs. Bassett hound eyes wide open behind the tiny panes of spectacles riding low on his nose. Arched brows. A high forehead giving way to locks falling to his shoulders.

"What a pleasure to meet you, Mr. Franklin," Lincoln beamed, extending his hand.

"'A wise man will make more opportunities than he finds,'" Franklin intoned.

"Francis Bacon?" Lincoln hesitated.

Franklin poked a finger in the air. "'A proverb,' sir," he said, "'is the wisdom of many and the wit of one.'"

"Well, that was Lord Russell," Lincoln said. "You don't hear Russell quoted much."

"Because he hasn't been born yet," Franklin said, getting a little agitated. "On the other hand, I have always said, sir, that 'a fly may sting a stately horse and make him wince; but one is but an insect, and the other is a horse still.'"

"Samuel Johnson, for sure," Lincoln said.

Franklin gave Lincoln a look. "'Great fleas,' sir, 'have little fleas upon their backs to bite 'em. And little fleas have lesser fleas, and so ad infinitum.'"

"Uh-huh. Augustus de Morgan."

"'No man is demolished but by himself!'"

"Bently!"

Franklin lashed his cane down on Lincoln's desk.

"Confound it, Lincoln, 'to everything there is a season!'"

"Ecclesiastes!" the President got around behind his rocker.

Franklin began pursuing. "'The race is not to the swift, sir, nor the battle to the strong!'"

"Sounds like either George McClellan or the Senate Appropriations Committee," Lincoln said. He was wondering if he could defend himself with an ink bottle.

"'Die Politik ist keine exakte Wissenschaft!'" Franklin waved his cane around.

"Bismarck," Lincoln puffed. "But we're getting a little ahead of ourselves."

At that, Franklin gave a cry and chased Lincoln around

his desk. "'Discretion is the better part of valor,'" Lincoln said, trying to keep up appearances as he retreated.

"Shakespeare!" Franklin cried, taking a swing at the air with the cane. "Henry IV, Act One."

"Lord," Lincoln muttered.

Franklin pointed his cane at him. "'I had rather be a dog,'" he sputtered, "'and bay the moon, than such a Roman.'"

"Julius Caesar," Lincoln explained. "But what about 'Eye of the newt and toe of the frog, wool of bat and tongue of dog.'"

"Hamlet!" Franklin said.

"Uh, no, Macbeth!"

"You're sure?"

"Positive."

"I always thought it was Hamlet."

Lincoln plopped down in a chair and Franklin claimed the rocker.

"'Oh vanity of vanities!'" Franklin said. "'How wayward the decrees of Fate are; How very weak the very wise, how very small the very great are!'"

"Thackeray," Lincoln said. "But how about this one: 'He makes no friend who never made a foe.'"

"Macauley?"

"Tennyson."

Franklin narrowed his eyes. "Here's one that will stump you: 'The thing is certain because it is impossible.'"

"Tertullian." Lincoln sighed. "Why don't you just give up?"

Franklin looked agitated. "I have not yet begun to quote! Chew on this one: 'The mass of men lead lives of quiet desperation.'"

"Thoreau. Too easy. But here's one you'll like: "'Three may keep a secret, if two of them are dead.'"

"Benjamin Franklin!" Franklin hooted. "You thought I wouldn't remember?" He narrowed his eyes at Lincoln. "I was saving this next one for last, and I'll wager that you'll miss it. Shall we bet $10?"

"No tricks?"

"Absolutely none."

"Cross your heart?"

"And hope to die! Who said, 'A penny saved is a penny earned?'"

Lincoln threw back his head and laughed. "Why you flim-flamming old rascal," he said, "you just swore and crossed your heart that you wouldn't pull a cheap stunt like that, and you thought I'd think it was your quotation. But it was by your father - the real Benjamin Franklin."

"You're sure?"

"Positive."

"Then pay up!" said Franklin Junior. "The quotation is really mine! Father said 'A penny saved is a penny got.' Look it up."

Lincoln paid the ten.

19.
Fiddle

Fiddle came to Mr. Lincoln's office every Tuesday except when he came on Wednesday, or sometimes Monday.

Fiddle was an elderly black gentleman with cloudy eyes and straight white hair. His hair looked like it was blowing toward the back of his head, and he carried an expensive fiddle in a case, and drove Cooper to distraction when he played it. Not because of the fiddle music but because of the way Fiddle tapped his foot to keep time. Fiddle's foot would go up and down and then Cooper's eyes would go up and down and then his ears would go up and down and then his whole head would go up and down, and then he'd smell the tasty smell of leather and couldn't resist.

One day, Fiddle showed up to play, and soon the up-and-down business got going, and Cooper got carried away by the tasty smell of leather and latched on to Fiddle's left shoe. He couldn't make himself let go, despite Fiddle's entreaties. "Let go, dog!" Fiddle said. But Cooper couldn't quite do it even when Fiddle danced around the room with Cooper still attached. The dancing and Fiddle's "let go's" made so much noise that here came the President.

"Lord have mercy," Lincoln said to Cooper, wrestling with his jaws. "What's got into you? Let go of the man's wingtip!"

"Dang!" Fiddle said. "He be makin' a bunch of holes this time! And I paid big money for them shoes!"

"Come on, Coop," Lincoln pulled on the dog.

"Dang!" Fiddle said.

Lincoln finally got Cooper to come to his senses, but Fiddle was in high dudgeon.

"I don't feel like playin no mo'," Fiddle muttered.

"Sorry," the President said.

"It ain't worth no dollar and a half to give a private concert if your shoes is gonna get tore up."

"I'll make it two dollars this time, Fiddle."

"It ought to be three."

"All right, three."

Fiddle kept muttering, but tuned up his fiddle again and played 'John Brown's Body.'

The President sat with his eyes half-closed, tapping his foot. Cooper was afraid to look.

Then Fiddle put his entire talent into 'Aura Lee', a Cooper favorite, next to shoe leather.

Then Fiddle played a little Beethoven and Mozart.

But halfway through 'Turkey in the Straw,' a string on Fiddle's fiddle broke with a *thoinnngg*, bringing the concert to a premature close.

"I still got three dollars coming," Fiddle said, "seeing as how it wasn't my fault the string broke."

"I'll get it," Lincoln said. He sat down at his desk and found three greenbacks in a purse, which he counted out to Fiddle.

"I guess this is legal," Fiddle said, taking a long look at it. He did not much believe in paper money.

Lincoln fell silent for a moment.

"Fiddle," Lincoln said. "I need to ask you a question."

"Like what?"

"Like some advice. I've got a proclamation right here in my desk and wonder if you think I should sign it right now, like some people think, or wait for a better time?"

"Whoa," Fiddle said. "I get four dollars to give advice."

20.
Fiddling with Angels

So that's how it happened.

But Fiddle never told anybody what he said and never came back and never played another concert. That's because he died that very next Sunday morning while he was getting ready for church, the same one Florence attended. Florence said Fiddle played at church every Sunday without fail except when he got into it with the preacher over what was Sunday music and what wasn't Sunday music, with Fiddle's opinion being that every kind of music was Sunday music if you tapped your foot the right way.

Still, the White House wasn't the same without Fiddle, especially at Christmastime, which it now was. Something always happened on a crystal night that Cooper looked forward to, and he couldn't understand why nobody else stayed up to watch. Not even Mr. Lincoln.

The President, in his nightshirt, let Cooper out the back door.

"Don't run off, now."

Along about midnight, maybe closer to one o'clock, Cooper's ears perked up. Barking, he ran in circles, then to the top of the kitchen steps. He watched the air above the apple tree.

The first angel turned a somersault with a golden harp. Then came another with a banjo. Suddenly there were dozens.

Cooper's tongue fell out in excitement as angels filled the tree, and they were singing. They sang against a background of stars, and shone like starlight.

Cooper was surprised to see Fiddle. But now Fiddle didn't look like himself. He was more like starlight, with a starlight fiddle.

Cooper cocked his head. He could hardly believe it. Fiddle played beautifully. He tapped his foot the right way, and the angels played 'Turkey in the Straw.'

Then Cooper saw something else he had never seen before. The stars danced. They danced from one end of heaven to the other.

Then the angels went away. Before they did, they left some apples for the birds.

21.
A Strong Lady

The Strongest Woman in the World came calling on Mr. Lincoln.

She told the President that her name was Emma Toff. She traveled with the circus, and spoke with a thick Russian accent.

General Abernethy had heard that she'd tried to join the Army.

"Not true! It is made-up propaganda!" Emma Toff told Abernethy.

Cooper did not think that Emma Toff looked all that unusual. She was as wide as a barrel, of course, and her arms and neck were like country hams.

But her feet were quite small, and her hands were dainty and dimpled.

"What would you like to see me do?" asked Emma Toff.

"Well-l-l," said the President, taken aback. "What do you do?"

"I will show my iron bar," Emma Toff said.

Disappearing into the hallway for a moment, Emma Toff

came back with a wagon axle. She spat into her hands, put the bar on top of her head and slowly bent it into an upside-down horseshoe. A very big upside-down horseshoe.

"Mercy," Lincoln said.

She handed the bent bar to Abernethy who nearly toppled over. He looked at it carefully.

"It is no trick," said Emma Toff, as if reading Abernethy's thoughts. "Go ahead. Bend it back."

"There's a war on, madam," Abernethy flustered. "I can't beat the Rebs by tying knots in wagon axles!"

"Mighty good thing," Lincoln said under his breath.

"I spit on war," Emma Toff said.

Cooper stood back, expecting her to spit.

Lincoln nodded. "I'd spit on war myself, if I thought it would do any good."

Just then, the Lincoln children and Mrs. Lincoln came into the room to meet Emma Toff. They looked at the bent bar. They had never seen such a thing. They listened as Mrs. Toff told how she had emigrated to America, educated herself with borrowed books, and married a circus strongman with whom she'd had three sons and a happy life.

Then, one by one, her husband and her sons had been killed in the war.

"That is why I came to see you," Emma Toff said. "We must stop this foolishness."

Mary Lincoln sat down with her and patted her hand. Emma Toff looked in her purse and found pictures of her family. All three sons had attended Ohio University. She pointed to her youngest, who had also been strong, she said. The last picture was one taken of her on a tour of her homeland, lifting a grand piano over her head with Alexander II and Tchaikovsky seated on top.

Mr. Lincoln watched the pictures go back in her purse. "We are mighty sorry, Mrs. Toff."

"So am I."

Before she left, she took several horseshoe nails from her purse and bent them into rings for each of the Lincoln children. She made a double ring for Mrs. Lincoln, and a matching one for the President, and even made one for Cooper.

22.
Aunt Agnes and the Egg Lady

There were two women who occasionally came to the White House, always dressed in black.

One was a large, plump, jolly woman with a ruddy face. Everybody in Washington called her "Aunt Agnes." The other visitor was a bent little sparrow of a woman who wore a large black hat with a veil, and a black coat and shoes. Everybody called her "the Egg Lady" because she sold eggs.

Most of Washington knew Aunt Agnes and the Egg Lady, but hardly anyone knew much about them. For instance, nobody could recall whose aunt Aunt Agnes was - if indeed she was anybody's aunt. There was a rumor, never substantiated, that Agnes was a grand-niece of John Quincy Adams. But nobody knew, really. Or how she happened to enjoy the status of a regular caller at the White House. Supposedly she had been given the run of the place by James K. Polk, whatever that meant, but most certainly - and there is no doubt on this point - she was no relative of the Lincolns.

So, Aunt Agnes would arrive regularly at the White House, mostly on Friday afternoons, and join in any tea that happened to be in progress, and talk to anyone who happened to be present, whether she knew them or not. But mostly she did know them.

If Mr. Lincoln wasn't busy, he enjoyed spending a few minutes with her because she was a non-stop cheerful talker and said the most unexpected things. For perhaps the same reason, Mrs. Lincoln also enjoyed her company. And the upshot of all this was that Aunt Agnes went anywhere in the White House she pleased, just as she had always done.

One thing Aunt Agnes did that made her indispensable was to play cards with the Lincoln children. She knew all kinds of games. She would also tell them stories about growing up on a farm in Massachusetts, and finding the bones of giant prehistoric creatures she had dreamed about.

Aunt Agnes always had money in her pocket, whose source was also a bit of a mystery. When she walked around Washington, she would meet people she thought were needy and she would give them money. Nobody could recall her ever expressing a religious sentiment, so that was discounted as a motive. Her one strong belief, to the extent that she ever discussed it, was that snuff was greatly overrated as a vice.

The Egg Lady was as quiet and controlled as Aunt Agnes was loud and impulsive. The children did look forward to her visits, but in a different way than they looked forward to Agnes's.

Saturday was the Egg Lady's day. She always arrived at one o'clock in the afternoon precisely, and always asked Florence or Mrs. Lincoln exactly the same question: "How many eggs do we want today?"

The order, whatever it was, went into the Egg Lady's small black book. She would write it down in a careful hand, in pencil, and put the book back in her black purse. Then she would go outside where her horse waited patiently with the egg wagon, and she would look in her book and put the exact number of eggs that she had written down, just a few minutes before, into a basket, and then she would count the eggs and check her figures again, and only then would she bring the basket into the kitchen where she would count the eggs out, very carefully, once more, one at a time.

It took the Egg Lady forever to do this, but nobody showed impatience.

Finally, with the lengthy transaction completed, the Egg Lady would look around the kitchen with her small, bright eyes and ask, "Well now, how many children do we have here today?"

When the number was given - it usually varied because of visitors - the Egg Lady would reach into her coat and pull out a sack of peppermints, giving a piece to each child. The Egg Lady also gave Cooper a peppermint.

There was something extraordinary about the Egg Lady's peppermints, and Mrs. Lincoln asked more than once where she got them. But the Egg Lady never told. The truth was, they were just ordinary pieces of candy that came from a store on K Street, but no one would have believed it.

It was in January, right after New Year's Day, that both Aunt Agnes and the Egg Lady - who, so far as anyone knew, never met each other - quit coming to the White House.

Nobody thought much about it, at first, but then Mr. Hay learned that Aunt Agnes had died in her sleep. Her home, it seemed, had been a room not too far from Capitol Hill. When Hay told Lincoln about the death, it was too late to attend her funeral, and in fact she hadn't had one. They were both surprised to hear that, despite her habit of giving away money, she had very little of it, and not enough, in fact, to pay her own funeral expenses.

The Egg Lady, Hay learned a short time later, had suffered a stroke coincidentally the same week that Aunt Agnes died. All Hay could learn was that the Egg Lady had been taken to live with a relative in Pennsylvania. Somebody thought it was a cousin, but Lincoln never found out for sure who it was.

23.
A Familiar Pose

The visitors were still downstairs when their footsteps reached Cooper's ears. His left ear rose first. Then the right. He sat up straighter. He barked. He looked at Mr. Lincoln who was sitting quite still, in his formal clothes, in front of Mr. Brady's camera. Mr. Brady was showing Marcia Bantom how the camera worked - how one caught an image by removing the lens cap and holding it in the left hand, never the right, while reciting a verse of poetry, at the end of which the exposure would be perfect and the cap could be replaced.

"What shall I recite?" Marcia asked, a twinkle in her eye.

"I never give away trade secrets," Brady said.

"Browning," Lincoln intoned, scarcely moving his lips. "The same four lines, every time."

"Now you've ruined my reputation as well as Browning's, Mr. President," Brady said.

"Then I shall give you Thomas More," Marcia said

merrily. She removed the lens cap and spoke, "'The Minstrel Boy to the war is gone, In the ranks of death you'll find him; His father's sword he has girded on, And his wild harp slung behind him.'"

Lincoln looked at Marcia more sharply than he usually did. Brady nodded. He counted up the syllables and said he wouldn't be surprised if the picture turned out to be one of Mr. Lincoln's best. Then he gave a cry. The glass plate, he said, had cracked.

"Hold still just a minute longer, Mr. President," Brady said, "and we'll take another."

Lincoln shook his head. "No, that's the last, Mathew."

"Oh dear," Marcia said. "I didn't do the poem right."

Lincoln laughed and said, "No, no, it was perfect."

Marcia reached for her bonnet and coat. "I must go, Mr. President," she said, but he wouldn't hear of it, and took the bonnet and coat away from her.

"You must stay long enough," he said, "to meet the great inventor."

Cooper ran under the couch as the visitor approached from down the hall. His name was Karp. He was escorted by John Hay, who thought he was the strangest looking man he'd ever seen, but of course did not say that aloud.

Karp was tall - taller even than Mr. Lincoln, and thinner. He wore a beard that was longer than Mr. Lincoln's, a beard as black as it was long and as long as it was black, which, together with his long black coat and long black trousers gave the impression of a man aspiring to be an implement for cleaning chimneys. Even his eyes were as black as coal. Buttons of coal.

Karp stopped in mid-stride as he entered the room, cocking an eye at the window shade behind Lincoln that seemed thoroughly agitated and spun furiously on its axis.

Flap flap flap flap flapflapflap!

"Pleased to see you again," Lincoln said.

The inventor bowed shortly, glaring at the shade. He also bowed to, but did not shake hands with, Mrs. Bantom and Mr. Brady. In fact, he said nothing except that he had a new machine to show the President.

With a quick motion, Karp motioned to an assistant in the hall who brought in a black box with a crank sticking out of it. Karp took the box and positioned it carefully on top of the piano and stepped back.

"It's a talking machine," Hay blurted out.

"A which?" Lincoln looked startled.

"If you please," Karp shot a black glance at Hay, whose smile disappeared.

"It is a machine vot collects sound," Karp explained. "Und den ve hear vot sound it collects."

"How marvelous," Marcia Bantom exclaimed.

"Der technical details I still am kevorking," Karp said, getting between Mrs. Bantom and the box.

Hay waved his arms. "I can't wait to hear it!"

"Can we hear it, professor?" Lincoln said, intrigued.

"I must varn it may be spitzensparken!"

"Heck, just wind it up and let fly," Lincoln said. Karp blinked and gave the crank several rapid turns.

While holding on to the crank, he instructed Mr. Lincoln to step close and speak into a hole in the box.

"What do you want me to say?" Mr. Lincoln said.

"Vatever you please," Karp said.

"It's hard to think."

"Vell, just say someting."

"I feel like a fool," Lincoln said. "I can't think of a thing."

"Arf," said Cooper.

"How about that poem about two blind mice?" Hay suggested.

"What two blind mice?" Lincoln said.

"The two blind mice that ran up the clock."

Marcia Bantom laughed. "No, no, Mr. Hay, that was three blind mice!"

"Seems like it was just two," Hay said.

Karp fumed. "Two mice, three mice, chust give me vun mouse but say somesing!"

Lincoln started reciting.

"Hickory dickory dock - "

"Two mice ran up the clock." Hay added.

Lincoln paused. "I'm sure it was three."

Karp snatched the voice-catcher away before there could be further discussion of rodents. "Vun, two, who cares?" Karp said, "Ve just see how dey run."

As everyone watched, Karp adjusted something inside the box and turned the crank again. When he let go, the box emitted faint scratching noises that sounded, more or less, like termites.

"It worked this morning," Hay's face was fallen.

"I can't hear anything," Lincoln shook his head.

"Perhaps the sound is just too soft," offered Marcia.

Lincoln turned to Cooper. "Come here, boy, and listen."

Cooper came over and listened.

"Dogs listen better than people listen," Lincoln said. "At least the people I generally deal with."

Cooper listened to the noises coming out of the Karp's machine, wiggling his ears.

"He hears something, it's just hard to say what," the President said.

"Can you make it talk louder?" Marcia asked Karp, who said his machine was not at fault and that the dog should listen louder.

"Oh fiddlesticks," Marcia said, looking around the room, fastening a pretty eye on Lincoln's desk where a battle map lay open.

"Would you mind?" she said, and took the map and rolled it into a cone which she inserted into the talking box's hole where the sound came out.

"Professor Karp?" she said firmly, pointing at the machine.

Karp cranked it up, and this time an eerie sound filled the room: the wavering but unmistakable voice of Lincoln reciting "Hickory dickory dock."

Everyone cheered, encouraging Lincoln to go to the piano and sing a tune as the box listened. When Karp made the box talk again, it emitted the scratchy sound of Lincoln singing and playing the piano.

Cooper's ears flew up. He sat in front of the cone, peering into it curiously as the music came out.

"Arrrrrrr! Arrrrrrrr!" Cooper sang along with the President. "Arrrrr arrrrr a-wooooooo, a-woooo!"

24.
Miss Dahlia Van Buren

Miss Dahlia Van Buren waddled out of the White House kitchen, shooing Tad and Amy ahead of her.

"You chirrens stay out 'o my cookies or lawd God I'm moan wear you out!" Miss Dahlia said. "I mean I moan wahhh you out, I ketch you tiptoe in my kitchen one mo time lak I tole you not to! Them cookies is fo yo momma's party! That woman bout run me slap crazy."

"Yessum," they said.

Miss Dahlia, as she preferred to be called - insisted on it, in fact - was the other cook besides Florence. She went back in the kitchen muttering to herself and checking the cookies that cooled on a big tin sheet. She took the cookie icer and squeezed a bit of pink decoration on one or two of the cookies and went away to attend to other chores.

The kitchen grew still.

After awhile, the door from the hallway opened. Cooper's face poked in. Then came the faces of General Abernethy and Mr. Lincoln.

"The field is ours," Abernethy whispered, tiptoeing rapidly to the cookie sheet.

"I could eat a dozen o' them anisettes," whispered Lincoln, trying one. "Here, Coop," he tossed a cookie to Cooper who caught it and gulped it down in one quick motion.

Abernethy raked a line of cookies into his hat.

"Take two lines," Lincoln licked his lips.

"Lord have mercy, you're gonna get us shot at sunrise!" Abernethy said, reaching for the cookies.

Miss Dahlia's voice was behind them. "Naw, you ain gon git shot at no sunrise, you gon git shot rat now!"

Abernethy and Lincoln both yelped. Cooper hid behind Abernethy, who hid his cookie-filled hat behind his back.

"Ah, Miss Dahlia!" Abernethy said, "we were just, uh, looking for you. Weren't we, Mr. President?"

"Yes, that's what we were doing," Lincoln said.

"Absolutely," Abernethy said.

"Uh-huh," Miss Dahlia said. "And now you done found me, what you found me fo?"

"Well - " Lincoln said.

"Well - " Abernethy said.

"Well - " Lincoln said.

"Well what?" Miss Dahlia said.

"Well... we were just wondering if you need a new well," Abernethy said.

"That's what it was, a new well," Lincoln said.

"We ain't got a well in the first place," Miss Dahlia said.

"That's why we wondered if you needed one," Abernethy said.

"And that's the truth," Lincoln said.

Miss Dahlia looked suspiciously at the cookie sheet. She walked over and began counting with a plump finger. "They bed be nineyeight cookies on that sheet 'r I gon see Miz Lincoln and she gon take a broom upside sombody head!"

"No need for alarm, Miss Van Buren," Abernethy's eyes bulged. "It just so happens that I counted your cookies just now - in fact, both Mr. Lincoln and I counted your cookies - "

" - and that's the truth - " Lincoln grinned sincerely.

" - and I can give you my solemn word as a three-star Army general and graduate of West Point and chief military adviser to the President of the United States and as a Loyal Moose - "

" - I fixin to Loyal yo Moose!" Miss Dahlia fumed.

"I swear upon my sacred military honor, Miss Dahlia, that all ninety-eight cookies are present and accounted for. Isn't that so, Mr. President?"

"Absolutely. Upon my solemn oath as, uh, a solemn oath taker," Lincoln sweated.

Behind him, Abernethy could feel Cooper nuzzling into the hat of cookies.

"Well I tells you what," Miss Dahlia said. "I kin see without countin nothin that they ain't no nineyeight cookies on det sheet and det woman been driving me crazy is gon have a fit and - Gennal Abanathy, what dat you holdin fo behan yo back?"

"Why, it's nothing!" Abernethy said.

"If it aint nothin put cho hans out chiah wah ah kin seeum."

"It's nothing but my hat, Miss Dahlia."

Miss Dahlia put her hands on her hips.

Abernethy felt Cooper snatch the last cookie. With a sick grin, he held out his empty hat. Miss Dahlia peered inside, then narrowed her eyes at Cooper. Cooper wagged his tail, feigning innocence.

"Look at det no-count dog!" Miss Dahlia shook a finger at him. "His sides is all cooched out full of cookies! Lawd help us, I'm gon tell the missus you done took all her party fixins and fed them to that no-good-fer-nothin and then gone and lied about it - what all you didn't eat yoselfs and swo on whole stacks of Bibles and I don know whatall, two so-call crissun gennamens!"

Lincoln tried his best grin. Then he ran after Abernethy who bolted down the hall and took refuge in Lincoln's study with the President right behind him.

"What are we gonna do?" Lincoln said.

"Do?" Abernethy re-gathered his dignity and drew up in a huff and poked a finger in the air. "You, sir, are still the President of the United States of America and I am still the chief of staff of the largest Army in the world, in full command of 528,256 infantry troops well-armed, 141,680 cavalry troops fully equipped, and 136,974 pieces of artillery."

"Then why are we hiding from Miss Dahlia?" Lincoln said.

"It's unseemly and I refuse to do it for another minute!" Abernethy thundered, shaking his fist.

"You're right! Lincoln said. "Let's put our foot down! Both feet!"

"Declare martial law!" Abernethy said.

"Well wait a minute, general," Lincoln said. "I've already declared war and that includes martial law."

"Declare something else!"

"I declare executive privilege!" Lincoln said.

"No quarter asked or given!" Abernethy saluted.

Just then they heard Miss Dahlia's voice down the hall. And the click-click-click of Mrs. Lincoln's footsteps coming their way.

Moments later, Private Simmons looked up from his guard post to see the President and General Abernethy climbing out the office window.

25.
Professional Poise

Lincoln was reading the *New York Tribune*. "Dang," he said loudly.

Mr. Hay, who was in the other room answering correspondence, looked up. "Sir?"

"It's Editor Greeley, again," Lincoln said, throwing the paper to the floor.

Cooper fetched it, then got busy with a flea.

"Greeley, my so-called friend!" Lincoln hollered. "He takes up the whole front page of his so-called newspaper to call me an uninformed ape! The whole front page!"

Lincoln threw the paper across the room. Cooper brought it back.

"Just look," Lincoln shouted to the empty room because everybody had fled but Cooper. "He misquotes me six times just on the subject of monetary policy which he spells m-o-n-i-t-e-r-y. It might as well be monastery policy! And then he gets a dozen facts wrong and finishes off by calling me a babboon with two b's!"

"Woof," Cooper said, happy to see Hay come in just as the President was inhaling so he could holler some more.

"So that's a nice how-do-you-do!" Lincoln railed to Hay. "I go and invite Greeley to the White House and show him every courtesy and he can't even spell baboon right, let alone monastery!"

Cooper listened to this, then scratched his left ear.

Hay said, "Shall I cancel the *Tribune*, sir?"

"No," Lincoln slumped in his rocker. "The *Times* is even worse. You know, Hay, I am resolved from now on to never get mad over something I read in a newspaper. That, I will refuse to do. Like I've always said, you can't get mad about the press and stay long in politics."

"Woof," Cooper agreed.

"I say that when you're the President," Lincoln poked a finger in the air, "you're bound to be a lightning rod. You're going to get blamed for everything, but you refuse to lose your temper. You control yourself even when an ignoramus with a newspaper calls you a baboon. Or a gibbon."

"Wisest thing to do, sir," Hay said.

"Woof," Cooper agreed.

"Criticism of the President," Lincoln poked a finger even higher into the air, "is something you just have to expect in a democracy. Fair or foul. A great leader stays calm."

"Absolutely sir."

"Woof."

"Keep your shirt on, is my motto."

"You could not be more correct, Mr. President."

"Woof."

"Misspelling baboon and printing malicious and unfounded rumors are just par for the course."

"Right once again, sir."

"Woof."

"That's why you don't see me holding a grudge just because the press lies about me all the time and Greeley kicks me while I'm down!"

Hay looked at his watch. "Speaking of the press, sir, it's time for your press conference. They're all outside now, in fact.

The whole national press corps."

"Everybody?"

"Greeley's in the front row. It's your chance to show him, sir, how little you care about his criticism."

"Greeley's here?"

"Ready to take notes."

Lincoln's eyes went big.

Hay had to dive and grab the President by the foot as he sprang for the door.

"Let me go!" Lincoln hollered, dragging Hay across the floor along with Cooper who had the President by a pant leg.

"Remember! Self-control, sir!" Hay pleaded, grabbing a coat rack that got dragged as well.

Abernethy ran in with two guards just in time to help Hay pry the President's fingers off the doorknob.

"And cancel my subscription!" Lincoln hollered.

"Moderation sir, remember!"

"And arrest Greeley!"

"I didn't hear that, sir!"

26.
Poker Plans

General Abernethy decided to have a poker game.

"Seven o'clock. My quarters." Abernethy handed Sergeant Clancy some invitations to take around.

An hour later, Clancy was back. "All done," he said, "and I'm positive the darlin' general would have me spare no expense on his account for six bottles of the very best Irish whiskey money can buy, seein's how Himself will attend."

"Lincoln?" Abernethy's jaw hung open. "Lincoln doesn't even drink."

"Oh, I was referrin' to your favorite card player, general, namely Mr. Salmon P. Chase of the Treasury Department."

"Oh ho! Chase wants to come back for more punishment, does he?" Abernethy rubbed his hands together.

"That he does, and he wished me to say that your generalship will be well advised, on this auspicious occasion, to kiss all your money goodbye because - I wrote down Mr. Chase's exact words which I hereby quote – 'because when I'm done with that bottom-dealin' sneak' - referrin' of course to yourself - 'the only thing left of him will be his belt buckle.'"

"Chase said that?"

"His very words, sir."

"Salmon P. for Pusillanimous Chase!" Abernethy beamed. "And to think he's the secretary of the treasury! Last time he vowed to clean me out, I had to lend him a bedspread to walk home in. Who are our other suckers, Clancy?"

"The Wall Street banker Jay Cooke has accepted."

"Cooke the Crook!"

"One and the same, sir! And he lets on how he'll skin you alive, too."

"Worst poker player I ever saw, next to Chase," Abernethy threw back his head and laughed. "He and Chase always try to team up and cheat. And never catches on that I can see their signals going back and forth! Why, it's like they've got their hands laid out. I'll bag 'em both with one shot!"

"And - " Clancy snapped the invitation smartly, "your fourth hand is Mr. Clively J.J. Byrd."

"Byrd the Third? Where'd you find him?"

"Fallin' off a barstool at Willard's."

"I'm already counting his money! But speaking of counting, if there's only four of us playing, why do I need six bottles of whiskey, Clancy?"

"I was thinking of stealing two," Clancy said, "for keeping me mouth shut."

"You can keep it shut for one. Put it on my tab."

"I already took that liberty, your eminence, and I'm thankin' you for bein' the generous soul you are. And by the way, sir, if I might ask, how are you fixed for poker supplies?"

"I'll need the usual," Abernethy said. "Six marked decks and a shoe mirror."

"Would you want the aces shaved as well?"

"Do you take me for a cheap riverboat gambler, Sergeant Clancy? Just make sure the backs of the cards have clocks big enough for me to read. Hour hand for suit and minute hand for deuce through ace."

"I'll see to it."

"And by the way, sergeant, what about my poker jacket - is it back from the tailor's?"

"Just arrived. Goldberg had a bit of trouble getting the royal flush tucked in the sleeve so it wouldn't show."

"But he fixed it?"

"Did indeed, your eminence. But five cards are the very devil to put in a silk lining so he had to charge a little extra."

"And what about my spare deuces and one-eyed jacks?"

"I was just coming to that, sir. When you find yourself short of wildcards, all you do is pull the handkerchief out of your left breast pocket and blow yourself a new hand."

Abernethy nodded. "But what do I do if the room is hot and nobody wears a jacket?"

"Goldberg has anticipated that very situation ahead of time and in advance, your reverence."

"And?"

"He fixed up some special suspenders with extra aces at the collarbone, extra kings around the heart, extra queens at the stomach and one-eyed jacks at the belly button."

"What about Jokers?" Abernethy demanded. "Just in case."

"Jokers wild?"

"What other kind of Joker would I want?"

"I'm afraid there won't be any Jokers."

"Why not?"

"Goldberg doesn't believe in Jokers."

27.
A Friendly Game

Flap flap flap flapflap flap!

"I'll see your five and raise you twenty," Abernethy crowed, tossing a crumpled bill into the pot.

"It's your funeral," Chase said.

"Maybe!" Abernethy had been studying Chase's marked hand, trying not to laugh.

"I'll stay," said Jay Cooke, the banker, tossing another bill on the heap in the middle of the table.

"Too rich for my blood," Seward folded his cards and began slapping at a small fire in his pants cuff.

"You in or out, Byrd the Third?" Abernethy paused with the deck.

"I'm thinking."

"Think faster."

The five men examined their cards. Clouds of cigar smoke rose into the overhead lamp. Whiskey sloshed on the table.

Cooper sat near Lincoln. The President of the United States was in long white shirtsleeves, the heels of his shoes hooked in the chair rungs. Although coatless, he wore his stovepipe hat, a suspected repository of spare aces.

"Why don't you take off your hat and stay awhile?" Chase was vigilant whenever Lincoln's hand went above his shoulders.

"My head is chilly," Lincoln said.

"Why does that worry me?" Chase said.

Byrd the Third threw fifty dollars on the pile. "Let's cut the bull."

"You're bluffing." Abernethy matched the raise, and so did Chase.

"Lincoln?"

"I'm thinking," Lincoln said.

Abernethy dealt Byrd the Third two cards. Lincoln drew a strange look by standing pat. Chase raised the pot another fifty, and Abernethy matched that fifty and raised another fifty.

Abernethy stared casually at the backs of Cooke's marked cards. The little clock faces woven into the curlicue design indicated he had a trio of kings, ace high. Byrd the Third, mysteriously, had a pair of sixes. Lincoln had zippo. Chase gloated over three jacks and a wildcard. Abernethy reached for the handkerchief in his breast pocket and blew himself a full house.

"Read 'em and weep!" Abernethy said. Chase sighed.

"Beats me," Byrd said.

Seward shrugged.

Abernethy reached for the pot. "I want to thank you, gentlemen," he said, "for your total and complete lack of poker-playing ability."

"Hold it, general," Lincoln said, poker-faced. Abernethy gave Lincoln a quizzical look.

"A straight-flush beats all," Lincoln grinned.

"You don't have a straight flush!" Abernethy blurted.

"How do you know that, Horatio?" Lincoln said slowly.

"Well, I, er...."

Four pairs of eyes riveted Abernethy.

"A crooked deck!" Byrd the Third jumped to his feet.

"Hold on, Byrd," Lincoln said, "Crooked deck or not,

my straight will beat any hand on the table!"

"Wait a minute - " Seward cried.

"Shut up, Seward, you folded," said Chase. "But let's see your cards, Lincoln, although no one doubts the word of Honest Abe."

"Goes without saying," Seward said.

"Well, all right," the President said, straightening up from petting Cooper. "Here's my cards."

Lincoln spread the hand out on the table - an unbeatable straight. "Just as I said!"

Abernethy suddenly lunged across and grabbed the cards, wrestling them away and turning them over to show a Mississippi riverboat design. "This is an outrage! Not even the same deck of cards!"

"Cheater!" Seward shouted, "and the dog was in on it!" Cooper bolted from the room, spilling a royal flush from his collar just as Byrd's pistol fell out of his waistband and fired wildly into the ceiling.

They all froze.

Suddenly from upstairs: *thumpity thump thump....*

Seward said, "What was that?"

"What was what?" Abernethy paused in the middle of trying to seize Lincoln's hat.

"*That,*" Seward hissed.

Female footsteps.

Lincoln's eyes grew large. "Oh Lord...."

"Sounds like.... " Chase said.

"Quick," Lincoln said, "straighten this mess up!"

***

The poker players barely had time to grab stuff and get things looking halfway normal as a gaggle of feet click-clacked in the hallway.

Alma Seward was first in the door. "Oh dear, ladies, oh dear!" Alma said, "we've interrupted a meeting of the Army

Chaplains Charity Board!" She cocked an eye at her husband.

"Oh!" Seward gulped. "Right!"

Kate Chase rushed past Mrs. Seward, oohing and ahhing and taking a seat beside her husband. "Such a good cause, dear!" she said. "Just look at all the money you've raised!"

The ladies came forward to look at the table where the men sat bug-eyed with hands hovering en flagrante over scattered piles of greenbacks, cards and two spilt bottles they hadn't had time to clean up.

"Do I smell liquor?" Mary Lincoln sniffed the air.

"Surely not," Mrs. Abernethy fanned her bosom. "The chaplaincy board is a very sober affair - isn't it, Horatio?"

"Totally," Abernethy hastened.

"Whatever kind of cards are these?" Mary Lincoln picked up the demolished hand in front of the secretary of state and showed it to Mrs. Seward.

"Poker?" Mrs. Seward said sweetly. "A game for gentlemen!"

"Oh, father, would you teach us to play poker?" Kate Chase pinched the treasury secretary's ear.

"Ow! Well, dear, I don't know. There are such complicated rules."

"Complicated rules?"

"Extremely complicated," Abernethy added. "Dear."

"What sorts of rules? Dear?" Kate smiled sweetly.

"Whatever ones we agree on." Chase said.

"We can make up our own rules?"

"Yes and no," Chase improvised. "We can make up variations, but must stay within limits, of course."

Mrs. Seward smiled happily. "Variations within limits! I like that!" She picked up the deck and cut it and gathered the two stacks and made a fan in each hand. Then she flipped the fans in the air and caught them without missing a beat, and melded the halves and did a one-handed shuffle and slapped the deck back on the table.

"Five dollars to open?" Mary Lincoln asked sweetly, helping herself to one of the President's greenbacks.

"Wait a minute," Lincoln hollered, "you can't ante up with somebody else's money!"

"Variation on the rule," Mrs. Lincoln said. "You in or out, Abraham?"

"In," Lincoln mumbled. He reached over and appropriated a greenback from Chase.

"Have you lost your senses, Lincoln?" Chase said.

"I kind of like these new rules," the President said.

Seward studied his hand. "I'll take three."

"Three what?" Alma frowned.

"Cards." Seward was bewildered.

"Don't be silly," Alma said. "I already gave you some."

"I discarded three cards and I want three!" Seward insisted.

"What three do you want?"

"Well," Seward hesitated. Then his face took on a sly look. "I would like two queens and one king."

"Let me see your hand."

"No. Are you crazy?"

"Then you're not getting any new cards."

"Variation!" Abernethy snickered.

"Cards?" Alma asked him.

"No," Abernethy said, "I'm pat."

"Just one or two?"

"No... I don't need any."

"Well, we all think you should have some. Otherwise, you forfeit."

"This is cheating!"

"No, no it's not," Mary Lincoln said. "We have the same variation for everyone, and if Mr. Seward takes a card, you must take a card."

"But Seward didn't take a card! He wanted a card and you wouldn't give it to him."

"That's my point."

"All right! All right! Give me a card!"

"Here's a Joker."

"I don't want a Joker!" Abernethy hollered "We don't even use Jokers! I don't want anything and especially I do not want a Joker!" He threw the card on the floor and stamped on it and said a cussword.

"Oh, now really, General," Mrs. Lincoln said.

"Maybe you should give him another card," Kate Chase said.

"Well, if you want him to have another card," Mrs. Lincoln said, "you can give him one of yours."

Kate found a four of spades and poked it into Abernethy's cards. "There," she said.

"Does anyone have the ten of diamonds?" Mary Lincoln said.

"I've got the nine of diamonds," Kate said.

"No, it's got to be a ten. I need the ten and the king of diamonds."

"I've got the king," Alma Seward raised her hand, and gave the card to Mrs. Lincoln, who repaid her with a jack of clubs.

"Does anyone have the ace of hearts?" Kate said.

"I'll look in the deck," Kate said. "There are lots of cards left."

"Royal flush beats everything!" Mrs. Lincoln said, collecting the pot from the table.

"Oh, let me have a turn!" said Alma Seward excitedly.

Chase stood. Or staggered. "I'm taking my money and leaving," he declared.

"Me, too," Lincoln said.

"You can't leave when you're ahead," Alma Seward said. "It's a variation."

"My variation is no more variations!" Lincoln hollered, setting off a ruckus among the women.

"All right," he backed down. "You get just one more variation, and that's it!"

"Very well," Mary Lincoln said, "stick 'em up."

"What?"

"Hand over all your money."

"Mother, you can't stick us up! You don't even have a gun."

"Variation," Mrs. Lincoln said.

28.
Essential Government

Florence, still in her apron, stood at President Lincoln's desk and recited the ingredients that Marcia Bantom had asked for.

"Four cups o' flour, a cup and a half o' sugar, a tablespoon o' baking powder - "

"Hang on," said Lincoln, "I need something to write on." He rummaged around the papers on his desk, turned one over and jotted down what she'd told him.

"A tablespoon o' baking powder?"

"You got to use that much or it won't rise, honey."

"...OK, got it. What else?"

"A teaspoon o' salt and a teaspoon 'o nutmeg."

"OK," Lincoln said, adjusting his spectacles, "I've written four cups o' flour, a cup and a half o' sugar, a tablespoon o' baking powder, a teaspoon o' salt and a teaspoon o' nutmeg."

Florence nodded and left. Lincoln put the paper in his "out" basket, so that he wouldn't forget it. Then he forgot it and took Cooper out for a walk.

***

John Nicolay, who was shuttling bills up to Congress because John Hay was out with the miseries, went into Lincoln's office and collected the one paper waiting in the out-basket and carried it up to House Speaker Gubble's office. Two days later, the Speaker sent a final version to the floor. With recess coming on it shot through both Houses like a cannonball. It only needed Lincoln's signature.

"They just made one small change in conference committee," Nicolay said.

"Change to what?"

"The bill you sent up, sir. The Senate said a teaspoon of nutmeg was too much and would only go for half a teaspoon."

"Nutmeg?" Lincoln looked bewildered. "What are you talking about, Nicolay?"

"Your bill, sir. the House tried to get you three-quarters of a teaspoon but the Senate said it was a matter of principle, and didn't cave until nine members broke off from the majority and did some dealing in the cloakroom and agreed to half a teaspoon in conference."

"Congress is up there debating nutmeg while I'm down here with holes in my britches fighting three million Rebs?"

"To be fair, Mr. President," Nicolay said, "the House was ready to go along with a whole teaspoon - we had the votes on our side of the aisle plus three crossovers from the opposition, but the Senate minority leader threatened a filibuster. The only way that was avoided was Senator Shaw crossing the aisle and threatening to blow up the filibuster because he's from Connecticut and feels very deeply about nutmeg."

Lincoln held out his hand. Nicolay handed him the legislation.

"They enacted the wrong side of the paper!" Lincoln hollered. "Didn't the Speaker notice?"

"Actually, he did, sir," Nicolay said, "but he said the other

136

side would be too hard to pass."

Lincoln flipped through the bill. "This thing must weigh ten pounds," he said. "What are all these other pages besides the one about nutmeg?"

"Riders," Nicolay said.

29.
Late Work

The clock in Lincoln's study struck twelve midnight.
Nobody was there but Cooper. He was asleep.
Flap flap flap went the window shade.
Cooper opened one eye and looked at it.
Flap.
He waited.
Nothing.
He scratched a flea.
Nothing.
He stretched his left hind leg.
Nothing.
He turned around three times.
Nothing.
He went back to sleep.

30.
The Leader

Mr. Lincoln dangled a hand and Cooper came over and pushed his head against it.

The President was sitting at his desk. Soon his eyes were half closed as he stroked Cooper's muzzle and pulled gently on his ears. After napping for a bit, Lincoln took Cooper for a walk down by the Potomac. In the late afternoon sun, Lincoln could see the considerable silhouette of Dr. Hunt approaching.

"I didn't like the way your chest sounded," Hunt said.

Lincoln threw a stick for Cooper. "When was that?"

"The other day."

"What did it sound like?"

"I forget. But I didn't like it."

Lincoln looked at Dr. Hunt closely. "All right, what medicine did you bring?"

"Not a thing."

Lincoln took off his coat and sat down on the grass by the river.

"That grass is damp, Lincoln!"

"No, it's dry."

"Don't tell me. I can see it."

Lincoln lay back and let the sun shine down unseasonably warm on his face. "Reminds me of when I was a boy."

Cooper came up and put a cold nose on the President who reached out and rubbed the friendly head, listening to the soft panting.

"You and Cooper are a pair," Hunt shook his head. "Two no-accounts if I ever saw the like."

"Why don't you throw the stick for him?"

Hunt mumbled something, drawing in a breath so that he could lean over his paunch and reach down on the ground. "Fetch!" Hunt said, throwing the stick.

Cooper sat down and busied himself with an itch.

"Thunderation," Hunt said, shading his eyes with a hand. "The stick went in the river."

Lincoln smiled happily, his own eyes closed. "Your trouble is, Hunt, you don't recognize a valuable trained flea-dog when you see one."

"He don't mind," Hunt said.

"Mind what?"

"I mean he don't mind. He won't do a thing you tell him to."

"Why, he minds all the time."

"Thunderation."

Lincoln opened one eye. "Hunt, I'll bet you anything you care to bet, such as your hat, that Cooper will mind anything I tell him."

"What would you put up?" Hunt snorted.

"My hat."

"It wouldn't fit me."

"You don't need to worry. But when I win, and take that hat of yours, I intend on building a birdhouse."

Hunt reached down so Lincoln could shake his hand.

"You aim to make that dog mind or not?" Hunt said.

Lincoln got up and called Cooper over. "Now boy," he said, "you better listen to me this time and you better mind or I'll lose my hat. You hear me? Now I'm fixin' to give you an order and you have to mind and do what I tell you. All set? Eat this!"

The President pulled a cracker out of his pocket and tossed it to Cooper who snatched it in mid-air and swallowed it with scarcely a gulp.

"Why, you low-down fraud!" cried Hunt. "That's not minding!"

"Now, Hunt, be a good sport," the President chortled. "Give me your hat."

The doctor grumbled and took off his hat but held on to it. "All you did, Lincoln, was tell that no-good hound to do something he would have done anyway even if you told him not to!"

"First thing I learned in politics," Lincoln said, holding out his hand. "I'm gonna enjoy your hat."

"Well, you're not getting it," Hunt said.

"But we made a deal and you promised."

"I do not deny that," Hunt raised a finger skyward. "But I have hung around you too long not to pick up some lawyering myself, so I refer you to the fact that we did not specify a time for delivery of said hat, so I am hereby as the party of the first part, notifying you, as the party of the second part, that I am invoking the whereases and fine print of our agreement which means you can go fly a kite."

"Give me that hat," Lincoln snatched at it but Hunt pulled it away.

"Admit you were out-lawyered," Hunt said, "and I'll give it to you."

Laughing, the President, the doctor and the dog walked back to the White House.

31.
Wild Blue Yonder

Lincoln and Cooper went straight up. The President held on to his hat with one hand. With the other, he gripped the side of the gondola basket that hung beneath the big blue balloon.

"Do not worry, Monsieur le President," said Blaise La Mousse, the balloon master. "We shall rise to one hundred meters only! Then I, Blaise La Mousse, the world's greatest balloonist, will bring us back to Earth so gently that we will not wake le fly!" He added, "If, of course, all goes le well...."

"Oh Lord," Lincoln said.

All did not go le well.

As fast as the blue balloon went up, it came back down with a thump. Two sandbags broke away from the gondola, causing the blue balloon to shudder and shake and drag the gondola along the ground at a reckless pace as it tried to rise again. Cooper barked but it did no good. Then he scooted through M. La Mousse's legs, causing the world's greatest balloonist to lose his footing and fall overboard in a heap, followed by another sandbag.

That did it.

The blue balloon took off in earnest. Lincoln sprawled backwards on top of Cooper, his hat down over his eyes. All they could hear, from far below on the White House lawn, was La Mousse's imprecations in French and General Abernethy yelling, "Come back down here, Lincoln, confound it!"

Cooper peered cautiously over the side. The landscape was fast turning into a checkerboard of green and brown. Lincoln saw the White House get smaller and smaller.

"Cooper," Mr. Lincoln gulped. "I hope you know how to fly a blue balloon, because I don't."

Cooper, now that the excitement was over, was beginning to enjoy the ride. He could see the Treasury Building. He could see two small figures near the Presbyterian Church. He barked at a passing hawk.

Lincoln thought the Capitol dome seemed to be getting smaller.

"Lord have mercy," the President's eyes got big. "We're in a south breeze, Coop!"

Cooper's tongue hung out as he frowned at the lazy, chocolate sweep of the Potomac. Soon they were drifting over Confederate Virginia. Several rockets and cannonballs rose toward them, but they were up too high.

Off in the haze, Cooper could see the steeple of Richmond's tallest church.

"Lordy," repeated Mr. Lincoln, holding on to his hat. Cooper barked.

Soon, Cooper and the President beheld a strange sight. Another balloon, a big gray one, was rising slowly into the air just north of Richmond. Lincoln found a spyglass and spied on the balloon.

"Blue blazes, it's the Beauregard!" the President said. "This could be trouble."

As they drifted closer, Cooper could see the Confederate flag floating from the other airship.

"Well, Coop," Lincoln said, "since we can't run and we

can't hide, we might as well pretend we're brave."

The President was busy hanging out Old Glory when the first bullet whizzed by. It went past Cooper's nose, and the next one passed through Mr. Lincoln's tall hat.

"Hey!" protested Mr. Lincoln.

More bullets hummed around the gondola as the two balloons drifted closer and closer together. The wind was blowing hard, and Lincoln and Cooper jumped from one side of the gondola to the other, dodging bullets. Then a Confederate sharpshooter took aim at Lincoln's stovepipe and made several more holes in it for the wind to whistle through. Laughter rang out from the gray balloon as the President's hat whistled 'Dixie.'

"Durn your hides!" Lincoln said, although he enjoyed the music.

A sudden, swirling gust interrupted the Confederate tune and brought the two balloons together like a waltzing couple, gray and blue. Lincoln and Cooper went sprawling as their basket met the Confederate basket dangling from the Beauregard, sending it into a spin. The Rebs were trying to untangle themselves when Cooper leaned out and bit the Reb balloon.

Whooosh! went the Beauregard, and it sank toward Richmond at a dizzy rate.

Lincoln did a dance and yelled over the side, "Check this out, Rebs!" as he fingered the holes in his hat and played a lively rendition of 'Yankee Doodle.'

After the Reb balloon was gone, Lincoln gave Cooper such a hug that the dog could only groan.

"We done it, Cooper," the President said. "Or, rather, you done it. You are the first American to win a victory in aerial combat!"

Cooper's ears rose. He looked at Lincoln's hat, but the hat wasn't doing anything. He raised his ears some more.

"What's wrong, boy?" Lincoln said.

Cooper woofed and pointed, with his nose, at a small raggedy hole in the blue balloon.

"Uh-oh," Lincoln said. "Bullet hole." He crawled up the ropes and tried to plug it with a handkerchief, but the blue balloon continued leaking.

"Cooper," Lincoln said, "I hadn't planned on us visiting General Lee just now. But if the wind don't change direction, we might."

***

The wind did change direction and the President and Cooper blew back to Washington and made a perfect landing on the Executive Mansion's north lawn, except for squashing two rose bushes that Mrs. Lincoln was particularly fond of.

Lincoln and Cooper ran as fast as they could, and Monsieur le Blaise left town.

32.
The Cookie War Heats Up

Miss Dahlia drew a large sheet of cookies out of the oven and put them on top of the cutlery table to cool.

In the library, Cooper raised his nose. A warm smell of vanilla and anisette was poking under the door. Abernethy was first to get up.

"I can't take it," Abernethy mumbled.

Lincoln said, "Bring me one, Horatio."

"One what?"

"A cookie. And better not let Miss Dahlia catch you." Cooper followed the general down to the kitchen. First, Abernethy sneaked along the back corridor. Then he sneaked along the front corridor. Then he tiptoed carefully through a door that led to a corridor through the pantry to a door to the kitchen. Cooper stuck his head through the door to make sure the coast was clear, then Abernethy dashed inside and grabbed cookies off the cookie sheet with both fists, stuffing them into every pocket.

Back in the study, the general gave Lincoln a cookie, and had to give Cooper one to keep him quiet, while keeping the rest in his pockets.

"I only dared take two," Abernethy lied. "Miss Dahlia is on the warpath."

"I could eat a dozen," Lincoln moaned.

"Me too," Abernethy said.

Out in the hall, Cooper threatened to sing, so Abernethy gave him another cookie, which Cooper swallowed in one gulp.

"General!" Lincoln called from the study, still nibbling on his one cookie.

"Yes sir." Abernethy returned.

"General," Lincoln said, "Am I not the President?"

"Yes sir, you are."

"The President of the United States of America?"

"You are indeed, yes sir."

"And of Republic for which we stand, one nation indivisible?" Lincoln smacked a fist into his palm.

"Of course, sir."

"Then I want another cookie."

"No way," Abernethy shook his head. "Miss Dahlia has her eye out."

"Dang it!" Lincoln pounded on the arms of his chair. "Elections have consequences, and being President ought to mean I can have a cookie if I want one!"

Abernethy nodded vigorously, "You're right, sir! Elections are what makes this country great. And you were elected President, the most powerful man in the world! You need fear no one! But that woman in the kitchen has got eyes like a hawk and a memory like an elephant."

"And Mrs. Lincoln's ear, and also a rolling pin," Lincoln sighed. "All right, Abernethy, forget the cookie."

Later, as Lincoln napped, Abernethy snuck out and tiptoed down the hall again.

He was eating cookies off the tray when Miss Dahlia

caught him. All of Abernethy's bluster, and, finally, his entreaties, did him no good.

"If I tole you once I tole you two times," Miss Dahlia shook her finger at him, "and now I'm tellin' Miz Lincoln."

"Madam!" Abernethy drew himself to attention, "It is my duty to warn you that you are about to blow the cover on a top-secret mission ordered by the President himself. My instructions are to take all military steps deemed necessary to implement Presidential culinary as authorized by Executive Order WD-40 and you have my solemn word on that as a general with three stars!"

"Well you fixin' to see stars when I tells Miz Lincoln," Miss Dahlia said. "And the debbil's fixin' to get you, too, fuh telling big stories."

Miss Dahlia strode off to find Mrs. Lincoln and Abernethy ran after her. "Egad, Miss Dahlia," Abernethy croaked, "can't we be sensible about this?"

Mrs. Lincoln of course was fairly fit to be tied because the cookie shortage ruined plans for her tea. She barged into the presidential study and did some shouting, a lot of it, regarding General Abernethy.

"What do you want me to do?" Lincoln said.

"Court-martial him!" Mary shouted.

"Court-martial Abernethy?"

"He took all my party cookies!"

"Now, mother."

"Don't 'mother' me, Abraham! Miss Dahlia caught him red-handed with both hands full plus his big mouth and three big pockets."

"Wait a minute," Lincoln sat bolt upright in his rocker. "His hands and mouth and three pockets were full of cookies?"

"Had to be two dozen!"

"Two dozen cookies?"

"At least."

"Not just two cookies?"

"He had twelve just in his mouth, Abraham!"

"I've been swindled!" Lincoln hollered and ran for the door. "I'm gonna bust him down to buck private!"

33.
The Strategy Meeting

Of all the cabinet members who gave Lincoln advice, Secretary T.B. Burbridge was the worst, or so everyone thought except Secretary T.B. Burbridge.

Whenever T.B. got the urge to advise the President, he would stick his hands in his pockets and say "I was just thinking, Mr. President." Or sometimes he would say "I was just thinking," without putting his hands in his pockets or saying "Mr. President." Either way, T.B. had a nearly perfect record of coming up with awful ideas while Lincoln had a nearly perfect record of listening to them.

At Friday morning's cabinet meeting, T.B. rose and said, "I was just thinking, Mr. President," but this time used his thumbs to hitch up his pants and reveal spats, nearly as loud as Dr. Hunt's.

"Go ahead, T.B.," Lincoln nodded, alerting Stanton who nudged Seward who woke up cussing and slapping at his beard, which he assumed was on fire.

"Whatever it is, I vote no," Seward said.

T.B. appealed to Lincoln. "May I proceed, Mr. President?"

"By all means," Lincoln said, knowing he'd regret it, which he soon did.

"Here we go!" Seward inhaled.

T.B. drew out a bunch of papers that he said contained some polls that showed the President could raise his numbers by delivering a snappy comeback to any attack by a newspaper, no matter how scurrilous. "That way," T.B. said, "you can go high when they go low! For instance, when the *Times* calls you a monkey or the *Tribune* calls you a nitwit, you can come back with a witty rejoinder."

Secretary Chase raised a hand, "Sounds good, but I think you've got it the wrong way around, T.B. It was the *Tribune* that called the President a monkey."

"No, I'm sure it was baboon," Seward shook his head.

"Baboon sounds right to me, too," Chase looked in his notebook.

"I think you're both wrong," Stanton said. "The *Tribune* called the President an orang-utang, so it had to be the *Times* that said baboon. And by the way, baboons are apes, not monkeys."

"As long as we're getting our facts straight," Seward said, "there's a big difference between a baboon and an orang-utang."

"Utan, Seward, not utang."

"What?"

"It's utan without a 'g.' Orang-utans come from Sumatra, whereas the President comes from Kentucky," Stanton said.

"So which paper called the President a monkey?"

"I don't remember," T.B. said, "The Boston paper called him a dodo."

"Which paper said 'gorilla?'"

"Baltimore, I'm pretty sure," Chase said.

"No, that was Boston," Seward insisted. "Baltimore said jackass, or numbskull. One of those."

T.B. rapped the table. "Gentlemen, can we just agree on the right term for the President? I think it's numbskull." Lincoln started to speak but Chase interrupted.

"As long as we're looking for facts, T.B., why don't we start with one we all agree on and say 'babboon' with two b's?"

Seward raised a hand, "Second the motion."

"You're seconding Mr. Chase's motion to call the President a baboon?" T.B. said.

"No, I'm just saying we all agree on it."

"Now wait a minute!" Lincoln said.

"Call for the question," Stanton slapped the table.

"I object!" Seward said.

"You have to be recognized first," T.B. said.

"Fiddlesticks!" Lincoln got out of his chair.

"You're out of order, Seward," T.B. rapped his gavel.

Chase protested. "I move the chair's ruling on the previous motion!"

"The chair will entertain the previous motion," T.B. said.

"Then I move to take the motion on the motion off the table," Seward said.

"It was never on the table!" said Stanton. "I move we adopt Chase's motion that the President is a 'babboon' with two b's."

"All in favor?" T.B. said.

"Point of order - to clarify the motion on Chase's motion," Stanton cried.

"The chair," T.B. said, "exercises its prerogative to amend. The chair moves to amend Mr. Stanton's statement that the President is not monkey but a nitwit and a numbskull."

"Re-state my objection," Stanton called.

"I do, too," Lincoln said.

"The chair recognizes Mr. Stanton," said T.B.

"I object to calling the President a nitwit, and move to amend the spelling of baboon."

"Overruled, out of order. You can only move to amend your motion."

"Without objection!"

"In that case," said Seward, "I move we adopt 'orang-utang.'"

T.B. rapped for order. "Gentlemen, if I may! In the spirit of compromise, can the cabinet simply agree on orang-utan as the proper way to describe the President?"

"Here, here!" Chase said.

"All in favor?"

"Aye, aye, aye, aye."

"I object!" Lincoln hollered.

"Motion carries," T.B. said.

34.
Culture Revisited

Stanton hurried to Lincoln's office with research of his own. "What it says," Stanton explained, "is that you'll lose New York unless you overcome this 'orang-utang' thing."

Cooper opened one eye.

Lincoln rared back in his chair. "All right, Stanton," he said, "I'll confess to just being a regular gibbon."

"I wish you would take this matter of image more seriously, Mr. President," Stanton shook his head. "And by the way, a gibbon, as in ape, is pronounced with a soft g. The other Gibbon, with a hard g, is an English historian who wrote *The History of the Decline and Fall of the Roman Empire.*"

"I thought his name was Gibbons."

"No, gibbons is more than one ape, the way you're saying it."

"Stanton...."

"Yes sir?"

"Stanton, why are we sitting here in the midst of the

greatest crisis in the history of the United States of America talking about monkeys?"

"We're not," Stanton said, "We're talking about apes, and more specifically the elusive New York voter."

"Cream of the American electorate," Seward nodded. "Everybody there subscribes to the *New York Times*."

"Or Mr. Greeley's *Tribune*," Stanton pointed out.

"Or both," Lincoln sighed. "They're all culture hounds and think we could use a little more of it. Did we ever decide whether it was the *Times* or the *Tribune* that called me a baboon?"

"The *Times*."

"Pretty sure that was monkey, Mr. President. But shall I go on?" Stanton said.

"Wouldn't stop you for the world."

"There's quite a bit of difference between *Times* and *Tribune* readers, in our polls. Nearly a fourth of *Tribune* readers never heard of you, four percent think you're actually a monkey and another four percent are unsure It's fifty-fifty, in other words, on that last one."

"I'll take all the good news I can get."

"Then I'll skip the readers who've heard of you."

"All right, Stanton," Lincoln waved a hand, "what's the bottom line with those New York voters overall?"

"Well, sir, just rounding off the numbers, three-fourths say they will vote for you unless they change their mind and don't, two-thirds are definitely undecided whether they agree with the three-fourths, and eighty percent think you cheat on your wife."

"Arf," Cooper said.

35.
A Fine Idea

Lincoln couldn't sleep. He paced the floor. He thought about his poll numbers. Cooper paced with him.

"What'll we do, Coop?"

Coop didn't know.

They kept on pacing.

***

Two days later Lincoln sent for his cabinet. He hoped they had some new ideas. Burbridge stretched out on a chair and put his hands in his pockets, but did not say anything. Seward put an unlit cigar in his mouth. Stanton arrived late, carrying another research report.

"Our options are limited, sir," Stanton told the President. The 'orang-utang' attack is gaining traction, which means our best chance of winning is if the other party doesn't run anybody against you. In that case you win by three percent, which unfortunately is still within the margin of error."

"Then what's Plan B?"

"Plan B is to go immediately to Plan C," Stanton rustled through his papers.

"What's Plan C?"

"The Hail Mary."

"Those are my choices?" Lincoln paced again.

"Well," Stanton said slowly, "New York is still the key, and our number crunchers came up with a plan that shows you winning by double digits."

"Is any part of it legal?"

"Completely, sir. It may take a little fibbing, prevaricating and weasel-wording, but no more than strictly necessary to impress New York's culture hounds."

"What exactly are you talking about, Stanton?"

"We did the focus group thing, sir," Stanton said, "and are positive you could get past this 'orang-utang' thing by creating a Presidential prize for poetry."

"That's all there is to it?"

"Pretty much, sir. The more high-flown the poetry you claim to enjoy, the better."

"But nobody reads high-flown poetry anymore, Stanton, unless they're incarcerated in a high school English class! So how will the New York culture hounds know whether the poet I give the Presidential prize to is high-flown enough?"

"You've answered your own question, Mr. President. The beauty of high-flown poetry is that a culture hound would not admit under torture that he has no idea whether it's any good or not even if he's read it, which he probably hasn't."

"What's our next step?"

"We have to make the prize a media event," Stanton said. "We'll bring you the youngest poet we can find - hopefully a young prodigy under twelve."

"Why under twelve?"

"The reporters need an angle that they can write about without having to read anything."

"And not knowing the first thing about poetry?"

"Bingo."

"Stanton," Lincoln grinned, "you are a true friend of culture. But just in case they ask, who's my all-time favorite poet?"

"How about Peter Abelard?"

"Never heard of him."

"Didn't expect you had. He was born 1079 and died in 1142. Wrote everything in Latin, so I can practically guarantee that the culture hound voters haven't heard of him, either. Which is why they'll be even more impressed."

Lincoln later sent to the Jefferson Library for a volume containing an Abelard poem, a hymn.

"Listen to this, Cooper," Lincoln began singing softly, adjusting his glasses: "O quanta qualia sunt illa sabbata, Quae semper celebrat superna curia!"

Cooper barked.

36.
A Highly Precise Poll

Time was getting short. Stanton hurried to Lincoln's office with the latest research from Barker & Bumble, tripping over long streamers of paper as he ran and causing some to blow away, which caused Cooper to bark and chase them.

"It's our greatest scientific poll, yet, Mr. President," Stanton assured Lincoln.

Seward grunted and stretched out on the library table, smoking a cigar. He waved a long ash in Stanton's direction.

"And no one's invited your opinion on these opinions, Seward," Stanton said.

"I didn't say a word," Seward said. He puffed on his cigar, neglecting an ember that was causing his necktie to smolder. "I just want to know what all this scientific snooping is costing us."

"I prefer to think in terms of benefits," the secretary of war said. "Mr. Lincoln, we're finding out in great detail exactly how and why and on whose account you are in dire peril of your political life. Knowing what the voters have on their minds will give you a great advantage in the election."

"How much money?" Seward repeated.

"Just rounding it off," Stanton said, "about eighty-seven thousand."

"Dollars?" Lincoln said.

Seward opened his eyes "I think I just had a stroke."

"Go ahead with your report, Stanton." Lincoln sat down.

Stanton polished the small lenses of his spectacles and began flipping through reams of figures. "To understand the high precision of our results," he said, "you must first know that we conducted individual interviews, in-depth, of likely voters in six hundred and seventy bellwether precincts in three bellwether geographic areas in fourteen bellwether states and three major cities. In New York City, for instance, we surveyed one thousand two hundred and four voters in two hundred and thirty-two precincts - Poles in Brooklyn, the Irish in Queens, Italians on Staten Island, and Jews on the East Side. We also polled Minnesota to see what the Swedes are thinking, Mr. President."

"Where else?"

"And Arkansas."

"Arkansas?" Lincoln blinked.

"Yes, sir."

"Stanton, why on earth did you take a poll in a Confederate state?"

"I'm sure the statisticians had a reason, Mr. President."

"I hope so," Lincoln said. "So, what did you find out overall?"

"Well, in New York, Mr. President, we are absolutely sure that two-thirds of the likely voters want you to cut their taxes. Three-fourths are either moderately worried or greatly worried about crime. Three-fourths want you to cut out welfare, immigration and foreign aid, and eighty-two percent think you cheat on your wife."

"What about Minnesota?"

"Well, as far as the Swedes are concerned, two-thirds want you to cut their taxes, three-fourths are worried about crime, three-fourths want you to cut welfare and foreign aid, and eighty-one percent think you cheat on your wife."

"What about Arkansas?"

"Well, Mr. President, two-thirds of the people in Arkansas want you to cut their taxes, three-fourths are worried about crime, three-fourths want to cut foreign aid and welfare, and eighty percent think you cheat on your wife."

"And this is all scientific?" Lincoln said.

"Absolutely Mr. President. When we do all the derivations and cube root analysis of the party of the first part and eliminate the squared empty set integral of Z-factor bias for the party of the second part and multiply that by one-half your height times your base, we can absolutely confirm that voters are triangulating."

"I need to lie down for a minute," the President said.

"Eighty-seven thousand bucks shot," Seward mumbled.

"Did you say buckshot?" Lincoln opened an eye."

"No," Seward said, batting at the small fire that was making progress in his necktie, "I'd just like for us to conduct a small but instructive mental exercise."

"What's that?"

"Let's say this country has a population of what, twenty million, roughly?

"About. Just the Union states."

"Round it off to twenty. By definition, half our population is of above-average intelligence and half is below-average, which means ten million of our people are dumber than normal."

"Never thought about it."

"Next, medical men estimate that ten percent of the population is deranged in some way. They have manias and delusions. Can't think straight, in other words. So two million of us are, to some extent, nuts."

"What are you getting at, Seward?"

"That's twelve million dumb or deranged people out of twenty million."

"Surely that can't be!"

"The numbers don't lie, I'm afraid, sir. To go on, I have it on absolute authority that five percent of the people are in jail, or have been in jail, or are doing things that might put them in jail at any moment. So that comes to a million crooks, jailbirds and no-goods, which brings the total to fifteen million."

"Seward, you're being preposterous."

"No, I'm not. Of the five million people left, at least twelve million are women, Indians and free blacks and poor people who are not allowed to vote, and three million drunks, dope-heads and crazy people who can't figure out how to vote, so many voters do we have left?"

"That's more than a hundred percent, Seward!" Lincoln objected.

"My very point, sir," Seward was vigorously slapping his smoldering tie. "When we add up all our ineligibles, dimwits, lunatics, women, Indians, black people, drunks and jailbirds, it comes to more than the number of voters."

"Dammit, Seward!" Stanton yelled.

Seward tut-tutted, raising his head to check his fire suppression efforts. "I realize, Stanton, that my statistics are disappointing for you, but you might want to take a look at this poll I did, on my own, that shows how well your thinking matches up with reality on Main Street. You know, to see whether we mandarins of the inner circles of government are moved by the same political issues as a million convicts and nincompoops in Minnesota."

"And?" Lincoln looked up.

Seward pulled out a piece of paper. "My own scientific poll shows that three out of four cabinet members and ninety percent of our most senior and experienced government officials want a tax cut."

Seward shoved the paper back in his pocket.

"That's it?" Lincoln said.

"They also think you cheat on your wife."

37.
Poet Laureate

"You're sure this will work?" Lincoln was nervous.

"Absolutely," Stanton said. "We've run the numbers backwards and forwards. And we're sure you can lock down the culture hound vote and lock up the election by naming a poet laureate."

"Seems too simple," Lincoln mumbled.

Seward, searching through his vest for a match, stared cross-eyed at his unlit cigar. "Nothing is ever too simple," he said.

"Go ahead and say it!" Stanton grew red in the face. "Go ahead!"

"Say what?" Seward affected to look puzzled.

"That there's nothing too simple for me to get wrong! You're always saying it."

"Really? I had no idea. Say, Stanton, you wouldn't have a light, would you?"

"No." Stanton moved his papers away.

Lincoln lay on the couch massaging his corns. "You said

we needed to name somebody under twelve so the reporters would have something to write about. What's our young prodigy's name, again?"

"Archibald MacLeish."

"Have I heard of him?"

"Well, he's ten and he's a prodigy and a Harvard man. Or boy, I guess."

"Do I shake his hand or pat him on the head?"

"I'd shake his hand. He's also the world's youngest professor."

"Then I give him the award or what?"

"Better make it a What. That'll give the story some legs so it's not just a one-day wonder. Offer him a job as curator of poetry at the Library of Congress

"What would he do?"

"It's a government job," Seward wagged his cigar, "so we should pray that he doesn't do anything."

"Always the cynic," Stanton shook his jowels.

"I have to agree with Seward to some extent," Lincoln said. "Any time the government does something, it's generally a bad sign. We certainly would rather that the Army do nothing, because if it does something it means we're in a war or getting ready for one! And do we want the surgeon general to stay busy? Of course not. If the surgeon general is earning his paycheck, it could mean we're having an epidemic. Same thing for the Justice Department. Do we want our government lawyers giving us a full day's work for a day's pay? You've got to be joking! If they're busy at Justice, it means people are breaking laws right and left and need to be in the penitentiary. I, personally, would breathe a sigh of relief if every public servant in Washington napped on the job for eight hours and went home."

Stanton rolled his eyes.

"Seriously Stanton," Lincoln began working on his whole foot, "Seward does have a point. We should not even want the Supreme Court to stay busy. If a case gets to the Supreme Court, it means Congress or some legislature has so fuddled a law that nobody can agree what it means or whether in all particulars it follows the Constitution. So, people have to hire expensive lawyers to carry the broken thing to the Supreme Court to see if nine other lawyers can dress up in robes and make sense of it, which would not have been necessary if Congress had spent its time loafing and raising campaign funds instead of staying busy."

"About the poet laureate," Stanton said, "my plan is to let the reporters in, then bring in young MacLeish about a minute before you make a grand entrance and astonish the press with a witty, well informed discourse with the poet laureate that will last about fifteen minutes. The New York culture hounds will eat it up!"

"Do I give the reporters plenty of time to write their dispatches and get them on the train to New York?"

"We thought this out carefully," Stanton said. "They should have just enough time to write, but not think. We don't want reporters thinking."

Cooper barked and rolled over.

***

At two o'clock in the afternoon, Stanton brought in young MacLeish, who was answering questions for reporters when Lincoln entered.

"How do, young man!" Lincoln said, shaking his hand.

"A poem should not mean, but be," said MacLeish.

"I was just thinking the same thing," Lincoln said, fishing surreptitiously for his notes.

"Poetry is a means of knowing," MacLeish said.

"Whenever I want to know something, I ask Cooper," Lincoln patted the dog.

"A poem is a dog," MacLeish said.

Lincoln quickly searched through his pockets and found a paper in his vest which, with practiced aplomb, he secreted in an open desk drawer where he could see it.

"Uh, would you mind repeating that?" Lincoln said.

"A poem is a dog."

"Take drapes to laundry" Lincoln said, glancing at the note.

The reporters scribbled.

"Hard to believe you're just ten," Lincoln said.

MacLeish threw back his head. "Poetry...is a means to know the kind of thing that can only be known emotionally...that can't be analyzed, taken apart, spelled out and put back together again."

Lincoln glanced into the drawer. "Two cords of firewood before Friday."

"Once," MacLeish said, "a Senator told me that he had read one of my poems and could not find a meaning. I told him that others have had the same difficulty."

Lincoln said, "Two cans of beeswax for pine floors."

"I had not finished," MacLeish cried. "Robert Browning admitted that, at the time he wrote a verse, only he and God knew the meaning - and that later on only God knew."

"Re-do wallpaper in hall."

Stanton stepped forward, applauding. "Marvelous! Marvelous!"

The reporters also applauded, stumbling over one another as Seward herded them out.

Later, Seward said, "What were you reading, anyway, Lincoln? You had them all buffaloed!"

"I don't know," Lincoln said. "The dog ate it."

38.
The Liberation of Women

Lincoln and Cooper went down to the Potomac late one afternoon to throw the stick. Abernethy heard about it and went after them, riding his horse. He was determined to have the hide and hair of every man in Lincoln's bodyguard.

"Don't you know there could be Confederate sappers around here?" Abernethy yelled at the hapless lieutenant-in-charge when he reached the river. He grabbed the young man's swagger stick and broke it over his knee.

The lieutenant hurried along at Abernethy's heels, explaining that the President wouldn't listen. "He's my commander-in-chief," the young man pleaded.

Abernethy fumed, "If he won't listen, hog-tie him! That's an order!"

Up ahead, on the banks of the brown river, Mr. Lincoln's tall hat was in silhouette against the sun in downward arc.

"Come join us," Lincoln called, poised with a stick to throw. Cooper barked.

"Get it, boy!" the President said. The stick sailed above the caramel water. Cooper launched himself from the bank.

"Mr. Lincoln," Abernethy slapped his gloves in his palm. "Sir, you are taking an awful chance. That other side over there is Virginia."

Lincoln stuck a jimson weed in his teeth. He waited until Cooper splashed back with the stick. Dripping with water, his coat slicked down, Cooper barked and waited expectantly as the President picked up the stick again and threw it.

Cooper took off.

"I swear, I think Coop would chase that stick til the world ended."

Abernethy, thinking of the danger, only shook his head.

Lincoln was in shirt sleeves; his coat was spread on the grass above the river and he lay down on it, adjusting his hat so that the brim fell over his eyes. Several notes and folded papers slipped from the hat and rested down around his temples. He ignored them, lacing his hands behind his head, letting out a contented sigh.

Cooper came back, barking, and dropped the stick once more.

"You throw it for him, Horatio," Lincoln murmured, sensing rather than seeing the dog. "I'm gonna shut my eyes awhile."

Abernethy hesitated, picked up the stick and looked at it. "Mr. President, this is foolishness, pardon me for saying so. Hush up, Cooper."

"Horatio," Lincoln's voice was muffled underneath the hat. "Don't you ever like to daydream? Just for a little while I'm daydreaming there's no war."

Abernethy looked at Lincoln. "I'm not good at daydreaming."

"Me neither. I'm practicing."

The general caught the lieutenant's eye. "Get your men together. You're going to escort the President out of here." He handed the stick to the lieutenant who, perhaps thoughtlessly, tossed it end-over-end toward the middle of the river. Cooper sprang in pursuit before it had time to splash down, dog-paddling furiously to reach the spot at the same time as the stick, and about this same time a shot rang out. It came from the Virginia side. A geyser of water rose six inches from Cooper's head. Abernethy's ham fist went to his holster and came back with a pistol in it, gray and gold and fully loaded. The young federal guards unslung their rifles and dropped to their knees to form a skirmish line, but there was nothing to shoot at. They aimed around uncertainly, looking to Abernethy and then to their lieutenant, for guidance as to what to do.

"Look," called one of the guards, pointing into the river.

Near Cooper, the coil of a newly-headless cottonmouth twisted slowly downstream.

And came a voice from the trees:

"Hope yo dawg's awright!"

It was a young woman's voice.

Nobody could think what to answer. Abernethy cupped a hand to the brim of his hat, squinting into the strong light.

"Fine shot."

"I was aimin fer the mockerson's left eye but I struck the right," the voice said. "I was scar't that ol snake mighta bit yer dawg."

Abernethy looked at Cooper.

Cooper barked.

"He's all right, ma'am" Abernethy called.

The voice said, "You gotter watch am-air cottonies this time o' day."

"We're much obliged," Abernethy said. "And I'd be pleased to thank you more properly, ma'am, if you'd stand so's we can see you."

"I might be a tad slow," the woman said, "but I ain't dumb."

"Union soldiers do not shoot women."

The next shot - from where was unseen - tore off Abernethy's hat.

"Womenfolk's got as much right to get shot as anybody else! Yankee!"

Lincoln raised the top hat from his eyes. "Horatio, did she call you a Yankee?"

"She did."

"I thought she did. You must have riled her pretty bad."

"And I'm still riled!" The voice called from across the river. "Men thinks they the only ones can do anything!"

Lincoln raised his arms. "Is it safe for me to get up?"

"Awright."

Lincoln slowly rose to his feet and fastened his tall hat on his head.

"You look like that Yankee President!"

"That's what my wife thinks."

"I bet you 'air that Yankee President! I seen yo picture in that big hat. That hat's a mighty temptin target!"

"Do you specialize mostly in hats, or is it snakes?"

"I was aimin to specialize in you 'til I seen that cottonie swimmin for yo dawg."

"The dog's much obliged."

"Well."

"Is it all right for us to go?"

"I reckon. But would you answer a question for me?"

"If I can."

"Is it true you aimin to free the slaves?"

"It's true."

"Well, you a tad slow. Halfa mine's already free."

"You freed half your slaves?"

"Naw, they run off on me. But now it's got me thinkin."

"About freeing the rest?"

"No, about shootin you fer stirrin up trouble. And you don't think I will, just 'cause I'm a woman?"

"I guess we better go."

As Lincoln walked Abernethy back toward the White House, he said, "Horatio, I swanny that future generations will talk about us for years and years for freeing the slaves. But freeing the women is going to be a sight more complicated."

39.
The Nanny

"Abraham," Mary said. "Do you know that you are talking to yourself?"

"Huh."

"Abraham, you are carrying on a regular conversation."

"Huh."

"Abraham, do you hear me?"

"I can't find it." Lincoln was turning pages in his Bible.

"Abraham, are you listening?"

"What?"

"I said you are talking to yourself."

Lincoln looked up, resting the Bible on his lap.

"Abraham, you were talking just now."

"I didn't know I said anything."

"I told you, but you weren't listening."

"What was I talking about?"

"I don't know, Abraham."

"I didn't even know I was talking."

"You were, though, just now."

"Huh." Lincoln leafed through his Bible some more. "Senator Cameron quoted a Psalm today and I'm sure it was Shakespeare."

"What quote?"

"That's the trouble. I don't recall, exactly, but I think I'll recognize it if I see it."

"Dear, don't you think if it's Shakespeare, you won't find it in the Bible?"

"I don't remember it being in the Bible. Which is why I'm looking for it and don't see it. I wish I could remember what he said. What time is it?"

"Nine o'clock, lacking a few minutes."

"I've been feeling like a banana all week. I got one on my mind Sunday, and I can't quit."

"You've always been fond of them. I never was."

"Why don't we have any?"

"Abraham, I have not seen banana one since the war. I have not seen one in the whole city."

"Most people in Washington don't seem to favor bananas. They're mostly a matter of where the railroads are. You can only take a banana so far, and it starts to turn on you. When I was a young lawyer for the Illinois Central, I would get bananas delivered on my desk right there in Springfield. I didn't even have to ask. The bananas would just show up, and everybody would want one. Remember Judge Roland Hankins? He represented the I.C. before I did, and he said it was the railroad's way of doing business. Another railroad that didn't have as much sense as the I.C. would have ruint it. So, you had your I.C. bringing bananas up from New Orleans, Louisiana, by the trainload, and the entire city of Chicago would get busy eating bananas, and before everybody got done with that trainload, the I.C. would bring another trainload and people would start eating bananas all over again. Half of the economy, it seemed like, was bananas."

"Yes, Abraham."

"I guess if it wasn't bananas it would be something else, but it wouldn't be near as good as bananas."

***

Later that same evening, around ten, Mary brought up the subject of a "nanny." She had heard about other women, mainly wives of senators and bankers and so forth, hiring full-time caretakers for their children. They were called "nannies," and their main purpose was to indicate the family's social and financial status. Mary thought they might get a nanny themselves.

"All right," Lincoln said at last.

"It's not as if we're abandoning the children," Mary said.

"No, no."

"There are just so many other demands."

"True."

"They want me visiting hospitals. They want me to join committees and go to committee meetings. They want this and they want that."

"To be expected."

"Florence tries to help me out, but she's busy."

"She certainly is."

"So, you agree we need a nanny."

"Go right ahead," Lincoln said.

"Just for a time," Mary said.

***

Not too long after that, a carriage brought Miss Eleanor Cochran. She was a nanny. Hay met her at the curb. He looked at her, didn't know what to say, so he said, "My compliments."

Miss Cochran peered at Hay through a pince nez that sat smartly on her small, upturned nose. Hay had never seen a more perfect nose. Very small nostrils that were just the right shade of pink and quivered just the right amount when she breathed. Hay was certain he had never seen finer nostrils. She was also blonde.

"Sir?" Miss Cochran said. "Were you about to say something else?"

Hay swallowed. His Adam's apple bobbed. "Sorry, what was that?"

"You were about to say something?"

"No. What?"

"May I get down?"

"Oh. Yes ma'am." He helped her down, touching her arm. It was clad in a silk sleeve. He felt the blood drain from his face.

"I'm thirty, Mr. Hay. Mr. Hay, is it not?"

"Yes. But John is, uh...call me John."

"How old are you, John Hay?"

"Twenty-two. But going on twenty-three."

A slight, speculative smile toyed with her lips. She swayed as if to say something, but did not.

"Will all our conversations be like this, Mr. Hay?"

"Like what?"

"Inappropriate. Don't you think this conversation is inappropriate?" She pointed to her luggage. "You can carry those."

Hay followed, hobbling, trailing her into the Executive Mansion. "Inappropriate, how?"

"You asked how old I was."

"I did not!"

"And did I answer you honestly?"

"You told me thirty."

"It was a lie. I'm thirty-one. As of last week."

"You're - "

"And am I attracted to you?"

"Excuse me, Miss Cochran?"

"You're going on twenty-three. That's what you said. You told me everything when you held my arm to help me down."

"I told you how old I was, after you asked. I wouldn't lie to you about that, Miss Cochran."

"Which way do we go, Mr. Hay?"

"Right, at the top of the stairs."

He followed her up, catching a glimpse of ankle, and stumbling.

"And you did not lie to me?" she asked without

turning around.

"No! I would never lie to you. It's the last door on the left."

She opened the door on the right.

"Miss Cochran, that's the President's bedroom, Miss Cochran!"

He trailed in with the luggage. She stood there looking at the four-poster bed.

"I see," she said. "I see indeed."

Then she turned and went across the hall to her own room and thereafter took up the duties of White House nanny.

40.
The Mystery

The day after Miss Cochran arrived, General Abernethy decided that his uniform was too tight.

"Sergeant Clancy!" he shouted.

Clancy ran in.

"Confound it, Clancy," Abernethy fumed, "this uniform is too tight. Which cleaner did you take it to?"

"The same one as always, your generalness," Clancy said.

"Well it's too tight and I want to know the reason!"

"I couldn't swear what it is, sir, unless I was to swear on me Bible which I must have left in me other pants, sir."

"Confound it, sergeant, I don't want you swearing on a Bible! I want to find out what that cleaner is doing to it."

Clancy ran out and came right back and said, "I asked them straight-up to give me the low-down, sir, and they did."

"Well what was it?"

"They said you're getting fat."

"That's not so, sergeant!" Abernethy shouted. "I am not

getting fat!"

"Their exact words was, 'he's two good axe handles across the beam and his uniform is just an axe handle and a half.'"

"This is wartime, Clancy!" Abernethy said. "I could have them shot for treason!"

"In that case, sir," Clancy said, "it would be incumbent upon meself to quote to his generalship the exact reply, which is another way of sayin' verbatim accordin' to me best memory, which is excellent and somethin' I took from me great-uncle Seamus who could remember anything, which is, to wit, 'the general could lose thirty pounds off his middle and still be a holy blivet, but he would have a fightin' chance to button his uniform if he drew in his breath and held it. Takin' a chance, of course, that the buttons would pop off anyways and go flyin' and cause casualties the Union can scarcely afford under the circumstances, which are already somethin' awful, which is why the general might want to reinforce the buttons with a stouter bit of thread.' To the best of me recollection."

"Clancy!"

41.
Two Days Later

Knock knock knock-knock-knock. Knock knock.

"Go away Clancy!" Abernethy shouted.

"How's your diet coming along, your worship?" Clancy strolled in.

Abernethy flung his pen down on his desk. "Sergeant Clancy, have you forgotten how to report properly to a commanding officer?"

"Not a'tall sir."

"Then do it!"

"Shall I go outside and come in again, sir?"

"No, confound it, Clancy! Stand at attention! Heels together!"

"Which I hereby do exactly to the very best of me ability, sir, and however long the general wishes, knowin' as certain as the awful snakes was drove out of Ireland that consideration is bein' paid to me poor bunions that hurt somethin' fierce. Near as bad as me corns."

"Stop blathering about corn Clancy! Never mention

corn! Or butter!"

"It was more about me bunions, sir."

"You're not making sense, Clancy! Why are you even in my office?"

"To deliver a notice regarding General McClellan, sir - "

"What notice?" Abernethy sat back. "What's that pipsqueak McClellan done now?"

"It's on this paper, which I'm hereby and therefore deliverin' in person as ordered."

"Then deliver it, Sergeant Clancy, and do it properly!"

"Yes sir!" Clancy raked off his cap. "I, Sergeant Major Timothy O. - for O'Neill, which was me mother's maiden name - Clancy, United States Regular Army, hereby report with a proper salute and standin' straight at attention, accordin' to regulations, to the right honorable Horatio K. Abernethy, adjutant general of the Army, the horrible news of a mistake by none other than the commanding general of Army of the Potomac, General George McClellan."

Abernethy's mouth hung open.

"That sawed-off peacock is admitting a mistake?"

"Not him, exactly."

"What are you talking about, Clancy?"

"General McClellan's gone and sentenced poor Private Ian McIver to be hung."

"Who the devil's Private McIvan?"

"McIver, sir - me sister Mary Margaret's youngest and unfortunately not too awful bright although he's me second cousin."

"You just said he's your nephew, Clancy, and now you're saying he's your second cousin?"

"Yes sir, second or third, I could never find out which one."

"Never mind what kind of kin, Sergeant Clancy! Why did McClellan order him hanged?"

"Because they wouldn't do it, otherwise."

"Clancy, you're making my head spin. Just tell me what the devil this is about!"

"Well, to begin at the beginning, sir - "

"Begin in the middle, Clancy!" Abernethy yelled, "I don't have all day. I haven't had lunch."

"Yes sir. To start with the main subject, General McClellan signed poor Ian's death warrant while he - meanin' the general and not Ian - was having a fine hot breakfast and enjoyin' a second stack of pancakes."

"Pancakes?" Abernethy licked his lips.

"And a side of apple-cured sausage, as was told to me. They said the smell was all delicate-like and the cakes in front of the general was golden brown and soaked through in hot butter and maple syrup - "

"Stop talking about pancakes!" roared Abernethy. "And maple syrup!"

"Yes sir. But would yez also want me to skip the part about baked ham - "

"Clancy!"

"Yes sir."

"Give me that warrant!"

Abernethy peered at it. "What's this? It says, 'Sentence to be carried out after full observance of Prisoner McIver's request for last meal, per Army Regulation A-103-102!' I never heard of any such regulation, Clancy!"

"Oh, the Army has a regulation for everything, sir."

"This says 'The Condemned asks for two platters of southern fried chicken, a dozen hot dinner rolls with fresh butter, prime rib of beef with au juice and horseradish cream sauce, and five pounds of planked halibut!' For the first course? And we have to go along with this?"

"A man's last meal and all, sir. It's regulations."

"And it's an outrage, Clancy! It even talks about chocolate cake and lemon meringue pie! How can I sign such a thing?"

Clancy saluted again. "I already anticipated your generalship's reluctance ahead of time and in advance, and took the liberty of signing it meself on your behalf of yourself, and throwing in a dozen Honduran cigars for the sake of mercy."

"What are you talking about, Clancy? McIver didn't even order cigars!"

"He forgot, sir," Clancy said, "so I filled it in. Right underneath 'chocolate cake.'"

"Clancy, if it wasn't for regulations, I'd have you and

McClellan both hung alongside McEwan or whatever his name is for sponsoring this bacchanal! Think what it'll do to his waistline, Clancy! A military man should watch his trim even if he's to be hanged."

"My very thought, sir."

"And you never did say what this McIwan did to get the death penalty!"

"It's all there in the fine-print, your sirship."

Abernethy looked at the order again and jumped to his feet. "Confound it, Clancy, this order is a complete mess! It says it's McClellan who's to be shot at sunrise, not McIvers! And I though you said McIvers was to be hung."

"I meant shot. And its McIver. Sir."

"Get the details right, sergeant! No detail is too small for an Army man to foul up! And don't think for a minute, that you can play on my sympathies to save your second-cousin. Desertion is serious business! Bang! Firing squad! Only way to maintain discipline."

"True, sir."

Abernethy rapped on the paper. "Whatever else we may think of this capital sentence, Clancy, General McClellan has your cousin dead to rights!"

"Nephew, to me best recollection, sir."

"Admit your nephew committed a serious offense, Clancy! ...But wait a minute!" Abernethy frowned at the paper. "This says Private McIan ran away to Atlanta while he was supposed to be on picket duty in Mississippi."

"I thought I wrote Alabama."

"Confound it, Clancy, he couldn't have been on picket duty in either place. They're both in the Confederacy!"

"It does sound fishy all right."

"Fishy's not the word for it!"

"Prime ribby, then?"

Abernethy's stomach rumbled.

"Sergeant Clancy, stop talking about fish and prime rib and tell me what Army regulations say about a prisoner's last meal if he gets a reprieve?"

"Yes sir."

"Yes sir, what?"

"In that case, the darlin' regulations say all unexpended food, victuals, provisions, edibles, comestibles and such and so forth are declared thereby ipso facto under statutes provided by writ of habeas corpus to be official Army surplus and disposed of according to procedure adjudicated by the adjutant general."

"Well, in that case, Clancy, since you have been an exemplary sergeant and a credit to the Army, I have decided to take those facts into account and grant your nephew clemency!"

"You are a paragon of incontinence, your honor, and if I hadn't heard it right with me own eyes I would have swore on Bibles piled clear up to the ceiling that you and the word mercy didn't belong in the same sentence."

"Thank you, Clancy."

"What happens to me nephew now, your excellency, since you're granting him a pardon?"

"Don't put words in my mouth, Clancy! I said clemency, not pardon! I'll have McIvers breaking rocks and eating bread and water until he's a hundred years old!"

"He'll be down on his knees thankin' you, sir."

Abernethy strolled to the window and looked out. "After all, any boy can make a mistake - "

"Yes, sir, Ian's not too awful bright."

"How did his commander get him back from Atlanta, anyway?"

"I can't think how, sir."

Abernethy roared, "What do you mean you can't think how?"

"It was an awful job just thinkin' up everything else."

"Clancy, confound it, are you telling me you concocted this whole wild tale to cover a food order that could put us both in the stockade!"

"I'm sure to get ten Our Fathers and ten Hail Marys at me next confession, sir, counting the penalty for the lobsters."

"You ordered lobsters, too?" Abernethy hollered. "How could you do such a thing!"

"Oh, it was very devil fillin' out the paperwork, sir, but me reasonin' and way of thinkin' was, as long as I was signin' a death warrant for Ian and a requisition for his last meal, I might as throw in fresh lobsters before I looked for a way to cancel the hangman because I'm almost positive that Ian wouldn't wish to get hung, even for a fine meal."

"Your cousin doesn't even know he's facing the hangman?"

"Oh, it would come as a terrible shock, your generalship, so we'll have to do somethin' with the paperwork to make sure he doesn't find out and nobody ever sees it."

Abernethy turned the warrant over and picked up a pen. "Life on the rock-pile sound about right, for the record?"

"As long as Ian don't hear about it.

"He won't. Nobody will. This is the Army, Clancy. Once these papers get filed, they're forgotten. Now let's start with that prime rib."

42.
The Efficiency Expert

When Mr. Hay got to work at seven o'clock in the morning, Miss Cochran was there. She was perched on a tall stool at a borrowed kitchen table.

"What happened to your desk?" asked Mr. Hay.

"I had the servants take it out," replied Miss Cochran.

"But why?"

"It was rubbish. The chair was worse."

"I'll order you another," Hay said, embarrassed. "I mean a desk and chair both."

"Don't bother," Miss Cochran said, "I've already done it."

"But it takes special authorization!"

"From Senator Flegel, you mean?"

"Well, yes. He's chairman of Appropriations, and watches our office like a hawk. You have to negotiate with him, sort of."

"I've already negotiated," Miss Cochran said. "He's sending his butler to Baltimore to pick up something appropriate."

"Flegel?"

"Yes."

"How on earth did you manage that?"

"I sent him an address."

"An address?"

"Yes. The one I wrote down on this paper."

Miss Cochran handed Hay a slip of paper with a notation in her neat handwriting: 32 Harrison Avenue.

"What's this?"

"The address of a woman who has long been found by the senator to be very charming."

43.
A Fine Fettle

"Professor Doubleday to see you, Mr. President."

"Send him in."

Lincoln put the war dispatches on his desk and turned around just in time to see Doubleday walk in. As usual, the bow-legged professor was carrying some type of sporting equipment.

"What is it this time, Abner?" Lincoln said.

"Something for the troops," Doubleday enthused. "Keep them in fine fettle!"

Doubleday laid out on the President's desk a medium-length club of polished hickory, a small cage with a padded leather fringe, a fat leather glove with stubby fingers, and a hard ball sewn tightly into a pigskin cover.

Cooper came in and sniffed the ball.

"What is it boy?" Lincoln tousled Cooper's head.

"Oh, Cooper knows what it's for!" Doubleday chortled, putting the leather glove on one hand and pounding the palm with his fist to make a dent. "It's for a ball game, and I got the idea from

Cooper - watching him run and catch a stick you threw."

"This is a mighty big stick for him to fetch," Lincoln frowned as he picked up Doubleday's wooden club.

"Oh, you don't throw that," Doubleday said, handing Lincoln the glove.

"You throw the glove?" Lincoln grinned. "Coop does like leather!"

"No, no," Doubleday said, "you wear the glove."

"What for?"

"To catch the ball."

"Cooper has to throw a ball?"

"No, I forgot to mention that dogs can't play."

"So, I throw the ball."

"Sometimes."

"Then what do you do with the stick?"

"You throw the stick down."

"I thought you said you didn't throw the stick."

"Well, you don't," the professor said. "You just sort of drop it."

"Drop it?"

"After you hit the ball."

"But I thought you caught the ball with the glove."

"Yes, but sometimes you try to hit it with the stick."

"Hit the ball?"

"Yes." Doubleday led them outside for a demonstration. Lincoln removed his coat despite the fall chill, but left his stovepipe hat in place.

"Let's see now," said the President, "do I wear the glove when I hold the stick, or just when I catch the ball?"

"I haven't got that far," allowed the professor. "But probably you should take the glove off when you hold the stick."

Cooper barked and wagged his tail as Doubleday gripped the ball.

"I'm going to throw you the ball," Doubleday said, "and you try to hit it. I'll wear the glove and catch it."

"Ready," Lincoln said, taking a few axe swings with the wood.

Doubleday tossed the ball and Lincoln brought the stick

around smoothly and tapped the missile back over the professor's head. Almost before Doubleday could turn around, Cooper flew after it and caught the ball on first bounce at the edge of the lawn.

"What are you calling this game?" Lincoln said.

"Base Ball," Doubleday said. "And, despite my earlier statement, it appears that dogs can, indeed, play."

Cooper hurried back to the professor with the ball and received a pat on the head. "I might have to revise the rules," Doubleday made a note to himself, "to put several dogs on each team."

"Throw it again," Lincoln said.

Doubleday threw a little harder this time, and Lincoln connected and sent the ball arcing onto Pennsylvania Avenue where Cooper retrieved it in a cloud of dust."

"This is kinda fun," Lincoln said, admiring the wooden club. "Back home when we were kids, we used to see how far we could bat a rock with a stick of stove wood. Pretty far, sometimes."

Cooper barked impatiently.

Doubleday gripped the ball. "Now then," the professor smiled wickedly, "I'm going to throw you a special throw I've invented which I call my curve throw, and I will pay you five dollars if you hit it."

"And I'll pay you five if I don't," rejoined Lincoln.

"You won't see it," sneered Doubleday, "but you may feel the breeze."

"Weenie arm!" sneered Lincoln.

Doubleday spat tobacco in the direction of his toes, glared vengefully at the President, wrapped two fingers along the seams of the ball and kicked one foot high in the air and cut loose with his curve throw that failed to curve.

Lincoln brought the stick around and hit the ball with a resounding crack, sending it on a soaring journey across the avenue where, with an expensive tinkle of glass, it crashed through the upstairs window of Montgomery Tillicot's fine mansion.

Doubleday and Cooper were fleeing the scene before the President could even move. Then the President joined the foot race, holding onto his tall hat and just managing to round the corner before an irate Mrs. Tillicot appeared on her front porch with the ball.

"Think she saw us?" Lincoln panted.

"One of the hazards of the game," Doubleday puffed.

"I meant to ask you," Lincoln said, "I know what the stick is for, and what the glove is for, and what the ball is for. But you never did say what that little wire cage was that you brought?"

"Catcher's mask," Doubleday said.

Lincoln nodded. "We better wear one next time, then, so we don't get caught."

44.
The Generals

General Abernethy got so mad at General McClellan one day that he tried to throw him out a second story window at the White House. Seward stopped him, and Lincoln remarked later to Hay, "it was the only time I ever saw Seward do anything against the public interest."

Needless to say, not much love was lost between the two generals. Behind his back, General McClellan called Abernethy "a flaming incompetent! A rum-head!" While Abernethy would get sidetracked at staff meetings and rant that "Little Napoleon knows less about infantry tactics than I know about green cheese on the moon - and his only expertise with a horse is imitating the south end of one!" Which, of course, got back to McClellan.

Flapflap flapflapflap!

45.
Stonefence Cooper

Cooper chased the rabbit from the White House to the river. The river was a sheet of brown ice.

Dog and rabbit ran three times around Ambassador Odegaard who was out skating with his skates, his ears muffed, a pipe in his mouth.

"Here, gol darnit you, Cooper!" called Mr. Odegaard. "You leave that rabbit alone or I tell Mr. Lincoln and Missus Lincoln, too!"

Cooper and the rabbit paid no attention. Third time around, the rabbit made a blur into Confederate territory and Cooper was right behind him. They ran and ran. Cooper slowly closed the gap. Desperately, the rabbit darted left across a field but soon encountered a stone fence. A leap did not carry him over the top, and he fell back down, his eyes big, and Cooper practically on top of him.

"Sacre bleu! Wait un minute!" the rabbit cried.

Cooper put on the brakes so fast that his ears flapped

together in front of him.

Napoleon?

"Of le course," groused the rabbit. "Now please close your le mouth, s'il vous plait, as I do not care to count your le teeth."

Cooper closed his le mouth.

"Listen to moi," said the rabbit, "we don't have much time. It is trés important that we get right away to the headquarters of this Confederacy general, the one they call Monsieur le Stone Wall. No? Yes? That's why I led you across the river. There was no other way."

Cooper looked puzzled.

The situation, as Napoleon explained it to the dog, was a disaster in the making. The summer before, Napoleon had given Abernethy the idea of luring part of Lee's army across the Rapidan River where even McClellan might manage to destroy it. The key was the river - it would be a barrier to keep Stonewall Jackson's troops from marching to Lee's rescue.

"But sacre bleu!" - the rabbit was twitching his nose angrily - "when I put forth this brilliant le plan, it was hot summ-air! But now it is cold wint-air! The riv-air, she is frozen! It is like a highway! This Monsieur Jackson, this Stone Wall, he can cross le riv-air anywhere! But there are le fools in Washington who insist on going ahead with my le summer plan. I tell you, Cooper, they are all mad, I tell you!"

Cooper helped the rabbit over the fence.

As the rabbit hopped along, Cooper followed.

"The key to le past," the rabbit said mysteriously, "is le future."

After about an hour, Napoleon - or the rabbit, rather - stopped and stood up on his hind legs and sniffed the air. Cooper sniffed too.

"Do not sniff while I am le sniffing!" the rabbit said. "It is impolite!"

Soon they came to another stone fence, and Napoleon found a small hole and crawled through it.

"Wait for me le there," Napoleon's voice was le muffled.

In a few moments, Cooper heard a scratching sound near the hole and saw the dead winter grass stir.

"Be careful where you step," said the tinny French voice down underneath the matted grass.

Napoleon?

Cooper put his nose to the moving spot and came face-to-face with a field mouse.

"Coop-air," the mouse said wearily, "please again to quit le sniffing. It is tiresome."

The mouse could not run as fast as the rabbit, so Cooper gave it a ride, taking this direction, and that, from small whisperings that the mouse put in his ear. Ever southward they went at a steady pace, and soon they crossed the frozen Rapidan, and Cooper became aware of soldiers strangely dressed in raggedy coats. The coats were mostly gray, but some were different colors; the pants underneath were gray and also ragged and often stuffed into boots that were coming apart. Some of the soldiers huddled around campfires. In a snowy hollow, one group loaded grapeshot for twenty cannons hidden in the trees. Cooper saw many of the soldiers reading books, and, here and there, some knelt in circles as one read aloud.

"Bibles," Napoleon whispered to Cooper.

Bibles?

"My plan," Napoleon said impatiently, "should be clear at this point, even to you."

46.
The Breakfast

Mr. Lincoln didn't say much at breakfast.

"Is something wrong, dear?" Mary buttered her toast.

"No," Lincoln snapped, and kept looking at the paper.

"Well," she pursed her lips, "you've been so quiet."

Lincoln adjusted his eyeglasses and turned the page.
Then turned the page back.

Mary watched him, sipping her coffee.

Lincoln looked at the page some more.

Mary said, "Did you hear that Martha Groves is driving
her own carriage now? Can you imagine?"

Lincoln shook the paper, muttering. "Didn't William
leave the coffee pot?"

"I'll get it," said Mary.

But Lincoln was already on his feet, headed into the
kitchen. He came back a moment later without the pot.

"He's gone. No coffee."

"I could go and find him," Mary smiled.

"I don't want coffee," Lincoln said, picking up the paper again. The editorial page.

Mary said, "I wish you wouldn't look at those awful pictures they draw of you, dear. You know they upset you."

"I'm not upset," Lincoln muttered. "I don't give a fiddle-dee-dee what this Gaylord Goolsby has drawn!"

"I know you don't," Mary said, "and anyway those pictures don't even look like you. Or not very much."

Lincoln threw the paper down. He started to peel an egg, mumbling to himself. Then he picked up the paper again.

"Edna Foster's baby was a girl!" Mary said, hoping for distraction. "They say she looks just like Senator Foster's mother."

"Who does?" said Lincoln.

"The baby."

"What baby?"

"Abraham, you have not heard a word I've said."

"And when will Goolsby learn to spell baboon?"

"You haven't said a word about Mrs. Foster's baby."

"B-a-b-b-o-o-n!" Lincoln said.

Mary took her coffee and went into the pantry.

In a few minutes she stuck her head out. "Father," she said, "you can be very cruel. Comparing the Foster baby to a monkey!"

Then she disappeared back into the pantry, taking her coffee.

Lincoln drummed his fingers on the table, now wondering if baboon was supposed to have three b's. after all, or whether two b's was enough and how exactly you counted them. He wrote the word down both ways. Babboon looked better to him than baboon. "I think it's babboon," he said, but immediately started having doubts. He tried writing down different words of all kinds and pretty soon they all looked funny if he looked long enough.

"Confound it, Mary!" he hollered through the pantry door, "I forgot I have to go talk to a bunch of Tom, Dick and Harrys looking for postmaster jobs!"

Mrs. Lincoln opened the pantry door just a crack and slammed it for emphasis.

Lincoln hollered again, "And what do I care what Goolsby draws about me? I'll just show him! I'll read the paper anyway and not get all upset."

Mrs. Lincoln didn't answer.

"What Goolsby does or don't do don't bother me!" Lincoln said. "Doesn't."

Nothing. Door still shut.

"What if Goolsby says three times a week that I look like a monkey? I don't care one bit."

Mrs. Lincoln stuck her head out of the pantry and started to say something, but did not, and shut the door again.

"I mean it," Lincoln said. "I don't care. Goolsby can tell the world I'm the spitting image of an 'orang-utang,' and I just consider the source. All Goolsby is is a picture-drawer and his opinion does not matter to me in the least. It's like water off a duck's back!"

Mrs. Lincoln stuck her head out, finally.

"You heard right, mother," Lincoln said, "I'm no longer upset. From now on, my motto is 'Sticks and stones may break my bones but words will never hurt me! Nor pictures, neither.'"

Mary came out of the pantry, beaming. "That's the spirit, father! Show the world who you are - bigger than a newspaper scribbler calling you a gibbon!"

Lincoln's eyes narrowed. He looked at the paper again. "He's put an s on gibbon and made it gibbons and I gave him the dickens the last time because Gibbons was a historian. If some pencil pusher's going to call me an ape, he should get it right!"

"Abraham," Mary said, "Gibbons was not Gibbons, he was Gibbon - *The History of the Decline and Fall of the Roman Empire*, without an s but a capital G. A small g is a big ape. But it should be capital G if he calls you an ape and it's the first word in a sentence."

Lincoln grabbed for his hat and coat. "I'll capital Goolsby's G when I get ahold of him!" The President hollered. "I'll whup his hide til it won't hold shucks!"

"Guards!" Mary ran down the hall after her husband.

47.
The King of China

On Thursday Mr. Hay got sick, and nobody was left to do his work except General Abernethy, who always called Hay a "sneaky, pigeon toed pencil pusher." Behind Hay's back, of course, although it still got back to Hay.

Hay was mystified by Abernethy's epithet until he learned that Abernethy used it against anyone who did not wear scarred-up cavalry boots and prop them recklessly on top of a desk, papers and all, whosever's desk it was.

That morning, Cooper brought Abernethy a note in his teeth which turned out to be from Mrs. Lincoln. Abernethy roared and threw the note on the pile of to-do's he was handling mainly by yelling at Sergeant Clancy.

"Take care of it, Clancy!" Abernethy pointed at the note. "Top priority!"

"Aye sir!"

"Mrs. Lincoln's orders!"

"Aye, sir, it does look a bit like the old lady's scribbling. Wonder what it says?"

"Just do it," Abernethy yelled. "And be quick about it. And report back here on the double!"

"I won't lose a minute," Clancy said.

"See that you don't."

"And I'll be saluting you now, sir, and taking me leave, if you don't mind."

"You have your orders."

"As good as done," Clancy saluted and Abernethy saluted. "And I can tell you right off," Clancy said, "that you've got the right man for the job."

"Glad to hear it, Clancy. Now move it!"

"That I will, sir, seein' it's a mission to save the world! As sure as I'm standin' here, and you're sittin' there, it's highly important and not to be trifled with. Wild horses could not drag me from the slightest deviation from me orders, sir, and I'll neither be addin' to nor subtractin' from what your Honor has laid down to me like a holy writ. An order from the general is like all Ten Commandments and the Code of Hammurabi all rolled into one. Which is why I can assure his generalship, right here and now, of me complete and prompt attention to duty."

"Clancy!"

"A loyal soldier to the core, sir!"

"At ease, Clancy!"

"God bless you, sir. I never could stand at attention too long without me bunions hurtin'," Clancy resumed reading Mrs. Lincoln's note, moving his lips as Cooper wiggled his ears.

"Clancy, why are you still here?"

"Her ladyship has an awful hand, sir, like me Great Uncle Martin. He wrote a will that nobody a'tall could read, so they had to bring him back from the dead."

"Clancy!"

"It'll just take me a minute to run upstairs and clear it up with the Missus what she meant."

Abernethy jumped to his feet. "Stay where you are, sergeant! We don't want the First Lady stirred up!"

"Then if you don't mind, sir, I'll ask Mr. Hay his opinion since he has long experience with madam's writing."

"The Army does not crawl to civilians, Clancy!"

"Point well taken, sir," Clancy said, "but I may have to crouch a bit, because all I can make out on me own is three words and the time of day - four o'clock in the p.m. this afternoon."

Abernethy pulled out his watch. "An hour from now?"

"Aye, sir, and gettin' toward fifty-nine minutes as we stand here discussin', so the question that jumps out is what happens at four o'clock."

"What three words can you read?" Abernethy mopped perspiration from his brow.

"'King of China,' sir" said Sergeant Clancy, "as near as I can make out with me bare eyes. And there's some words before and after 'four o'clock' and a few teeth-marks from the dog, and after that I'm not a hundred percent sure what I'm seein'."

"Thunderation!" Abernethy put the note in front of him.

"We have to stay calm and fall back on military logic and analysis, sergeant, to determine the exact meaning of this note!"

"Aye, sir."

"It clearly concerns the King of China. But what about the King of China?"

"I think I can make out another word, sir, uh, 'silver.'"

"Silver?"

"Plain as day. It says 'King of China' and 'silver.' And 'Reg Room' - no, 'Red Room.' The Missus makes her d's look like g's. But 'four o'clock' is plain enough."

"So," Abernethy paced, looking at his watch. "King of China, Red Room, silver."

"And four o'clock."

"And something about vases."

Abernethy's eyes bulged. "Oh no!"

"What is it, sir?"

"It's got to be a state reception!" Abernethy snapped his fingers. "The King of China will arrive in the Red Room at four o'clock and the President and Mrs. Lincoln will present him with silver, for a gift."

"Silver?"

"Kings like silver, sergeant!" Abernethy said. "Or else gold but we don't have any. Now go get Mr. Lincoln! We have no time to lose!"

Momentarily, Clancy returned with the President and Cooper. Abernethy explained the emergency.

"Good Lord," Lincoln said, "why didn't mother tell me about this? Where are we going to get silver for the King of China in less than an hour?"

"Mr. Chase at the Treasury Department?"

Lincoln shook his head. "Chase is gone. Try Seward at the State Department. Grab anything you can. Meet us in the Red Room."

Clancy returned with Seward who wore a morning coat and carried a large silver punchbowl. Lincoln had changed into his formal clothing and was standing in the Red Room with white gloves held in one hand.

"What do you want with a silver punchbowl that says 'First Place Winner National Spelling Bee?'" Seward said.

"It's for the King of China," Lincoln whispered. "He's due at four o'clock and he's expecting some silver and I didn't have time to get any."

"China doesn't have a king," Seward said loudly. Just then, Mary Lincoln happened to walk through. Abernethy saluted. Seward bowed. Lincoln shifted uncomfortably in his patent leather shoes. Clancy gripped the punchbowl.

"What in the world are you men doing?" Mary waved her arms.

Lincoln showed her the note.

Mary read it. "For heaven's sakes, Abraham, I wanted to know what kind of china we could borrow for the dinner for the Italian ambassador tomorrow night, and whether it's too early in the season to get a vase of four o'clocks for a table decoration. I borrowed a vase because they keep disappearing every time tourists come through, but the flowers are a problem, and the ambassador is very partial to four o'clocks."

"China doesn't have a king?" Abernethy croaked.

Mary Lincoln rolled her eyes and left. Lincoln removed his gloves and strolled slowly from the room, followed by Seward carrying the silver punchbowl. The dog went the other direction.

"Clancy!" Abernethy yelled as the two of them went

back to Hay's office. "Clancy, if there's anything in the Army lower than buck private, I'm going to find out what it is and bust you down to it!"

"That would be civilian, sir," Clancy said, "if you wouldn't mind putting it in writing."

48.
Archives of State

"Have you seen the treaty with Guatemala?" Mr. Hay asked Lincoln.

"No," Lincoln said.

"I know it was around here someplace."

"What does it look like?"

"Big piece of paper. Red wax seal with some Spanish writing. Two big red ribbons."

"Sounds familiar," Lincoln said.

"It ought to. You signed it two weeks ago."

"Oh," Lincoln blinked.

"And now I can't find the treaty."

"Why are you looking for it?"

"I have to give it to the secretary of state."

"What does Seward want with it?"

"He has to file it."

"Well, it's probably here in my office, which is why we can't find it. What does the treaty say, anyhow?"

"It's in Spanish, but the English translation says the United States promises to sell Guatemala ten locomotives on credit, underwrite the Guatemalan peso, guarantee Guatemala's independence forever, and buy all the bananas the Guatemalans are willing to sell us."

"That's it?"

"Well," Hay said, "Guatemala agreed, in return, to maintain friendly relations with the United States."

"Glad to hear it," Lincoln nodded. "I was afraid for a minute that the Guatemalans had taken advantage of us."

"You haven't heard all of it," Hay said. "One reason Seward is looking for our copy of the treaty is that Guatemala has just hooked up with Mexico and they're planning to invade Texas while we're busy fighting the Rebs."

"But what about our treaty?"

Hay raised both palms. "The Guatemalan ambassador is telling Seward they're invoking the friendly relations clause."

"They're being friendly by invading the United States?"

"The phrase they used was 'removing the Confederate province of Texas so that it may cause no further disturbance to our valued ally.'"

"Texas is part of the United States, the way I look at it Hay! Invading the United States is not friendly!"

"That's not the way the Guatemalans and the Mexicans look at it, sir."

"Who got us into this mess, Hay?"

"I'll look into it, sir."

"I'm going to boil Seward in oil!"

"Yes sir. But you may not have to do it if we can find the treaty."

"Why not?"

"There's an escape clause."

"We can cancel the treaty?"

"Yes, sir. Either side can do it by notifying the other side. But you need an official copy of the treaty."

Lincoln wandered around his office with his hands in his pockets. He kept looking in drawers and in closets and hampers and bookshelves, muttering to himself.

Hay thought Cooper may have been playing with it. So they followed Cooper around for awhile, but Cooper didn't seem to know anything.

"Maybe it's in your dresser," Hay said at last.

Lincoln looked offended. "Why does everybody think that anything that gets lost around here is probably in my dresser?"

"Well...."

"There's no reason on earth why I would put a treaty with Guatemala in my dresser."

"True, sir."

Presently Mrs. Lincoln came along.

"What are you men looking for?" she said.

"A treaty," Lincoln said shortly.

"What sort of treaty?"

"A big treaty with red ribbons on it."

"In Spanish?"

Both men looked at her.

"Yes ma'am," Hay said.

"It just got back," Mrs. Lincoln said.

"Back from where?" Lincoln and Hay said together.

"From the laundry." Mrs. Lincoln took them to the dresser and opened the second drawer where the President's fresh white shirts were always returned by the laundry. "Why did you want it starched?"

***

The next day, Hay came back from Seward's office.

"Get that Guatemala business taken care of?" Lincoln looked up from his desk, glasses perched on the tip of his nose.

Hay nodded. "Seward straightened it out."

"No more treaty, huh?"

"Well, a different treaty."

Lincoln put his pen down. Hay slumped in a chair. "Well, it turned out that Guatemala controls two small islands off the tip of Honduras that are our chief source of niter."

"The niter we use to make gunpowder?"

Hay smiled grimly. "Friendly relations means the Guatemalans sell us niter but do not officially tell the Swiss who are officially neutral and officially own the niter mines and officially cannot allow their niter to be sold to us to pretend not to know the Guatemalans are selling us niter."

"The Swiss are selling us Guatemalan niter?"

"Through the Hondurans who ship it on ships registered in Panama."

"What do the Swiss get out of this, other than money from niter they can't sell us?"

"They want to stay square with the Guatemalans who want to keep selling bananas."

"How do we keep the Hondurans quiet, then?"

"They get half the locomotives we promised Guatemala."

"But they don't even have any track!"

"They're selling the locomotives to the Panamanians who lease them to the Guatemalans on condition that all they're used for is to haul our niter to a deepwater port in Honduras."

"I'm getting dizzy, Hay. What about the invasion of Texas?"

"That's off."

"What'd it cost us?"

"Ten more locomotives."

"Ten more? Where will they put ten more?"

"Oh," Hay said, "they won't take delivery. They've already sold them, before they're built, to the Baltimore and Ohio Railroad."

"B&O is buying them?"

"Well, not exactly. B&O is cancelling the orders and getting a refund."

"How can the B&O get a refund if it never pays for the locomotives?"

"Well, sir, the locomotive factory will invoke the clause in the contract that requires us to make good on a loan guarantee that kicks in if B&O reneges on the purchase which triggers a pass-through that gives the proceeds to B&O, while the factory gets reimbursed the full amount by government-backed re-insurance financed by commodity speculators who get a tax break on Guatemalan banana futures. What it all boils down to is a Wall Street thing."

Lincoln twirled his glasses. "Hay," he said, "I don't know how much of this friendly relations stuff we can stand."

"Me neither, sir."

Cooper wandered in, then wandered out again.

"Mr. President," Hay was hesitant. "How do we cover an un-appropriated $400,000 for nonexistent locomotives?"

"Tell Chase he needs to do some more experimenting with those fancy new greenback presses so they'll print right," Lincoln said. "I figure he'll have to run about a half-million to get them adjusted."

"We pay off the B&O with what is technically waste-paper? How do we enter it on the books, sir?"

"I didn't hear that question, Hay."

49.
The Affair

Lieutenant Ambrose was from a good family, and his family had known Mary Todd Lincoln's good family since he was a boy. Or, rather, it was the other way around: the Todds had known the Ambrose family forever, and Mary Todd had attended the future Lieutenant Dexter Radcliffe Ambrose's christening as well as other momentous events in his life including his graduation from West Point. The last-mentioned momentous event in Lt. Ambrose's life had taken place in the sunny spring of 1861, almost exactly coincident with the outbreak of the first Great War, the Great War to Preserve the Union.

For most young officers Ambrose's age, the War was an obsessive preoccupation although Ambrose's foremost obsession was with Ambrose, that is, with himself. In any conversation, Ambrose quickly found an opening, or created one, to mention outstanding facts about himself including the fact that he'd stood first in his class at the U.S. Military Academy, after which his store of conversation tended to drop off.

It was the close connection between the Ambroses and the Todds that had gotten the young lieutenant posted to the White House. There Ambrose made a highly favorable impression on himself, above all, and would always be seen wearing spotless uniforms in which he declined to sit lest he wrinkle his trousers, leaving it to the imagination whether his underwear was ironed to perfection as well. Dangling from his left shoulder was a gold-braid aiguillette denoting staff position, and therefore something Ambrose paid special attention to, lest it become tarnished or tangled, taking care to arrange a fresh supply from a New York sartorial establishment which specialized in gold braid and so forth and which shipped the aiguillettes to Ambrose on the first of every month, by train, unless it was a holiday when it would ship them on the second of the month.

Flawlessly clad and polished, Ambrose saw to it that General Abernethy's every wish and whim was perfectly catered to, keeping the general's dispatches in perfect order and never allowing the general's pencils to go unsharpened or his spittoon to go unpolished, or his field maps to jumble up, or his cigars to dry out, or his field orders to pile up unsent, or queries, from whatever quarter, to go unanswered, or medals to remain unawarded, or jokes to fall flat, or official visitors to remain un-flattered. Nor would Ambrose allow Abernethy's schedule ever to have a gap in it, or an error or a blunder or lapse of protocol. And neither would Ambrose allow the general ever to forget the most insignificant birthday, anniversary, or commemorative date affecting those in high positions, or allow him to overlook any obligation or stumble over anyone's name, or allow any appointment to be forgotten or mislaid, whether it was with the general's barber or his doctor or toenail trimmer, assuming that it was all of inestimable importance to important military persons of the general persuasion. Lastly, everything on Abernethy's agenda was timed to the minute or the half-minute, with no second being wasted or neglected upon any pretense whatsoever.

In other words, young Ambrose was driving Abernethy crazy.

Mary Lincoln was not aware that Abernethy was thinking he might strangle Ambrose with his bare hands or have him shanghaied by the Chinese Navy. But the President's wife, seeing the young man as she did through the eyes of a doting godmother, could not imagine he was less than precious to Abernethy as well. That is why she was pleased when Ambrose asked permission to call on Cissy, a tall, plain-ish niece of the First Lady who had come to the White House for an extended visit.

Cissy served tea to the young man in the Rose Room, giving a polite cry ("my word!" or "do tell!") when Ambrose mentioned his class standing for the ninety-ninth time.

"I hope, sir, that I'm not keeping you from your duties," Cissy added, hoping he'd take the hint.

"Oh, I think the general will not begrudge me an hour," Ambrose said, taking to the sofa and letting his head rest languidly on the back and throwing a handsome, booted leg over the overstuffed arm.

"Of course, of course," Cissy said, fanning herself rapidly and listening to the infernal ticktock of the clock.

***

Lieutenant Ambrose came back to see Cissy several times, always in the Rose Room, where she always served tea.

"Dear Cissy!" Ambrose exclaimed. "May I call you that?"

"Of course."

"Cissy, you must not concern yourself with my weariness."

"Weariness?"

"From my duties. Night and day. You must promise not to concern yourself."

"I promise."

"Cissy." Ambrose suddenly leapt from the sofa and went down on bended knee. "Cissy, may I kiss your hand?"

"Later," Cissy said. "First tell me about your duties again. They must be a dreadful burden, as they keep you constantly here in the parlor, so far from battle!"

Ambrose straightened his jacket. "I would rather have a cavalry command, of course. My greatest wish is to be in the very thick of the fight!"

"Say no more, sir, I will ask my uncle, the President!"

"On the other hand," Ambrose paced, "a soldier must serve where duty calls. This is war, after all. My bone spurs be damned."

Ambrose strode to the window where he clasped his hands behind his back and allowed a frown to knit his handsome brow. His clear eyes gazed southward, as if at the enemy. The muscles of his jaw flexed manfully. His new calfskin cavalry boots, polished to perfection that very morning by Private Greiman, and sent back once for additional buffing, creaked with each movement. The creaks attracted the attention of Cooper who had been napping under the piano until the third or fourth creak got him to his feet and caused him, by creaks No. 5 and 6, to walk over and plant his nose against the leather, which smelled delicious.

"Do now you understand why, Cissy, I must remain here?"

"In the Rose Room?"

"Working night and day for the general, I meant." Suddenly he took her hand.

"Stop that!" Cissy cried.

Flustered, Ambrose stopped.

"Not you, Lieutenant. I was talking to Cooper. I thought he was about to eat your boots."

Ambrose frowned at Cooper. "There's a good boy," he said, thinking no such thing.

Cooper growled.

"You were about to say, Lieutenant Ambrose?" Cissy fluttered her fan.

"Well, I was about to share with you, Cissy, a feeling so deep, so personal that I feel a need to ask your permission before I say it."

"Say what? Careful of the dog."

Ambrose's lips trembled. He seized Cissy's hand again, a grievous error on several accounts. Cooper, undone by the smell of leather, leapt forward and clamped his teeth on Ambrose's right foot, growling and improving his grip as Ambrose hopscotched with all possible dignity, which was not much.

"Grrrrrr!"

"Cooper! Let go!" Cissy cried.

"There's a good dog," Ambrose gasped, waving his foot around, with Cooper growling and maintaining a death grip.

"I do apologize on Cooper's behalf," Cissy said.

Ambrose staggered but kept jumping. "A dog cannot stop me," he cried. With Cooper on his foot, Ambrose reached the neighborhood of Cissy's hand, and then the hand itself, which he took, panting, and kissed it before Cooper jerked him off-balance.

"Why, Lieutenant Ambrose, I do think you're an athlete!" Cissy exclaimed, as Ambrose pranced.

"Damn you, let go!" he panted, grabbing her hand for balance as he tried to shake the dog loose.

"I beg your pardon sir?"

"Ow, not you - Son of a! - dammit dog! Let go of my foot you - you - !"

"I do declare, sir!" Cissy said, snatching her hand away. "I do declare!"

"Let go, you fleabag!" Ambrose cried.

"You really should not speak to Cooper in that tone, sir!"

Ambrose hobbled to the settee, his foot orbiting off the floor with each stride, the dog attached.

"What I was about to say - " Ambrose said.

"About your military duties - ?"

Ambrose seized her hand again. "Dear Cissy - " smack. He kissed it again. Smack. "You have no idea - " smack, smack - "what it is like to find a woman who understands me - " smack, smack, smack. "I may not have mentioned to you that I finished first in my class at West Point...."

"You did, actually."

"I did mention it?"

"Yes."

"Regardless. When one finishes first in one's class, as I said, it conveys an obligation that weighs heavily. Bone spurs notwithstanding."

"Noblesse oblige... with bone spurs."

"Yes, noblesse oblige - the noble obligation to remain on staff, close to the general, working night and day planning a brilliant victory. Whether or not the common masses appreciate it!"

"You're right," Cissy said, "they would not."

"Dear Cissy!" Ambrose leapt to his feet, or, rather, to his foot, the one Cooper wasn't holding captive.

"Cooper, let go! Ambrose said, shaking his foot.

The President came into the room. He stopped, surprised to see Ambrose and Cissy.

"Excuse me," Mr. Lincoln said, "I heard Cooper carrying on and I thought he mighta cornered a rat."

"Sir!" Ambrose tried to draw to attention and salute.

Cissy said, "Lieutenant Ambrose was talking about the obligations of duty, Uncle Abraham."

"Well, don't mind me." Lincoln stared at Cooper. "I guess you've noticed that Cooper favors boots."

"Yes sir."

"Likes the taste, I expect."

"Yes sir."

Cissy said, "Uncle, Lieutenant Ambrose is too proud to ask, but I now know for a fact that he would rather be on the front lines facing shot and shell, massed artillery, rebel yells, bayonets, miserable muddy trenches and paltry rations, than remain here in the White House."

"That so?"

"He told me so himself," Cissy nodded. "Of course, he would never speak up himself or mention his bone spurs, patriot that he is."

Lincoln looked at the young man with interest.

"You were first in your class a West Point, I keep hearing."

"I don't think sir," Ambrose said, a grin pasted to his face, "that I should receive any special treatment."

"I admire that you never asked for it."

"I shall serve here, sir, if the nation prefers it."

"Shoot, lieutenant, I'm not sure the nation even prefers that I serve here. I'll write the order myself."

"Please don't trouble yourself, sir!"

"No trouble." Lincoln got out a pen. "Let's see... the fifth New Hampshire is down to six men."

"Six?"

"As I recall. And two are still on crutches."

"I've never even been to New Hampshire, sir!"

"Doesn't matter," Lincoln said. "Now...if I can just find some ink to dip my pen in."

Cooper's grip kept Ambrose from keeping up with the President as he strode off in search of ink.

"Don't let me impose, sir!" Ambrose cried, as Lincoln outdistanced him. He shook his foot desperately "Dammit, dog, let go!"

Cissy called, "I found a bottle of ink, Uncle Abraham. "Can Army orders be in purple ink?"

"They have to be in black!" Ambrose cried desperately, running orbit-footed to the door. "Army regulations say absolutely positively black! Let go, dog!"

"Oh goody," Cissy held up the bottle. "This is black ink!"

As Ambrose hopped away down the hall as fast as he could hop with Cooper hanging on, Lincoln stared.

"Wonder if he's right about black ink?" Lincoln said.

"Probably," Cissy said. "He was first in his class."

50.
The Menace

"General Breaker is here, sir!"

Flap flapflapflap flap!

"Oh, Lord," Lincoln sighed. He threw his pen down on his desk and stashed his inkwell in the middle drawer.

Cooper crawled under the couch.

Hay got a frog in his throat. "Shall I put the Ming vases away, too, Mr. President?"

"What Ming vases?"

"A figure of speech, sir." Hay waved his arm to indicate the room's plethora of knickknacks - Tiffany statuettes, Faberge eggs, crystal whatchacallits and porcelain doodads, all foisted off on hapless Presidents by official visitors since the Adams administration.

"No, no, Hay," Lincoln said, "let's not start hiding things. General Breagher is a sensitive man and he notices things like us hiding the crockery when he shows up. And he hates being called Breaker! Besides, he hardly broke a thing the last time he was here."

"Because we put it all up," Hay wanted to tell the President, but did not. "Shall I show him in?" Hay said instead.

"Go ahead."

As Hay left to fetch the visitor, Lincoln muttered and took the ink bottle out of the middle drawer and locked it in the bottom drawer.

"MR. PRESIDENT!" Breaker's voice boomed down the hall like a military marching band. The door banged open and in strode the general, short and square, his beard bristling like a porcupine and his eyebrows flapping like unruly crows in a cornfield. Breaker's feet, two sizes too big by any reasonable reckoning, were the kind that didn't know their whereabouts at all times, which could explain why Breaker's left foot located the rear rocker - the right rear rocker to be exact - of Lincoln's empty rocking chair as he stomped forward, saluting.

"No, Breaker!" was all Lincoln had time to say as Breaker's king size hoof snapped the end off the rocker and flipped the chair upside down, all in one motion.

"NEVER FEAR, I'LL FIX IT!" Breaker boomed.

"No!" Lincoln shouted, imagining the chair's total destruction as he ran to collect the pieces. Breaker was doing the same thing and as he bent down to get the wood, his head met Lincoln's and sent the President backwards seeing stars.

"MR. PRESIDENT!" Breaker cried.

Lincoln held his noggin and grabbed a pedestal that held a third-century Greek bust of Julius Caesar, causing Caesar to crash to the floor.

Hay came running in. "What happened?"

"WE HIT HEADS IS ALL," Breaker said, picking up the bobtailed rocker and pieces of Caesar and trying to set the rocker down straight.

"I'm dizzy, Hay," Lincoln mumbled, and forgot and sat in the rocker which immediately rared backward and kept on raring until it and the President turned a complete flip.

"Mr. President!" cried Hay.

"Cancel my appointments," Lincoln said.

"I CAN FIX IT," Breaker cried, surveying the broken chair.

"Just let me lay here a minute," Lincoln said, motionless.

"I'll get Dr. Hunt," Hay said, racing out of the room.

Breaker helped Lincoln to his feet. "I'll have your chair fixed IN JUST A JIFFY," the general said, setting it precariously upright and checking to see if the broken pieces fit.

"I think I've got a concussion," Lincoln said.

Just then, Hay came in with Dr. Hunt who carried a large medical bag. "You shouldn't be on your feet, man!" Hunt said to Lincoln, pushing him back into the rocker, which rared back again and turned another flip with the President.

"You must give up that sort of thing," Hunt admonished, "while you've got a concussion."

"Let me stay on the floor," Lincoln said.

Hunt began rummaging in his bag. "What happened, Lincoln?"

"The chair turned a somersault," Lincoln explained.

"Thunderation," Hunt said, "no wonder it broke, with you carrying on like that! And fix that infernal window shade, Hay, while I find my castor oil."

"I'LL DO IT," Breaker said, and before Hay could stop him he jumped up on the windowsill with his big feet and grabbed for the shade which immediately rocketed to the very top, spinning rapidly with a *flappaflappa flapflapaflap* causing Breaker to lose his balance and fall through the window and into a large rose trellis that broke loose from the side of the White House and crashed down on the lawn like a giant fly swatter, swatting Corporal Shaffer whose musket fired inadvertently, setting off a general alarm among the guard force.

"Who is that shooting?" Hunt looked up from his bag.

"Breaker fell out the window and hit a sentry," Hay said.

"Who shot who?"

"Never mind. We've got to go down there and calm things before all heck breaks loose."

Hay and Hunt hurried down the hall and descended the back stairs so fast that the arriving secretary of state, Mr. Seward, didn't see who it was.

"What's the shooting about?" Seward said as he hurried

into Lincoln's study. "And what are you doing on the floor Mr. President?"

"Breaker was here."

"Are you hurt?" Seward helped Lincoln to his feet. "I think I got a concussion."

"A concussion? You shouldn't be on your feet, Mr. President." Seward pushed Lincoln back into the rocker and it rared all the way back again and turned another flip.

"Mr. President!"

"My spine, Seward!"

"Mr. President!"

Footsteps in the hall signaled the arrival of Mrs. Lincoln.

"Abraham," she said, "are you out of your mind?"

"Is that you, mother?"

"Of course it's me? Who were you expecting? Now, get up off of that nasty floor before you catch something." Lincoln clambered slowly to his feet.

"I thought I heard a shot," Mrs. Lincoln said.

"You did," Seward said.

"Who is shooting?"

"The sentry," Lincoln said. "The one that got hit by your rose trellis."

"What are you talking about?"

"He got hit because Hunt was looking for his castor oil."

"What's that got to do with the rose trellis?"

"Hunt wanted Hay to pull the shade down."

"What was Hunt doing here?"

"He was seeing about the rocker."

"What's that got to do with the shade?"

"Breaker was here."

"Breaker? Why didn't you say so?"

Suddenly and before anyone could stop her, Mrs. Lincoln sat down in the rocker. Nothing happened. She rocked unevenly and waited for the President to resume his explanation.

"Well," Lincoln said, "Breaker stepped on the rocker and broke it, and then Hunt came to give me a dose of castor oil."

"Abraham," Mrs. Lincoln studied the President. "You worry me sometimes."

She got up and left.

Lincoln looked closely at the rocker.

Seward lit a cigar.

Breaker and Hay soon returned, not much the worse for wear except that Breaker's uniform was in shreds and his hair was wild.

"General Breagher," Lincoln said, "do you recall, exactly, what you wanted to see me about?"

"TO PAY MY RESPECTS," Breaker said, pulling a trellis splinter from the seat of his pants. "IT'S MY COURTESY CALL!"

"And honored, I am, by your courtesy!" Lincoln said, extending his hand. "May you soon call on the enemy!"

"Hear, hear," Hay said.

Breaker stepped forward to shake the President's hand, creating a moment of suspense that ended in anticlimax because nothing untoward happened, and he soon saluted and left, allowing Lincoln to release the breath he'd been holding several minutes.

"Well," Seward said, blowing a smoke ring, "not too much harm done, considering. What happened to Hunt?"

"He's downstairs with Shaffer, trying to give him castor oil."

"If you don't need me, sir," Hay said to Lincoln, "I have some letters to catch up."

"Of course," Lincoln said.

Hay left, and Seward soon left, too, saying his business could wait.

With everybody gone, Lincoln looked cautiously at his rocking chair. He picked it up and set it in its usual place on the rug.

"I guess I have to get it fixed," Lincoln told Cooper, who had just crawled out from under the couch.

"I can't do without my rocker," Lincoln told the dog. Cooper looked at him.

"I could get it fixed, or maybe I could get a new rocker." Cooper looked at the chair.

"A new rocker," Lincoln said, "might be nice, but it wouldn't be my old rocker."

Cooper's tongue hung out.

"Maybe I can still sit in this one if I'm real careful. Mrs. Lincoln did."

Cooper rolled his eyes.

"I'll just mind how I sit," Lincoln said.

Cooper sat.

Lincoln wetted a fingertip and rocked the chair an inch or two.

"Just have to remember not to rock."

Cooper wrinkled his brow.

Carefully, Lincoln sat in the chair.

He rocked a little.

Nothing happened.

He rocked a little more.

Nothing happened.

"This is great, Cooper," said the President, and he went and got the briefing book out of his rolltop desk and went back to the rocker where he always sat to read.

Sitting carefully, he adjusted his glasses and opened the book. Nothing happened.

He relaxed. The shade went *flapflapflap*, and the chair rared back and turned him a somersault.

51.
Additional Military Matters

On Thursday, Hay brought the President a letter. It was in a gold envelope.

"From King Moghut of Siam, sir," Hay said.

"Really?" Lincoln said, looking up from the pile of military orders he was working on. "And what can I do for the king of Siam?"

"It's more the other way around, sir. The king is offering to send you some Siamese elephants to help win the war."

"Well, well," Lincoln nodded. "A herd of Siamese war elephants would sure scare the dickens out of the Rebs! How many elephants is the king talking about?"

"Two," Hay said.

"Dang it, Hay," Lincoln hollered, "what am I supposed to do with two elephants?"

"The king says just wait awhile and they'll multiply. Sir."

"Hay, do you know how long it takes elephants to multiply?"

"I never thought about it, sir."

"Well I can tell you exactly how long: too long!"

"Yes sir. I'll draft a polite letter declining the elephants. And what do I do with the other stuff that came with the letter?"

"What other stuff?"

"The gold-inlaid Siamese dagger and two elephant tusks."

Lincoln sat back in his rocker and massaged his temples. "Good Lord, Hay, I don't care, but get rid of them fast so I don't get impeached for violating the Emoluments Clause."

Cooper walked around the President's chair three times and plopped down for a nap.

52.
Graphic Tales

General Abernethy was reading *The Chicago Graphic.* His sister mailed him a copy at the White House every now and then. It was one of those newspapers that came in tabloid size and had big headlines and big pictures and a lot of unlikely tales.

"Thunderation!" roared the general, stirring Cooper out of a sound sleep. "How can they print this stuff?"

Taking the paper in hand, Abernethy stomped down the hall to Mr. Lincoln's office where he continued to rant and carry on.

"Just look, Mr. President!" Abernethy hollered.

Lincoln was busy with his corns and had one shoe off, but he nodded politely and took the paper from Abernethy.

"You talking about the Loch Ness Monster being seen in the Mississippi?" Lincoln said.

"No, no, Mr. President," Abernethy said. "Turn to the next page! The one with a headline that would knock the eyeballs out of a blind man! It's all nonsense and drivel! A so-called scientific public opinion poll!"

"Uh-huh. So, this professor says his scientific survey of just fifty-seven residents of Chicago shows I can't win the election?"

"Arrest the lot, I say!" Abernethy could not be calmed down.

"Now, now, Horatio. They might all be Democrats. Haw haw haw."

"But this is treason, Lincoln! It's wartime!"

The President leaned back in his rocker and continued to study the story. "This *is* kinda interesting, Horatio. The professor that did the poll, Professor Ham Herbert, says that he can interview a sample of voters in just a few bellwether precincts and tell without fail how an election will come out. Whether it's for dogcatcher or governor or President."

"Pshaw!" Abernethy grumped. "There's not a word of truth in that entire miserable rag of a newspaper. If you doubt me, just look at the rest of the articles!"

Lincoln reached for his glasses although they were not strictly necessary to read type sizes normally found on Wanted posters. "Are you still talking about the Loch Ness Monster or the one about Cuba disappearing into the Bermuda Triangle?"

"Either one," Abernethy fumed. "Or the woman walking down the street in Baltimore and bursting into flames for no apparent reason!"

Lincoln stared at the ceiling. "That one sounds familiar. But the last time they printed it, it was a Philadelphia woman walking her cat in Scranton and her sister's cat caught fire in Pittsburgh."

"Oh yeah," Abernethy scratched his head, "but the way I remember it, it was a man walking a woman down Biddle Street in St. Louis and the man caught fire, and the woman escaped with the dog."

"It was either a dog or a cat," Lincoln said.

"I wish they would settle on one story."

"I think we should padlock the paper for fraud," Abernethy said.

Lincoln put his feet on his desk. "Fraud," he said, "is a great tradition in this country, Horatio. I'm surprised it's not in the Constitution. While we might survive without free speech for a month, I don't think we could get by for a week without flim-flam."

"What are you talking about, Lincoln?"

"When Senator Joad called at my office the other day, what did I do?"

"Well," Abernethy scratched his head, "you pumped his hand until I thought he'd spout water, and you called him the greatest Senator since Cicero and your greatest friend outside of Cooper and the greatest political thinker since Plato, and you generally filled him with so much hot air and bull-hockey about his mental abilities and all around charm that he forgot himself and came out foursquare in favor of the War Bond Act, which he had been ready to defeat as a menace."

"Uh-huh. And did I mention a word about the senator being a miserable toad-frog and a two-faced lizard or any of the things he actually is?"

"Of course not, Mr. President."

"And when I was talking to the bankers the other day about our latest war bond issue, did I call them a thieving pack of grifters who would sell their mothers for a nickel?"

"No," Abernethy said, "you called them patriots and praised them to high heaven for remembering always the motto, 'God Bless America.' And I think you mentioned something about twelve percent interest."

"Well," Lincoln said, "the devil might not get me for the patriotism speech, but I could hear him sharpen his pitchfork when I said twelve percent."

"But the bankers will get rich!" Abernethy said.

"Yes," Lincoln said, "the bankers will get rich, but their investors and the stockholders in their banks will lose their shirts."

Abernethy arched a brow. "How's that?"

"Dry, dull stuff called monetizing a debt. Chase will print more paper money which will drive up inflation, and we'll pay off the bonds with cheap dollars. By the time the bonds mature, the banks will be lucky to get back fifty cents on the dollar."

"How does that make the bankers rich?"

Lincoln grinned ironically. "The bankers get their fees upfront for underwriting the bonds even though they know full well that everybody they sell them to will take a bath."

"That sounds downright illegal, Lincoln!"

"It was, until we got Joad to slip a small amendment into the War Harbors and Dredging Act that gives the underwriters a one-time exemption to the conflict of interest clause of the Interstate Bank Fraud and Embezzlement Act."

Abernethy sat down. "Lord, I hope the *Graphic* doesn't get wind of this."

"Oh," Lincoln said, "I doubt the *Graphic* would be interested unless we burst into flames."

Abernethy shook his head. "Well, some other paper, then. Lord, Mr. President, we'll all land in the stewpot if some nosy reporter ever figures this out. But I'd like to see Senator Joad burst into flames just as soon as he's done voting for the bonds."

53.
The Wallpaper Plan

Mary Lincoln got up one day, totally at war with all the wallpaper in the White House. For example, she hated the wallpaper in Mr. Lincoln's study.

"What's wrong with it?" Lincoln said.

Mary Lincoln rolled her eyes.

Before long, the White House was full of paperhangers in baggy overalls. They carried ladders and big sloppy buckets of paste and wide brushes and trestle boards that they strung between the ladders so they could slap paste on the new wallpaper that they hung in every room of the house.

The style of wallpaper that Mrs. Lincoln had picked for the Presidential study was a scarlet brocade, which General Abernethy said looked like a cheap Baltimore bordello although he did not say it where Mrs. Lincoln could hear him.

The wallpaper store did, in fact, have to send to Baltimore for the paper Mrs. Lincoln was set on, which caused no end of snickering on Abernethy's part although he did have to listen to her shout and harangue with the store managers because she wanted to change the wallpaper in the President's study, particularly, and would not rest until the managers vowed to send wild horses to Baltimore to pick up the desired pattern and deliver it on Thursday, which happened be the same day as Mr. Lincoln's war briefing.

"Thunderation," Abernethy fumed. He and General Sneath of the Pinkerton Bureau arrived with several other generals and Sergeant Clancy to find the study in a frenzy of wallpapering. There was nowhere to sit.

"Why don't we move to the East Room," Lincoln suggested. "Ol' Sneak needs a place to put his maps."

They went down to the East Room, but it was even worse. Painters were at work there, as well as paperhangers.

They tried the Oval Library, but the varnish on the floor wasn't dry. So, they all piled into the kitchen, but Florence soon ran them out.

They ended up back in Lincoln's study.

"You'll have to work around us," the President told the wallpaper men.

Sneak spread out the secret plan for attacking the Reb stronghold at Waterville, using a trestle board stretched between two paperhanger ladders. Abernethy, squinting around for a spittoon, accidentally fired a chaw into a paste bucket. Then he got some paste on his hands and got the map stuck to his hands and couldn't get it off. Sneak tried to help, but the map fell to the floor, and Sneak accidentally kicked over the paste bucket as he tried to catch the map, and got paste all over Cooper.

Lincoln held up the dripping map. "Here," he said, and took the plan and slapped it on a bare wall next to a newly-stuck roll of Mrs. Lincoln's scarlet brocade.

"Hit it a lick with that brush," Lincoln told a young paperhanger.

The young man brushed the plan flat on the wall. Lincoln and his generals gathered around.

"The Waterville attack will be simple," Sneak said. "We sneak up beside this creek and pound the Rebs with our artillery and then rush 'em at dawn."

"What about the Reb artillery?" Abernethy frowned.

"What Reb artillery?" Sneak examined the map.

"Right here," Abernethy poked a finger at a brown mark.

"I think that's your chaw of tobacco, Horatio," Lincoln said.

"Right," Sneak said.

"But Horatio may have a point about Reb artillery," Lincoln went on. "Where's Beauregard's 99th Cannonball Brigade? It's all artillery and they might sneak up on us while we're sneaking up on them."

"The 99th's clean off the map, sir," Sneak scoffed. "We think they'll be stuck in Froggy Bottoms."

"Where's that?"

The young paperhanger spoke up, "maybe I can help, sir. I had a cousin in Froggy Bottoms and we used to fish there for crawdads."

Lincoln handed the young paperhanger a pencil, and he drew a circle on the bare plaster next to the plastered map.

"Froggy Bottom's right about here, sir."

"Ten miles from Waterville?" Lincoln said.

"More like five," the paperhanger said.

Sneak scoffed some more. "They'd still never get to Waterville in time. Froggy Bottoms is a tidal marsh, and you can't move anything heavy on the road when the tide is in."

"I'm not so sure about that, sir," the paperhanger said. "There was a hurricane about a dozen years ago and it cut a new channel for the creek which is now a sizable river that flushes out the swamp. The old channel - can I draw a line on the wall here?"

"Certainly," Lincoln nodded.

"The old channel is hardpacked sand, and the farmers all use it for a road now. I know because me and my cousin used to hitch rides on their wagons when we went in there to go crawdadding. We would take that road to the far end of the marsh where the biggest crawdads were."

Lincoln glared at Sneak. "What about that old channel?"

Sneak's eyes looked shifty. "Well - "

Abernethy bit a plug of tobacco.

"May I, Mr. President?" the young paperhanger held up his pencil.

"Proceed," said Lincoln.

"Well, Mr. President," the paperhanger continued drawing, "there's sometimes a complication with the old channel bed. Two or three days a month when the moon's just right, the tide comes in extra high and the old channel floods again and you can't use it for a road at all. It's more like a river, which means a gun would disappear completely and a horse would drown. So, all you have to do is attack the Rebs when the tide is roaring up the old channel, which would keep the Reb artillery stuck in Froggy Bottoms."

Lincoln rubbed his whiskers and peered at Sneak.

"That's what you actually planned to do, wasn't it, general?"

"Absolutely sir," Sneak said. "Attack at high tide."

"Maximum high, sir," the paperhanger said. "Normal high's not high enough."

"I meant maximum high!" Sneak said. "That's what I meant!"

"And what shall I do with the general's top-secret battle plan, sir?" the young paperhanger said, pointing his brush at the wall.

"Slap something over it," Lincoln said, "before Mrs. Lincoln decides she likes it."

54.
How Cooper Saved the Blockade

Mary Lincoln was nervous about the party. She kept the servants running. Pretty soon the cook was upset. And Mr. Lincoln couldn't find his collar button. By the time the ambassadors arrived for dinner, the whole White House was in such a fettle that nobody could have a good time.

Cooper looked through the keyhole into the East Room. All he saw were long faces. Mr. Van Der Hooeven, the Dutch ambassador tried telling an improper joke. Mrs. Odegaard shrieked, but the other wives only looked at each other.

It was awful. Not even Lincoln could save the day. The President tried telling the British ambassador, Sir Cecil Moregrave, the story about the congressman and the elephant, but the ambassador only bared his teeth.

"Haw, haw, haw," said Lincoln. "Now, Sir Cecil, have you ever heard the one about the queen and the preacher?"

Sir Cecil stared glassy-eyed, and Lincoln couldn't find a way to get around to asking about the blockade runners, and how the Firth of Forth shipyard was planning to sell steam-driven sloops to the Confederates.

"Haw, haw, haw," Lincoln's laugh was high and thin. "And that puts me in mind of the one about the two traveling salesmen in Missouri...."

"Man the lifeboats," mumbled Secretary Seward. He slipped through the door to the foyer where Abernethy, looking stricken, was smoking a cigar. Seward unscrewed the head of his walking stick and poured them a brandy.

Cooper wagged his tail. He barked. He thought Seward might want to go out and toss the stick.

"Hush, Cooper," Seward put a finger to his lips, waving the stick. Cooper totally misunderstood this and cavorted backwards into the hat rack which toppled drunkenly and spilled a pile of ambassadorial top hats on the floor.

"Thunderation," exclaimed Abernethy. He and Seward grabbed for the rack and the hats as the dog kept barking, and suddenly the door opened from the East Room, flooding the foyer with ambassadors.

"Gott im Himmel!" cried the Prussian ambassador. "Mine hat! Der homberger ist on der floor gemixt mit hatzenderbyheimers und gernogginlidz!"

"No harm done, old boy," Sir Cecil said, picking up a derby and donning it, only to have it slide down over his eyes.

"Har, har, har," laughed Ole Odegaard. "Dot's mine!"

"No, I dink I got yours, Ole," said the Dutchman, Van Der Hooeven, exchanging a hat with the Norwegian but discovering that it perched on top of his head like a teacup.

"Yek yek yek," laughed the Prussian ambassador, who chose a hat that promptly covered his ears.

The foyer was full of ambassadors with hats that wouldn't go over their heads or slid down over their eyes, and one that fit perfectly but turned out to be a spittoon.

Now, everyone was laughing, including the ladies. They began trying on hats, too.

"Haw, haw, haw!" Sir Cecil was laughing now, too, in a laugh that sounded amazingly like Lincoln's. "Good show, Mr. President! Jolly good!"

Lincoln nudged Abernethy, gave him a quizzical look.

"Cooper," Abernethy whispered, "knocked the hat rack over."

"Well," Lincoln murmured, "he may have saved the blockade."

Later, as the party broke up, Cooper followed Seward out the door, his eye still on the walking stick that looked an awful lot like a regular stick, as far as he was concerned, and sticks were wonderful things.

Mr. Van Der Hooeven and Mrs. Van Der Hooeven drove off in a carriage. Ole Odegaard decided to walk with the Prussian ambassador. The unofficial legate from China joined the secret monsignor from the Vatican, and the Finnish head of mission strolled along with the ambassador from France.

Only Sir Cecil stayed behind. "I say, could you tell the one again about the traveling salesman, Mr. President?" he asked.

"The one with the elephant or the one about the farmer's daughter?" Lincoln said.

"I'll need both" - Sir Cecil leaned confidentially toward Lincoln and winked - "because the queen does love a good story."

"Queen Victoria?"

"Hah!" Sir Cecil lifted a brow, his eye twinkling. "You've no idea!"

"In that case I'll throw in another one with the two old maids, with my compliments."

"Jolly good, Mr. President! And by the way, you probably wouldn't object if I advised against selling those blockade runners to the Confederates?"

55.
Oopz

Boom!

The loud explosion from the basement woke Cooper. He jumped straight into Lincoln's lap.

"Whoa, boy," Lincoln said. "That sounds like the professor!"

Lincoln took Cooper down to the basement to see how the secret experiment was coming.

Cooper was wide-eyed as they clambered over a smoky pile of wrecked laboratory benches, broken test tubes and wrecked wreckage.

"Wolfgang?" Lincoln called out.

"Maybe it don't voik," muttered a voice from under a heap.

"Wolfgang!"

"Volfgank," muttered the voice. "Mit a 'V' is pronouncen."

"Volfgank, where are you?"

"How should I know? Someplace. Try digging."

"Talk so I can find you."

"I am spoken already. Tell Goldberg to talk. My assistant

talks all the time, even when he should be listening, like just now, in case anyone is interested in my opinion."

Cooper soon sniffed out Professor Von Oopz, and Lincoln removed a few boards to uncover his face.

"Are you all right, Volfgang?"

"Personally, I think I'm dead but I will feel a lot better if Goldberg is dead, too, because he would never listen. I can give you a qvote exactly. I was sayink to Goldberg, vatch out! So he don't vatch out."

"Where did you see him last?"

"Out der vindow flyink, and serves him right."

The basement didn't have a window, but Cooper peered at a hole in the wall and saw the assistant's long, pointed shoes stirring. Presently, Goldberg sat up, picking pieces of Bunsen burner out of his beard.

"If I told you once," Von Oopz shouted at him, "I told you two times, maybe it don't voik!"

"Vot don't voik?"

"Vot ve vos voiking on!"

"Mine atomic mess-kit?"

Von Oopz climbed out of the debris. "Now he remembers!"

Goldberg scratched his head. "Ve vas atoms in der skillet putting?"

"Ja, ja."

"Vot happenen to der skillet!?" Von Oopz demanded.

Lincoln blinked. "You were doing research on a skillet?"

Von Oopz put a finger to his lips. "Secret."

"Wolfgang," Lincoln's voice rose, "I gave you and Goldberg a pile of research money to build a secret weapon to win the war - and you were down here inventing a frying pan?"

"Not chust any frying pan, Mr. President," Goldberg said. "It's a known fact dat troops don't like to fight vitout having hot lunch first."

"What are you talking about?" Lincoln's voice rose some more. "Who cares about hot lunch?"

"It's no good fighting on empty stomach."

"Congress will eat me alive if it finds out I've spent all this money on a skillet!"

"Don't vorry, Mr. President," Von Oopz said, "like I told Goldberg, maybe it don't voik."

"Dot's vot I said," Goldberg shook his head. "I said maybe it don't voik and he says maybe it vill, but we don't know yet."

"But we already have skillets!" Lincoln hollered.

"Not vit atoms cookin! Der atom skillet stays red-hot and ve also put a gun in it!"

"You put a gun in a red-hot skillet?"

"People can have a hot lunch and shoot at same time."

Lincoln found a chair and sat in it.

"After der var is ofer," Von Oopz went on, "effryvun vill vant der new frying pan they don't haff to heat."

"Not if it costs a million dollars!"

"But don't forget it shoots, also!" Von Oopz enthused. "You can cook pancakes vitout a fire, and if der enemy attacks vile you're eating pancakes, don't vorry."

"How can I not worry? I've spent a pile of government money on a skillet that won't even make waffles!"

"Because Goldberg never fixed der atomschmascher fur der vafflemacher! Der atomsmasher is gebroken!"

"Hah," said Goldberg, "der atomaschmascher is kaput because der neutrons is gemixt vit der protons and make shpitzen sparken!"

"No no!" Von Oopz said, "der sparken ist shpitzen already und der nucleus is chumping up und down - "

"Und burning der pancakes and poppencorn!"

Lincoln yelled, "I am not paying for a popcorn maker!"

"Don't vorry," Von Oopz soothed the President, "I told Goldberg it don't vork. I told him two times."

"Hah! It vill vork ven ve do it right!" Goldberg said, pulling a blackboard out of the debris. "First, ve must take der X uff der hypoteneuse uff der isoceles and diffide by der cube root uff der density uff der nucleus...."

"Und add a few neutrons, vich you don't have," scoffed Von Oopz."

"I can get neutrons!"

"I tell you, Goldberg, it don't voik."

"Your mutter's mustache!" Goldberg cried.

"You vatch, I try it vit protons!"

Lincoln and Cooper ran from the basement.

Later that day, another explosion rattled Lincoln's study. Lincoln went to the window and saw Von Oopz and Goldberg lying on the lawn.

"What happened?" Lincoln called. "Nothink," said Goldberg.

"Maybe it don't voik," Von Oopz said.

"Don't listen to him," said Goldberg.

56.
The Epidemic

When Cooper woke up in the morning, his head hurt and his eyes were red.

"Dat dog has de pinkeye!" exclaimed Florence, putting her hands up to shield her eyes.

"Pinkeye?" said Abernethy. He had just come into the kitchen, hoping to steal a cookie.

"Don't look at him!" Florence warned. "Or you get de pinkeye too."

Abernethy put his hands over his eyes. "What's pinkeye?"

"Dat's wen yo eyes gits pink."

Word spread quickly through the White House that Cooper had the pinkeye, and that no one should look at him.

"Has anybody else caught it?" Lincoln asked Hay.

"I don't know, Mr. President," Hay said. "I've got my eyes covered up."

"Well, don't take any chances," Lincoln said. "It's pinkeye."

"What about your appointment with Commodore

Farragut, Mr. President? He's already here."

"Commodore Farragut? Who said 'Damn the torpedoes, full speed ahead?'"

"That's him."

"Better bring him in but make sure he keeps his eyes covered up just like I've got mine covered."

Farragut came in, wondering if it was really necessary to keep his Commodore hat over his face.

"We don't want you getting pinkeye, Captain," Lincoln explained.

"It's Commodore, Mr. President."

"I just promoted you."

"Captain would be demoting me, sir."

"I must have meant Admiral."

"Thank you, Mr. President."

"Great fight in Tampa Bay where you said 'Damn the torpedoes!'"

"I'm afraid the *Tribune* got the bay wrong, sir, it was Mobile Bay. And I don't remember anything about torpedoes."

"And then you said 'full steam ahead!' and inspired the whole country!"

"I think it was 'full speed,' I don't think I said steam."

"I'm just glad it's short enough to fit in a headline, Farragut!"

"I did yell a lot more than that, sir, but nothing you could print."

Seward came in with cigars and they all sat and had one. Lincoln assumed that Seward also had his eyes covered to avoid the pinkeye, but Seward, of course, did not have his eyes covered and was looking at Cooper.

"How is the pinkeye going, Seward?" Lincoln said.

"Hard to say," Seward said.

"What about Congress?" the President asked.

"Haven't heard of a case."

"Nobody?"

"Not a soul."

"What about the staff?"

"I don't know. They've all got their eyes covered."

Lincoln spread his fingers and looked at Seward who

looked back at him.

Farragut still had his hat over his face.

"Well admiral," Lincoln rose and took Farragut's arm.

"Nice to see you. Have a nice trip."

"Aye, aye, sir."

"Careful going down the stairs."

"Aye, sir."

Moments later, Seward and Lincoln heard some loud crashes and thumps.

Hay came in to report that Farragut had tumbled down the staircase. Dr. Hunt came with an ambulance to take the admiral to the hospital. The case was put down to pinkeye, and Farragut missed the rest of the war.

***

Later, when Seward was an old man resting in Alexandria, a blanket over his lap, a young historian visited him and asked about the Farragut incident.

"Farragut's place in history was saved by pinkeye," Seward said.

"What do you mean?"

"He fell down the stairs with his hat over his face and never got a chance to say anything after 'damn the torpedoes.' Suppose Nathan Hale had escaped the British hangman before saying 'I only regret that I have but one life to lose for my country,' and then lived on and become a blabby codger and said all kinds of extra words and then died in his bed. Nobody today would remember Nathan Hale. Same thing with Farragut. It was 'damn the torpedoes' and then nothing else because of his pinkeye accident."

The historian took a few notes. "By the way, Mr. Secretary, whatever happened to the dog? The one they called Lincoln's Doctor's Dog."

"Cooper?"

"Yes sir. The one that had pinkeye."

Seward raised his hands slightly then dropped them to his lap.

"I don't know."

57.
The Appointment

Lincoln couldn't find the report that General Meade sent. He would have looked in the Meade file, but he couldn't find the Meade file.

"Have you seen the Bragg report?" Lincoln asked Hay, fit to be tied.

"It's must be in the Meade file, sir," Hay said.

"Which I can't find."

"You did say Bragg report?" Hay scratched his head. "Which you think is in the Meade file."

"If we got a Bragg report from Meade," Hay said, "it would be in the Meade file."

"Hay," Lincoln stood still in the middle of the room, his arms straight down by his sides, "did we actually receive a Bragg report?"

"Yes sir, but it must have gotten into the Meade file which is why you can't find it."

Lincoln began rummaging again. He avoided looking

Hay in the eye, which Hay knew was a bad sign. Finally, Lincoln muttered, "We've got to do something about losing things, Hay."

Hay followed Lincoln around the room, his face red. Keeping up with files was his job. The wispy new mustache he was growing under his nose wiggled unhappily as he looked through the same drawers that Lincoln had just looked through and the same pigeonholes that Lincoln had just peered inside of, and the same teetery stacks of Presidential papers that Lincoln had just re-teetered.

Seward dropped by and watched this but soon left without lighting a cigar.

Lincoln gave up the search and moved on to a new subject.

"Look at this one, Hay," he said, pulling a paper off a collapsing stack on his desk. "The Army can't make next month's payroll without a new appropriations bill. But the bill has to go through Senator Freeble's committee and he'll attach a dozen porkpie strings to it."

"A dozen's not a lot, for Freebie."

Lincoln sank in his chair. "The country might have money enough for a million-man Army to save the Union, Hay, but it will surely go broke trying to hire every shirttail relative of Phil Freebie's. So...do you need an assistant?"

"Assistant what?"

"Assistant anything. Phil has a nephew."

"Another one?"

Lincoln pulled a notebook from his pocket. "Phil wants us to give this nephew a commission. "In the Union Army?"

"Navy, whatever."

"Lord."

"According to this here, the nephew's now the corporal in sole charge, and in fact is the sole member, of the 39th Terre Haute Terrors, guarding a livery stable for retired cavalry horses in Terre Haute, Indiana.

"Sounds like postmaster material to me, Mr. President."

"Freebie's nephew or a retired horse?" Lincoln shook his head. "The United States Post Office is already filled up with deadwood, Hay. One more relative of the senator's would bring the service to its knees, but we need 'ol Freebie's committee, so we have to find something for his nephew."

"Well," Hay sighed, "if he can shovel manure in a stable in Terre Haute, he might be able to shovel these files."

***

Cooper came out from under the sofa and stretched. He stretched one hind leg at a time, first one and then the other, holding each leg way out in back of him as far as he could stretch, and let it quiver as he grinned and showed his teeth.

Lincoln did some stretching himself as he sat in his chair, sticking his legs out straight so that pretty soon he was supported mainly by the back of his neck.

"Hay, remind me who that congressman was that just died?"

"Oh, Ed Graspers."

"The honorable Greedy T. Graspers. I never did appoint a replacement for him."

"Uh, the governor gets to do that, sir. You don't get to."

Lincoln looked sly, still holding his legs out stiff and balancing on his neck.

"That's just the way it works. Sir," Hay said.

"Well, I made a deal with the governor," Lincoln said.

"What deal?"

"I get to make the appointment if I get his nephew a cushy government job."

"What cushy job do you have in mind?" Hay gulped.

"Congressman." Lincoln said.

Seward had come in just in time to hear this exchange, which had rendered Hay speechless.

"Why," Seward asked the President, hauling out a cigar, "would you appoint the governor's nephew to Congress when he was already in over his head when he made corporal? And how does doing the governor a favor help you get your bills out of limbo in Senator Freebie's committee?"

"Well Seward," Lincoln said, "you know as well as I do that in politics an incrumbent has a much better chance of getting elected than a non-incrumbent, even if the incrumbent is a nincompoop and has a spine like a noodle. So, you can see the advantage of starting out in politics as an incrumbent."

"True," Seward nodded, taking a minute to slap out the small fire in his pants from the spark that fell off his stogie. "But surely you wouldn't appoint that doofus nephew to a seat in the U.S. House of Representatives!"

"Well, I sure don't want him in the post office," Lincoln said.

"But if you appoint the nephew to Congress," Seward said, "he'll be an incrumbent and stick to that seat like a barnacle and gum up the government for ages to come."

"You're right, Seward," Lincoln said, "which is why Freebie and I came to a meeting of the minds about the governor's nephew. What Freebie really wanted was to get that appointment for his wife. So, when I first brought up the nephew, he pounded his fist on my desk and jumped up and down and said it was treason and that I have to appoint his wife or else my bills are all sunk and will stay sunk!"

"What did you do?"

"I gave in," Lincoln said.

Seward's mouth hung open.

Lincoln got up and paced the room, swinging his watch fob around and around. "When all this first started, I was afraid I'd have to make the nephew an assistant to Hay, or, worse, put him in the post office. Then I realized I could solve everything by appointing Mrs. Freebie to the vacant congressional seat."

"But what about the governor's nephew?"

"Part of my deal with Freebie was that his wife puts the nephew on her staff. She can assign him to a broom closet."

"What now, Mr. President?" Hay said.

"A glass of water," Lincoln said. "Then wire General Meade and tell him he'll finally get the new artillery he needs."

"Yes sir. Water. Artillery. Wire Meade."

"Go."

Later that day, Lincoln found the Meade file. It was under Cooper who was sleeping on it. The file, it turned out, didn't contain anything important.

58.
The Tele-phone

On Thursday, two men came to install Mr. Lincoln's tele-phone. It took them two hours.

Afterwards, Lincoln went and got Abernethy so he could show it to him.

"They say I can talk on it," Lincoln said.

"Who do you talk to?"

"Nobody yet."

"If I get one," Abernethy said, "we could talk to each other."

They sat and looked at the tele-phone for a while.

Cooper also came and looked at it.

The great clock ticked.

"They say when you talk on the tele-phone," Lincoln said, "it's just as plain as talking to somebody, almost.

"Be mighty useful if you ever want to talk to somebody," Abernethy said.

Lincoln nodded. "The tele-phone men claim it's so easy to learn how to talk on the tele-phone that even a teenager can do it."

Hay stuck his head in the door and looked at the tele-phone while Abernethy took the tele-phone men down to his office to see if he himself could get a tele-phone to talk on.

Seward came by and sat down with the President.

"Any calls on your tele-phone yet, Lincoln?"

"Not so far."

Seward nodded. "Mind if I smoke?"

"Open that window, first," Lincoln said.

Seward set fire to his cigar. "Lincoln, how many tele-phones are there, roughly, altogether, in the country?" he asked, exhaling a cloud of smoke.

"Well," Lincoln said, "this is the only tele-phone I know of, so far, in Washington. They say they're planning on putting more in New York but they don't know where, just yet."

Cooper turned around and around on the rug and took a nap.

***

Sergeant Clancy rapped on the door.

"Beggin' your pardon, Mr. President, but General Abernethy wishes to inform yourself that a new tele-phone is now ready and waitin' in his generalship's office, so you can call him."

"Abernethy has a tele-phone?"

"He does, sir. And I quote the general exactly, so as not to make even the smallest sliver of a mistake that could cause a regrettable misunderstandin' with regard to it, namely the message I'm about to deliver to yourself, by your leave, and entirely from pure memory as me Great Uncle Givins, God rest his soul, taught me in the memory department when I was knee-deep in grasshoppers."

"You mean knee-high to a grasshopper?"

"We did have an awful lot of grasshoppers. But to resume me message, sir, it's a true fact that his generalship is waitin,' even as we speak, to receive on his tele-phone an order spoken by his commander-in-chief."

"Abernethy wants me to give him an order on the tele-phone?"

"What the general said was, and this is a quote from him exactly, 'I am ready now, as of this moment, to receive any and all orders from me President and commander-in-chief' - meanin' yourself - 'without undue aggravatin' delay in our official communications.' Unquote."

"But General Abernethy is just down the hall, Sergeant Clancy. If I want to talk to General Abernethy, I can just take six steps down the hall and do it."

"Oh, the general won't hear of it, sir! Far too inconvenient for your Lordship, and too hard on the feet."

"My corns do hurt," Lincoln admitted.

"So the general'll be standin' by for his orders, then."

"Fine."

"Meanin' he'll stand fast by his tele-phone as he waits, and won't budge an inch."

"Fine, sergeant. But I can't think of any orders for General Abernethy right now."

"He'll be sorely disappointed, sir, standin' there as he is and ready to remain all night if need be, to talk on the tele-phone, faithful soldier that he is."

"I'll try to think of something," Lincoln said.

Sergeant Clancy saluted twice and spun around on his heels and left.

Lincoln thought for awhile.

He scratched his head.

The clock on the wall ticked. It bonged.

Cooper got up and turned around and around the other way on the rug and resumed his nap.

Lincoln looked at his tele-phone.

That afternoon he stuck his head out the door and hollered, "I don't have anything, Horatio!"

***

Lincoln quit looking at his tele-phone. He got Cooper up from his nap.

"Let's go throw the stick, boy."

"Arf," said Cooper, and the two of them went downstairs and out the front door. They were headed for the river when the President's tele-phone rang. They could hear it jangle through the open window.

Private Shaugnessy came running. "Sir, sir! Your tele-phone's a'ringin and also a'janglin'!"

"Who is it?"

"I don't know, sir. I'm afraid as the devil to touch it."

"Come on, Coop," Lincoln said. They loped back to the office where the tele-phone jingled.

"Hello?" Lincoln said. "Hello? Hello?"

"I think you have to pick it up, sir," Private Shaugnessy said.

"Pick what up?"

"The talker part."

"I don't want to talk, I want to hear."

"That's what the talker is for, sir. You listen in the talker, and then you talk in the talker after you listened in the talker. Or you can talk first, if you want to."

Lincoln picked up the talker and shouted, "Hello! Hello!" He frowned at Shaugnessy. "I don't hear anything."

"Somebody has to listen to the other talker, sir. Try talking and then listening."

"I did."

"I think you're talking in the wrong end of the talker."

"What's the right end?"

"The other end."

"Here, you do it."

Shaugnessy handed Lincoln his musket and took the tele-phone. "I'm not hearing a thing, sir. Maybe they're listening 'cause they think I'm talking."

Cooper listened to the talker for awhile, and shrugged. The tele-phone didn't do anything.

***

Lincoln and Cooper started for the river again. Amy decided to go with them. When they got to the bottom of the stairs, the President's tele-phone jangled again.

"I'll get it!" Amy called, and ran past Lincoln.

"Dad, dad! It's General Abernethy."

Lincoln came and talked into the talker. "Hello! Hello!"

Amy poked him on the arm. "Listen, father."

Lincoln put the talker to his ear.

"It's me, Mr. President," came the thin voice. "I'm down the hall talking to you!"

"And I'm here talking to you," Lincoln said.

"Do you have any orders?"

"Any what?"

"Orders. For me."

"You have to talk louder!"

"Can you hear me?"

"I'm talking in the talker."

"Are you talking or listening?"

"It's me, Mr. President."

"Yes, I hear you. Wait a minute."

"Do what?"

"I'm listening. You have to talk."

"Are you down the hall?"

"I'm right here."

"Wait a minute! Wait!" Lincoln put down the tele-phone and stuck his head out the door. Abernethy did the same. They waved at each other.

"What were you talking about?"

"I was saying I didn't have any orders for you, Horatio."

"You have to tell me on the tele-phone."

They went back to their tele-phones.

"I said I didn't have any orders for you," Lincoln shouted. "Did you want to talk about anything else?"

"I can hear you better now that I know what you're saying."

"I can hear you better, too."

"It's just like you were right here."

"I am right here, Horatio. If we want to talk to each other, why don't we just talk?"

"The tele-phone saves a lot of time, Mr. President," Abernethy said.

"What was that?"

"Time. It saves a lot of time."

"I'll look," Lincoln said. "It's four o'clock."

"No, I said it saves time."

"Oh, all right. Now I can understand what you're saying."

"Why don't you try giving me an order and see if I can carry it out. Hello?"

"Do you have a pencil?"

"I'll get one."

"All right."

"I've got a pencil."

"Tell General McClellan," Lincoln said, "to march down to Richmond and capture it forthwith."

"Four? Your clock must be a little fast. Mine says three-thirty."

"I'll check my clock. But maybe it's your clock that's wrong."

"Just think," Mr. President!" Abernethy said, "Pretty soon the whole government will be like this."

59.
Hard News

Lincoln, Seward and Stanton were slumped in the cabinet room. Cooper was there. Montgomery Tillicot, the postmaster general, was there, and so was Salmon P. Chase, the Treasury secretary.

Pretty soon it was the whole cabinet. And Cooper.

Chase sat reading a Bible.

"How do you spell damnation?" Seward peered at Chase over his cigar.

"Take that dog turd someplace else!" Chase fanned a hand at the smoke without looking up.

Seward tipped a cone of ash onto the carpet.

"Honduran."

Stanton said, "Are we having a cabinet meeting or not?"

"Soon as Hoppy gets here," Lincoln nodded. "Senator A. Flagon Hopwood has demanded - " Lincoln fished a note from his breast pocket and adjusted his glasses - "let me quote, 'a most urgent meeting regarding constitutional national deportment.'"

"What the devil's Hopwood talking about?" Stanton threw some papers on the table so loudly that Cooper quit scratching a flea. Seward blew another smoke ring, and then started getting Chase's goat by leaning in to see what he was reading.

Lincoln tapped the table with a pencil. "Order, please, gentlemen, order."

"I'll have bourbon," Seward said. "And make it a double."

Stanton fumed, "What on earth does Senator Hopgoblin mean by 'constitutional national deportment?'"

"I guess you can ask him," Seward said.

"I don't have to ask!" Stanton shouted, red in the face. "It's gobbledegook! Means absolutely nothing! Show me one word in the Constitution about deportment! Yet we have all agreed to a full cabinet meeting to discuss it?" Stanton pounded the table so hard that his glasses fell down to his chin whiskers.

Lincoln started to say something but the war secretary had no intention of shutting up. "Am I the only sane person here," Stanton's chin whiskers wiggled as he retrieved his glasses, "who has actually read the Constitution, every buckle-slipper clause and powdered-wig amendment, even though I'm busier than the all rest of you put together, running a war despite the unending obstacles put up by the lunatics and field mice who make up the majority of Congress? I mean, I have work to do! And one thing I urgently do not need to do is sit around all day discussing the hallucinations of a nut like Hopwood!"

"A nut who's also a committee chairman," Seward said mildly.

"Has it ever entered anyone's mind," Stanton fussed, "that there should be serious qualifications for anyone wishing to hold public office? Why is it illegal in every state in the Union for a person to enter the barber trade and give people haircuts without a license, but no law against a complete nincompoop entering the United States Senate? I've got real challenges in the War Department - guns that won't shoot, explosives that won't explode and cavalry horses so old they can't fart, and I can't havecontractors hung by their thumbs because they're somebody's constituent! And who do I get for generals? Military peacocks and underemployed political hacks with state militia commissions looking to burnish their resumes! And right in the middle of this cavalcade of catastrophes comes a wackadoodle senator to waste my time! I know you know how crazy he is, Lincoln, because he writes to you all the time and you send the letters on to me with a note at the bottom, 'handle this.' How do I handle the ravings of a total nut? I tell you, sir, Hopwood is driving me crazy!"

Lincoln sighed. "All right, all right Stanton. We know Hoppy is a brick short of a full load, but his constituents keep sending him back to the Senate. It's their constitutional right, so Hopwood is now a loon with serious seniority, and chairman of a committee we need. So that's why I'm happy to meet with him to discuss - what was it again, Seward?"

"National deportment," Seward's cigar had unraveled to look like a brown flag.

"So," Lincoln said, "we'll all be highly concerned - " pointing a finger in turn at each cabinet secretary, " - War Department, State Department, Post Office and - " jabbing a thumb at himself, " - President. All sunk, otherwise."

Hay stuck his head in the door. "Senator Hopwood is here."

The senator appeared, trailed by three aides carrying armloads of files and papers. Chase and Seward pulled out a chair for him and Hopwood sat and hooked his thumbs in his lapels and harrumphed, "About this matter of national - "

"You're looking mighty good, senator," Stanton smiled at him.

"Thank you. As I was about to say - "

Seward reached over and adjusted the senator's bow tie, bringing it into symmetry. "It's amazing how you do it, sir! And we can't wait to hear your views on national compartment - "

"Comportment," Stanton kicked Seward under the table.

Hopwood cleared his throat again and opened a report. "As I was about to say - "

"You go right ahead, sir," Seward said, "we can't wait to hear!"

"About deportment, from a constitutional standpoint," Stanton exclaimed, waggling his chin whiskers.

"Has anybody read the *Washington Star*?" Seward said suddenly.

"I have," said Montgomery Tillicot.

"Notice all the mistakes?" Seward said.

Hopwood looked up from his report.

"Excuse me, senator," Seward waved his cigar. "I didn't mean to digress about the *Star's* abuse of semicolons, but I think it ties right in."

"Well," Hopwood's eyes went strange, "I was about to bring that up myself."

Stanton jumped in, "and some of the spelling was quite bad."

"I noticed that, too," Tillicot said.

Lincoln started to speak but Hopwood didn't notice. "The *Star*!" Hopwood groused, "I no longer even read - "

"Because of its flagrant flouting of national deportment," Seward nodded knowingly. "The constitutional kind in particular."

"You're concerned about that, too?"

"We were just discussing it," Seward said "Did I already mention how good you're looking?"

"Thank you," Hopwood rose from his chair. "I think that about covers it."

"We're much obliged," Lincoln said. "Come back soon!"

Hopwood took his aides and left.

"Whew," Stanton said.

Lincoln left.

Cooper scratched a flea.

Postmaster General Tillicot sat in the corner poring over new postages stamps. He found one that said "Statute of Liberty." Chase looked over his shoulder and said, "Maybe Hopgoblin has a point. Forget I said that."

Stanton cried, "For pity's sake, Seward, the *Star* has got Rhode Island spelled 'Road Island!' And Manassas doesn't have enough s's and they spelled cabinet with two b's."

Seward set his cigar afire and left.

60.
The Gettysburg Address: The True Story

"About five minutes, Mr. Lincoln," John Hay said nervously. He peeked out the window of the railroad car at the vast crowd bobbing up the hill to await a momentous Presidential address.

"Dang," Lincoln chewed his pen and threw another ball of paper on the floor.

Cooper chased it down and sniffed it.

"Maybe I'll just make a few notes," Lincoln said. "I'll write down the beginning of the speech and make up the rest as I go."

"Or not, sir!" Hay choked.

"Just wing it," Abernethy nodded, looking at his watch. "Nobody will hear it anyway," sighed Seward. "The only people close enough to catch what you're saying will be a gaggle of wannabes who are mainly here to be seen."

"But we do need to get going," Abernethy said.

"One more minute," Lincoln promised.

A knock on the door of the Presidential car sent Hay scurrying to the other end to answer. "No!" They could hear him say to someone outside. "Absolutely no advance copy. Not even for you, Beehan."

Cooper's ears went up at the mention of the name. Beehan, star reporter of *The Daily Double*, was always getting things wrong - "improving Lincoln's quotes" is how he put it - which gave Hay conniptions although it didn't bother Lincoln that much.

"Was that Beehan?" the President said.

"I threw him out," Hay said.

"Maybe you shouldn't have," Lincoln sighed.

Drawing a fresh sheet of paper, Lincoln wrote: *Eighty-some-odd years ago our forefathers established on this continent a new nation....*

Lincoln's pen came up. "Seward, when would you say our forefathers established the country? Was it 1776 with the Declaration of Independence, or 1789 with the Constitution?"

"Either one."

Abernethy continued to consult his watch. "Mr. President, I don't want to rush you but - "

"One more minute," Lincoln wadded up the paper and threw it on the floor. "I keep changing my mind between eighty-some-odd and eighty-seven."

"Why don't you say fourscore, instead of eighty?" Seward said. "Most people won't know what 'fourscore' means. Or by the time they figure it out, it won't matter."

"Yes, yes, anything, but hurry," Abernethy furiously shook his watch.

Fourscore and seven - Lincoln's pen scratched hurriedly. "No, wait. Maybe it should be just plain fourscore, or maybe I should keep it general and say 'several years ago.'"

Abernethy began swinging his watch in a circle.

"Do I hyphenate fourscore or not?" Lincoln chewed his trembling pen. Sweat was breaking out on his brow. A roar was rising from the crowd on the hill.

"Mr. President, please!" Abernethy shouted.

But the paper was a mess. Lincoln reached for a new sheet but there wasn't any. "Oh Lord!" he said, and searched his coat and found something to write on and set his pen sputtering across the page. Suddenly he quit. He looked at the paper. He stared at it, pen raised.

"We can't wait for inspiration!" Abernethy hollered. Lincoln continued to stare.

Seward walked over and took the paper.

"Fourscore and seven years," Seward read slowly "and a teaspoon of baking powder, six eggs, two cups of sugar, a cup of flour...."

Abernethy sat down.

Seward frowned. "You're writing on top of a cake recipe, Lincoln! Where's what you threw away?"

Hay jumped down on the floor and found a piece of paper with only the words Fourscore and seven written on it.

"Here, Mr. President," Hay said. "Here's your start. Just keep going and don't mention eggs or flour."

"My mind's a blank," Lincoln groaned.

***

Bundled up in topcoat and stovepipe hat, Lincoln let Hay and Abernethy lead him up the hill, the three of them stopping once or twice so that he could shake a hand or respond with word or gesture and wave his hat as three cheers rose from the crowd. At the summit, the wind was blowing so hard that it tore the paper out of his hands, and Cooper went racing for it.

Lincoln smiled and shook his head. The paper was lost, so Lincoln reached in his pocket to see what else he had. The only thing handy was the Baltimore and Ohio timetable. "Fourscore and seven," he ad-libbed. The wind blew his words away. Mathew Brady had to keep a grip on his camera as he tried to focus it.

"Fourscore and seven...years!" Lincoln repeated. Beehan, who had horned in next to Smithers of the *Times*, shouted in his colleague's ear, "What'd he say about a score?" Smithers shrugged, letting his notebook fall to his side.

With dramatic inflection, none of which could be heard,

Lincoln said, "Arrival times in boldface, departures in italic...
Washington 4:07 p.m., Baltimore 6:22, Harrisburg 11:10...."

Smithers leaned forward, then turned and looked at
Beehan. "I must not be able to hear, Beehan. I could swear the
President's reading a train timetable!"

"You'd better see a doctor," Beehan said, writing rapidly
in his notebook and holding it so Smithers couldn't see. Smithers
started to panic.

Downhill from them, Brady was having trouble steadying
his camera in the high wind. He got only one exposure before
Lincoln quit speaking and stuffed the timetable back in his pocket.

Seward started clapping wildly and then Abernethy
jumped up and did the same and then the crowd started
clapping like mad, and clapped all the more as Lincoln raised his
stovepipe hat. Smithers stared in panic at his notes.

As Hay followed the President back to his railcar,
through the crowd, he caught sight of Beehan. "Don't you think
it was his best?"

"Absolutely," Beehan nodded.

"Page One, Beehan?" Hay arched his brows.

"The only fit place for my byline," Beehan said. "And if
I can beat the *Times*" - he meant Smithers - "I get twice my usual
rate, plus bragging rights in every bar in town."

In the telegraph office, soon, Smithers was shouting into
the mouthpiece of a new tele-phone, trying to communicate
with his editor in New York who also had a tele-phone. "No,"
Smithers yelled, "we do not have a bad connection. I'm telling
you that all the President did was read the B&O train schedule!
No, I have not been drinking! I distinctly heard the President say
Washington 4:07 p.m., then something about Baltimore I didn't
quite catch, and then 'Harrisburg 11:10 p.m....' Yes, of course
I'm sure he said that! How can I help if it's preposterous?! I'm
just telling you what the President said! Hello? Are you still there?
Hello? Hello?"

Cooper came running into the office with a piece of paper.

"Here, boy!" Beehan said. Cooper gave him the torn
sheet and Beehan stared at the three words: "Fourscore and
seven? Fourscore and seven what, Cooper?"

"You're talking to a dog, Beehan, in case you didn't notice!" Smithers hollered. He shook the tele-phone at the clerk. "What's wrong with this thing? Get me New York again!" He glimpsed the paper Beehan was reading "What's that?"

"The President's speech, dear boy. The Gettysburg Address, he titles it!"

"He doesn't title it anything because there isn't any 'Address.' You got that from a dog!"

"He's the only one who had a copy."

"This is fraud, Beehan! I heard the President and you heard the President. He was reading a timetable!"

"Are you all right, Smithers? If you'll excuse me, I have a story to write. In fact, Lincoln's speech is so good that I'm sure the *Double* will carry it verbatim."

"Unspeakable!" Smithers yelled, and snatched the paper. "Aha! Just as I thought! This is no speech!"

"Well yes, it is. It's just in code. Only Cooper can translate."

"What are you talking about?"

"Just watch."

Beehan sat down at his new type-writing machine and looked at Cooper. "Go ahead, boy."

Cooper barked. Beehan typed rapidly. *Fourscore and seven years ago...*

Bow-wow!

...Our fathers brought forth on this continent a new nation...

Ruff-ruff!

...Conceived in liberty and dedicated to the proposition that all men are created equal....

Arf-arf!

Smithers grabbed a second tele-phone, heart pounding, envisioning his career going up in smoke. "I'm telling you," he croaked to his editor, "The *Daily Double's* story is a complete fabrication! What? F-a-b-r-i - What? Of course I know you know how to spell fabrication! But I'm telling you.... What? No, I'm not trying to cover up getting beaten on a major story! Beehan is sitting ten feet from me, taking dictation - from a dog! D-O-G! No, I have not been drinking!

Hello? Hello?"

61.
The Applicant

Hay went and got Smooth-Talking Smith, who Cooper could see was walleyed and shifty-looking, which is how a person looked who was a crook and a no-good who could talk a toadfrog out of his warts, or wiggle out of anything he wasn't trying to wiggle into in the first place unless you hemmed him in with strict legal language that would stand up in court. His eyes rolled around in his head like dice in a shaker, making Cooper dizzy when he tried to follow them.

"Why, M-mister Puh-President," Smooth-Talking exclaimed, pumping Mr. Lincoln's hand, "h-h-hit's awful nice to s-see you again."

"And you, too," Lincoln lied like a rug as Smooth-Talking pumped his hand.

"G-glad to hear it. M-mighty glad!" Smooth-Talking said, and kept pumping.

Lincoln took over the pumping. "Always a pleasure!"

"C-certainly is!" Smooth-Talking claimed, trying to let go.

Lincoln pumped for all he was worth. "When Mr. Hay told me the purpose of your visit, I was glad indeed, and am glad to be glad, and hereby incorporate in this paragraph as if re-stated in its entirety, as party of the first part, that I am glad pertaining to your visit here today, as party of the second part, on this auspicious occasion."

"Wuh-what occasion is thuh-that, Mr. P-President?"

"Paraguay."

"Pair of what?" Smooth-Talking frowned.

"Paraguay."

"I n-never heard such."

"Heard such what?"

"W-w-whatever t'was you said. Pair of gways?"

"No, Paraguay. It's a country that needs an ambassador."

"Yuh-you're aimin' t-t-to make me ambassa-d-dor to Puh-Paraguay?"

"Afraid not."

"W-well, how a-b-bout a puh-postmaster j-job, then? I asted to b-b-be a puh-postmaster."

"I already said no, as I recall."

"B-b-but y-you a-ch-ch-changin' your m-mind n-now?"

"Not exactly."

"W-well, I g-g-guess y-you c-could b-be thu-thinkin' about C-Customs. I asted y-you if I c-could be the C-Customs c-c-collector at the Port of C-Calumet."

"But I already had somebody."

"And th-then I said, w-well, Mr. P-President, if you wuh-won't give me a puh-postmaster job, nor a j-job collecting cuh-customs, I'd uh-uh-admire if you could just g-gimmie a job haulin' f-firewood for the Army. And durn if you didn't t-turn me down there, too."

"True," Lincoln said.

"W-well, I f-figgered b-before I c-came to s-see y-you this t-time that there wuh-wouldn't be n-no jobs, so I decided j-just t-to ask for a puh-Presidential s-souvenir."

"What kind of souvenir?"

"W-well, it w-would n-need to b-be s-something p-personal I c-could b-brag on. H-how about that gold watch f-fob?"

"I couldn't hardly part with that," Lincoln said. "Nor my watch, either."

"W-well, maybe y-you c-could spare y-your top hat."

"It's brand new!" Lincoln squirmed. "I'd as soon give you my pants!"

"W-well," Smooth-Talking said, "a puh-pair of puh-Presidential puh-pants would definitely b-be puh-personal and th-those old puh-pants d-do look all wore-out and puh-pitiful so it w-wouldn't h-hurt you n-none to p-part with 'em."

"They do look bad," Lincoln admitted.

Lincoln took his pants off and handed them to Smooth-Talking and finally pushed him out the door.

Hay came back in. "Seward's on his way over to see you, Mr. President. Uh, where's your pants, sir?"

"Just go find me another pair, Hay. I'll sit here behind the desk where nobody can see me."

Seward entered, fanning a smoldering cigar. "Was Smooth-Talking just here?"

"Yes. And gone, thank the Lord. What do you want, Seward? I'm going down to the river with Cooper, directly."

"Congratulate us first, Lincoln. We're rich men!"

"What do you mean, rich?"

"Smooth-Talking Smith has met his match. He got his comeuppance from me at the Supreme Court an hour ago. We made a wager."

"What wager?"

"A thousand dollars."

"You made a thousand-dollar bet with Smooth-Talking Smith?"

"I didn't. We did. You and I bet Smooth-Talking a thousand dollars each!"

"You bet Smooth-Talking a thousand dollars of my money?"

"It's a sure thing, Lincoln! And I got the chief justice to hold the money."

"You didn't!"

"I had to. Mr. Blowhard Smooth-Talking was standing drinks at Willard's bar and telling all the other blowhards what a great friend he is of yours. But obviously I knew different, so

I called his bluff and bet him a hundred dollars that he couldn't even get an appointment to see you. That put him on the spot, and everybody was looking at him, so he offered to bet me five hundred that he would not only get in but that you would grant him any favor that he wished, because you were such great friends."

"And you took the bet?"

"At first I played coy, but I had him where I wanted him. It was only a matter of playing out the line, like playing a bigmouth bass. I knew through the grapevine that he intended to ask you again to make him ambassador to Paraguay, which I knew you wouldn't do in a million years. So, I laughed and walked out, and he caught up with me in front of the court and said he'd raise the bet to a thousand, just to prove that he could smooth-talk you out of anything. All I had to do was get him an appointment so he could try. So, I called his bluff and got him in to see you - in case you were wondering how he got the appointment. But back to the bet, knowing what a sneak Smooth-Talking is, I made him write down on paper exactly what he was going to talk you out of, and seal it in an envelope and give it to me. And we both carried it directly to the chief justice to hold, along with our IOU's. I never let the envelope out of my sight, so I knew that Smooth-Talking had finally outsmarted himself! When Judge Bantom heard what the set-up was, he wanted in on the action and bet Smooth-Talking a thousand dollars himself. I signed a thousand-dollar IOU in your name, right then and there, to cover your bet, and the judge approved and signed as a witness! Smooth-Talking has finally met his Waterloo, Mr. President!"

Lincoln gave a frozen grin. "Seward, do you believe in psychic ability?"

"No," Seward said. "Why?"

"Because," Lincoln said, walking to the window in his long-johns, "I just had a psychic vision that we all three are going to need a thousand dollars as soon as we open that envelope."

62.
The Restaurant Incident

Cooper was curled up asleep under the open window. Lincoln was propped at his desk, wearing new pants and going over some papers.

Cooper began to moan in his sleep, twitching his feet and his nose all at the same time.

"Wake up, Coop," Lincoln said. "You're having a dream."

Cooper sat up.

"What was it, a rabbit?"

Cooper scratched, turned around several times, and lay back down.

Lincoln went back to his papers, scratching with his pen, watching Cooper out of the corner of his eye. Their eyes met. Cooper sat up and looked toward the window. His nose worked around in a circle. One ear lifted and he poked his nose forward.

"What's that?" Lincoln said.

Cooper's feet worked nervously and a small growl escaped his throat.

"What is it, boy?"

Abernethy shuffled past the doorway and noticed this tableau of President and dog. He came back to stare. "What's going on?"

"Cooper heard something," Lincoln said.

"Heard what?"

"I don't know, but he heard it. Look at him."

"Huh, I thought I heard something, myself," Abernethy said. "I just wasn't sure. I'll have Sergeant Clancy ask around and see if the guard heard anything."

Clancy came back and reported that one of Captain Dolan's men thought he heard something, but Dolan didn't know what."

After some discussion, Abernethy sent Clancy to tell Dolan to tell the gunboat to fire a few rounds.

Lincoln heard the shooting and got out of his chair and went and found Abernethy. "What was that?"

"We had the gunboat fire a few rounds."

"A few rounds at what?"

"Whichever way they thought they heard it from."

"Oh."

Things got quiet. Then the gunboat's guns started booming again. Lincoln grabbed the shutters on the window and closed them. "Abernethy!"

Abernethy hurried back into Lincoln's study, girded with pistol and sword.

"What are we shooting at?" Lincoln said.

"I thought you said do it."

"No, Horatio, all I did was ask you an hour ago if you heard something, and you thought you did, and now all hell is breaking loose."

"I'll tell them to stop," Abernethy said. "And I'll cancel the troop movements."

Presently the cannons stopped. Mary Lincoln went around shutting windows to keep the cannon smoke out.

***

Hay and Seward arrived in the President's study that evening, trailing pieces of paper.

"You'll be pleased," Seward said, "that the Senate passed a resolution unanimously supporting your firm action today. The House went along three to two, but the minority said you weren't firm enough."

"Lincoln nodded. "Let's wait and see how the *New York Times* handles it. Meantime can you tell me why Mr. Hop Lee is waiting in my vestibule?"

"Oh," Hay said, "he's madder than a hornet because our gunboat accidentally sunk the barge his restaurant was sitting on. The cook didn't know how to swim, and it scared him so bad that he quit, and now Hop Lee is going to have to cook all the noodles himself and buy a bicycle to do take-out."

Lincoln received Hop Lee and sent him over to collect a compensation payment from Chase. Later Hop Lee came back with take-out, after his cook agreed to resume work as long as he did not have to pedal around delivering food.

"This take-out ain't half bad," Lincoln said, manipulating the chopsticks.

Hay nodded. "Want an eggroll?"

Lincoln took one. "Wonder why they call it that when it don't look a bit like an egg?"

"One of the mysteries of the Orient," said Hay, "like why we're trying to eat with these sticks."

"Are these prawns?" Lincoln poked at one with a stick.

"I thought they were hushpuppies," Hay said.

"I'll swap you an eggroll for that prawn."

Lincoln took an eggroll and started to give half of it to Cooper, but decided not to.

Cooper whined.

The cook got a raise, by the way.

63.
How Cooper Got Lincoln Re-Elected

Mrs. Lincoln had an old chifforobe that she'd brought from Illinois, and Amy loved to meddle in it.

"Amy," Mrs. Lincoln would say, "please do not meddle in my chifforobe!"

"Yessum," Amy would promise.

"And that goes for you, too, Cooper," Mrs. Lincoln would say.

And Cooper would wag his tail agreeably.

But whenever a rainy afternoon got long and boring, Amy would sneak upstairs with Cooper to meddle in the chifforobe. She would get a chair and start with the top drawer where Mrs. Lincoln kept her old costume jewelry.

"Look, Cooper!" Amy would say, and Cooper would be shown a pearl necklace with a broken clasp, or a "diamond" bracelet with its gold turning black, or a ruby brooch with its pin missing. In the back of the top drawer was a small, oval tin box holding a gold coin, a locket with tiny painted portraits of a man and a woman, supposedly Lincoln's parents; a loose cameo, a polished square stone of an orange-ish color, and, mysteriously, a Masonic ring.

Cooper, to tell the truth, wasn't all that hot about looking at jewelry, but he liked it better than being forced to model women's clothes that Amy found in the lower drawers. One particular instrument of torture was a mighty corset of Mrs. Lincoln's which had been sequestered underneath assorted boxes of sashay and beauty powder and a glass jar of Epsom salts with a lid shaped like a bird.

Amy was holding the corset when Nancy Washington, the housekeeper, walked in.

"You chirren," Mrs. Washington stamped her foot, "you done been tole 'bout that chifforobe!"

"Well - " Amy always began a barefaced lie by saying "well," and putting her hands on her hips. "Well," she said, putting her hands on her hips, "mama said, uh, that I could play dress-up with Cooper. So there!"

"Amy Louise Lincoln!" Mrs. Washington said softly. "The debbil goan get you!"

"Well," Amy faltered a bit, but kept her hands on her hips. "Well, I guess he won't if I am telling the truth!"

Mrs. Washington did not have time to pursue that knotty theological question, so she left.

And Cooper eyed the dreaded corset.

***

Downstairs, Mathew Brady was having a terrible time taking a picture of Mr. Lincoln.

Already he had tried several times, but the product did not please him, and he was trying again.

He was crouched under the black curtain at the rear of his Foucault camera, the same one that had taken so many battlefield portraits and so many sad-faced likenesses of Lincoln.

"Mr. President," Brady came out from under the cloth,

gesturing helplessly. "Mr. President the voters want you smiling."

"I am smiling," Lincoln said.

"But you're not. And they want you smiling."

"Don't I have a smile on my face?"

"Not exactly, sir."

"Mr. Brady," Lincoln said, "I have been sitting here most of the afternoon, grinning like a jackass eating briars. I have grinned so long that my face is froze like the North Pole and the South Pole put together. I don't think I will ever be able to assume a normal expression for the rest of my life."

Brady stared. "You still have to smile, Mr. President."

"Help!"

"Okay," Brady sighed. "Let's rest a minute."

Lincoln began working his cheeks. "Why does the fate of the nation have to rest on my facial expression?"

"I don't know, sir," Brady said. "It's a mystery, really. I guess people just want their President to look happy, no matter what. So, if you want them to vote in your favor, you smile."

Lincoln wagged his head. "Are we really that dumb, Brady? Here I am, a modern President in the modern year of 1864 and in the middle of the worst war in American human history and everybody is telling me that I can't be President anymore unless I smile."

Brady shrugged.

"And I think you agree with them," Lincoln pulled at his beard. "I'd be angry, but I know you're right. I know they're right. The election is going to be close. And the future of this country, maybe, is hanging on how much I can grin - "

" - smile," Brady said.

"Smile," Lincoln nodded. "Whether I can smile for a gosh-darn picture."

"Shall we try it again, sir?" Brady got behind his camera.

"I'm doing it," Lincoln said.

"Is that your smile?"

"I don't know," Lincoln said.

At that moment, Amy's voice came piping down the hall. "Father! Father, I've got something to show you!"

"What is it, Amy?"

Lincoln's face relaxed a little.

Brady shifted under the hood. "That's a little better."

Amy came in. "Shut your eyes, father. I have something to show you!"

"What is it?"

"You have to close your eyes first!"

"Okay."

"And don't open 'til I say ready!"

"I promise."

"Cross your heart!"

Lincoln crossed his heart.

With a giggle and an excited whisper, Amy brought Cooper into the room.

"Okay, open your eyes!"

Lincoln took one look, and threw back his head and laughed.

Cooper was wearing a red satin bonnet with a bow tied under his chin, and gusseted in Mrs. Lincoln's corset.

"Haw, haw, haw!" Lincoln was slapping his knees.

Brady yelled, "there, Mr. President!" and began taking pictures.

After Amy and Cooper left (the bonnet fell underneath Cooper's head, and he began to walk out of the corset) Lincoln's amusement faded slowly into sadness.

But before that happened, Brady worked the shutter one last time and caught a happy image of the President. The expression was perfect, and the photograph appeared in all the newspapers soon thereafter, and in innumerable history books ever since.

Lincoln was re-elected. Whether the picture had much to do with it is one of those questions that can never be answered. But it was Brady's most famous portrait of Lincoln, and not many people know the story of how it happened.

64.
Cooper Dictates the Terms
at Appomattox

Grant studied the tired-looking general in the gray uniform.

Lee sat with his head back, his left hand touching his chin, his right playing absently with Cooper's ears.

"So!" Grant held out the box of Havanas. Lee shook his head.

"Mind if I do?"

"You are the victor," Lee smiled wryly.

"Not yet," Grant said.

Lee unbuckled his ornate sword and placed it on the table. "Now you are the victor."

Grant frowned at the sword. Shrugged. "You don't want to talk about terms?"

"Why?"

Cooper rolled over to have his belly scratched.

Grant obliged, with a light touch of his spur.

"A lot of people up North want your head," Grant said,

looking at the dog rather than Lee.

"I expect so," said Lee.

"If it was up to me," Grant said, "I might give it to 'em."

Lee got down on his knees to examine Cooper's muzzle. "This dog," he said, "would be a fine squirrel tracker."

"Squirrel tracker?"

"Keen sense of smell. And a fine climber."

"Climber?"

"Oh yes. Our Virginia dogs climb trees all the time."

"I had a dog once that snored."

"This one is definitely a climber."

"Think he's got much bloodhound in him?"

"None at all."

Grant put on his glasses. "I think he looks a little bit bloodhound, down around the feet."

"I don't think so," Lee said, holding up Cooper's feet, one by one to peer at them closely. "When the bloodhound bloodline gets spread out, bloodhound foot is easy to confused with redtick hound foot."

"Or bassett hound foot."

"Oh no," Grant said, "Look at the legs!"

"Say!" Lee put on his own spectacles. "This dog has legs like a pure-blooded...I can't think of the breed, but it's pure-blooded."

"Thalmatian?"

"No, thalmatians are extinct. How did you know about thalmatians?"

"My uncle had a half-thalmatian. Climbed trees like a monkey."

Cooper's eyes rolled from Grant to Lee and back. "All right," Lee said, "what about the terms?"

"I thought you didn't want to talk about terms."

"I don't, but let's talk about them anyway."

"They call me Unconditional Surrender," Grant said, puffing his cigar.

"So I've heard."

"That means no conditions."

"I've heard that."

"You believe it?"

"No."

"Well, you're right. It's a lot of horse manure thought up by the newspapers."

"What terms do you have in mind, then?"

"I want one of your uncle's tree-climbing half-thalmatian pups. Otherwise, everybody can go home."

"Will Northerners accept that?"

"Of course not," Grant ground out the cigar. "They want your tail in a sling. They want the South occupied and stomped on. They want revenge for all they've lost."

"But you don't agree."

"No." Grant toyed with the cigar stump. "This country has gone through four years of hell. If we act halfway smart, we might get over it in about a hundred years. If we're as dumb as I think we are, it'll take two hundred. Or longer."

"I'd bet on the longer time," Lee said. He sat back and crossed his legs, staring at Cooper who now rested a chin on his knee.

Grant nodded.

Lee sagged in his chair, scratching at Cooper's brow. "Well, we'd best get on with it," Grant said. He made no move, but took another cigar from the box, struck a match, let it burn out without lighting the cigar. Then, slowly, he rose to attention and scooped Lee's sword from the table.

"You'll hand this to me while Brady takes our picture," he said.

"And our dispatch to the newspapers will say what?"

"*My* dispatch will say 'unconditional surrender.'"

"Which will mean?"

"Unconditional surrender."

"Which will mean?"

"Go home. But don't forget my pup."

65.
The Sunday After the War

"Anything wrong, sir?"

William the butler asked the question softly, leaning over to adjust Mr. Lincoln's dessert plate. It held an untouched slice of chocolate cake.

"Am I what, William?" the President said, coming out of a reverie.

"I said, you haven't touched Florence's cake."

"Oh," Lincoln said. "I guess I haven't. Where is Mrs. Lincoln?"

"She went upstairs. That cake's mighty good."

"So it is," Lincoln said. "I'll polish it off by and by."

"Everything all right, sir?"

"Yes, yes." Lincoln smiled a bit, pulled out his watch. "I've kept you too late, William. You go on home. Send the others, too. I'll see the table gets cleared."

"But Mr. - "

"Go on now."

Later, Lincoln did something he had not done in years.

He began clearing the table, stacking the dishes, raking food scraps, collecting the silverware. It was a strange and pleasant sensation although, in truth, he had never cared for kitchen work and, in fact, had done very little of it since his youth.

But for now, he took a strange pleasure in hauling the dishes to the sink, putting the silverware in tall glasses and running water into the glasses from a tap that was the envy of Washington. He suddenly remembered his boyhood days in Kentucky, and how the enamel bucket bumped against his leg when he was about seven or eight years old, old enough to fetch water from the spring for his mother. He remembered an Indian moccasin print, once, at the spring. And there were sometimes signs of deer.

Now, for some reason, he could see in his mind's eye the nick in the rim of the bucket he had carried, a small flaw shaped like an eye, where someone had banged it and chipped the enamel. Maybe he'd hit it himself with the dipper while getting a drink of cold water. He didn't remember exactly. But for some reason he never forgot the nick.

He took his cake plate and put it down for Cooper. Later, Cooper followed him upstairs.

"Abraham?"

Mary had been trying on a formal dress, a black one, but was unsure whether it was the right thing to wear. She glanced at the President as he came into the room and sat on the bed. "Abraham, why aren't you dressed, yet?"

"Dressed?"

Mary rolled her eyes. "For the theater."

"Oh yes." Lincoln sagged. "I'll be ready directly."

"You did remember the tickets?"

"Yes, Chase sent them over."

"I hear it's a very amusing play, Abraham. A comedy, which you like. 'My American Cousin.'"

Lincoln nodded.

"The Bantoms saw it," Mary said as she smoothed her dress. "They adored it. How does this look, Abraham? I thought I'd wear the pearls, but maybe the gold locket...?"

"I heard the play was funny."

"Get dressed, dear, will you?"
Cooper barked.
"And make Cooper go away."
"Mary - "
"Yes?"
"Would you like to leave here and go back to Springfield?"
"Well," Mary tried on the gold locket. "I suppose when your term is up - "
"No, I mean now. Tomorrow. Maybe next week."
Mary looked at him sharply in the mirror. "What are you talking about, Abraham?"
"I'm thinking of resigning."
"You're not serious."
"I am. My job's done."
"Done?" Mary looked bewildered.
"I've thought about it, Mary, and I want to go back and just - " Lincoln paused, raised his hands, sagged again.
Cooper took a seat next to the President. Mary came over and put a hand on his shoulder, then sat next to him on the bed and gave him a hug. "You're just having a letdown, Abraham."
"Perhaps," Lincoln said. "But I looked around me tonight and all of a sudden I was wondering what I'm doing here. I belong in Springfield. We belong there. We were happy together, with the children, weren't we?"
"Of course we were. And we are happy here, even with all the tragedy. Even with losing Tad."
Lincoln sighed. "I really don't feel like going to the theater."
Cooper put his chin on the President's knee.
"Why don't I just stay here with Cooper and let you go? John Nicolay can take my ticket and escort you. I know he wants to see the play."
"Nonsense, Abraham! You are my escort and I will have none other."
Cooper whined and began limping around the room.
"What's wrong, boy?" Lincoln said, getting on the floor to examine the dog.
"Put him out, Abraham."

"He must have hurt his paw or something. Why don't you take the ticket and let John Nicolay see the play. I'll just stay here with Cooper."

Cooper began limping on two feet.

Mary shook her head.

"I'll go with you next time," Lincoln promised.

"All right," Mary said shortly.

Harriet, the maid, stuck her head in the door to tell the Lincolns that their carriage was ready.

A servant ran over to get Nicolay, but ran back to say that Nicolay was already on his way to the theater, escorting Kate Chase.

"Abraham, you must dress quickly and come with me," Mary commanded sternly. "I will not go alone and I will not leave you here moping with that dog."

Cooper whined and began limping on all four feet. Lincoln gave Cooper's head a tousle. "The hound of heav'n," he said, "doth not always catch his prey."

"Hurry or we'll be late," Mary said.

Lincoln got dressed quickly, and the two of them went down to the carriage as a servant held fast to Cooper's collar.

When the carriage was safely gone, and the door shut, the servant let go of the dog who ran to the window and looked into the empty street and barked.

Silence descended.

Slowly, Cooper walked up the stairs and plodded down the dark hallway and lay down on the cold hearth in Lincoln's study.

Flap flapflapflap flap!

About the Author

James O. Long is a Tennessee-born journalist and writer recommended many times for the Pulitzer Prize. Best-known for his investigative reporting, he was a staff writer for 41 years at *The Oregonian* newspaper in Portland, Oregon. His work also has appeared in *Newsweek* and the *Massachusetts Review*. He co-authored a book, *Killer: A Journal of Murder*, with Thomas E. Gaddis (*Birdman of Alcatraz*) that was turned into a movie starring James Woods. He is a U.S. Navy veteran and a graduate of the University of Portland. He has lived in Portland since 1962 and has three children and two grandchildren.

CPSIA information can be obtained
at www.ICGtesting.com
Printed in the USA
FSHW021212290220
67619FS

9 780984 811342